SILVER AND IRON

SAGE:
BOOK THREE

Books and stories by Marian Allen

Novels
Eel's Reverence
Force of Habit
SAGE Book 1: The Fall of Onagros
SAGE Book 2: Bargain With Fate
SAGE Book 3: Silver and Iron
Sideshow in the Center Ring

Short Story Collections
Lonnie, Me and the Hound of Hell
Turtle Feathers
The King of Cherokee Creek
MA's Monthly Hot Flashes: 2002-2009

Visit the author at
http://MarianAllen.com

SILVER AND IRON

SAGE: book three

A Novel
by

MARIAN ALLEN

Per Bastet

Silver and Iron Sage: Book Three

Second Edition

Copyright © 2014 Marian Allen

Published by Per Bastet Publications LLC, P.O. Box 3023 Corydon, IN 47112

Cover design by T. Lee Harris

ISBN 978-1-942166-54-2

DEDICATION:

This book is dedicated to my husband, who makes my writing possible and my life worth living.

SILVER AND IRON

SAGE: book three

PROLOGUE

On a rocky cliff above the Inland Sea, Dragon lifted her head and breathed a deep sound. No human could have heard her, but the fisherbirds all dove for their nests and fell silent, and the fish below darted this way and that with delight.

Dragon dug a stone from the rock, leaving a small hollow.

Tortoise, grumbling, stumped up the hollow and spat gummily into it.

Phoenix dropped a feather onto the bile. Feather and spittle shimmered and melted into pure water.

Tortoise turned on his brother with a vicious hiss. "Leave my spit alone! No interference! You promised!"

Unicorn planted a massive hoof between the two, so suddenly that Tortoise retracted his head.

Phoenix laughed. Tortoise, extending his head again, gave another hiss and turned away.

Unicorn tapped on his shell with her horn. "You've been busy, brother."

"I'm not the only one. I thought none of you were interested in the affairs of these mortals."

Dragon shook her head. "I care. I said so from the first."

"You don't count," said Tortoise.

Dragon shook her head again and gave a bubbly laugh.

Tortoise and Phoenix eyed one another from either side of Unicorn.

Phoenix said, "Why is it that everyone calls for you, but everyone comes to us? Could it be because they think you can be bought? Could it be that you *can*?"

If a tortoise can smirk, Tortoise smirked. "If the price is right." He swiveled his neck to meet the eyes of each sibling in turn. "Phoenix is sworn not to interfere. Unicorn sits on her haunches droning about life and death being the same thing. Dragon plays Happy Families with humans. I'm the only one the humans fear. I'm the one they come to in their weakness."

"And we," said Unicorn, "are who they come to in their strength."

With patently false surprise, Phoenix said, "Do you know: I think I *prefer* that?"

"Enjoy your philosophizing," said Tortoise. "The game's not over yet." With astonishing swiftness, he crawled to the edge of the cliff and threw himself into the water, far below.

CHAPTER 1
THE TRUE KINNINGER

Kinnan thought of himself as a man of action, yet he seemed to have done little these past ten years but wait. Wait for the uprising that never swelled, wait for answers from powerful men who always answered no, wait for Salali, wait for Brady.

He sat awake on his straw pallet in the goat shed. The animals were as restless as he was. They stirred in their dry straw bedding, bleating softly as if murmuring among themselves. The moon shone a cool silver light through the uncovered window, casting long impenetrable shadows.

Brady must return soon, or be done without. Meanwhile, Kinnan had Salali's word that his cause was fermenting within the populace. For no reason he could give, he trusted that word, and would wait on it and act on it. The time would ripen soon and he would move. Perhaps he would skirt the Kozabirian border to Istok, join with Anshar's band, and begin. Perhaps he would move among the people incognito, testing them for himself, revealing himself when he found the support he hoped for.

And then? Warfare, blood, and ruin. How many fighters could Landry field? The Swords, of course, but how many of the citizen militia would stand with Landry, and how many with Kinnan-called-beren-Ada? How many of the Thanes would stand with the current crown, and how many fighters could they bring with them? Would families divide and fight among themselves?

Landry must be deposed. Landry must be punished. For what he had done to the country, for what he had done to the people, for what he had done to Kinnan and Kinnan's friends and Kinnan's kin, Landry must be made to pay.

A slight noise from outside brought Kinnan to his knees, peering over the windowsill. He could see the garden and the stone privy. He could see the back of the cottage, its row of hives quiet in the relative cool of night; an angled view of the side with its chimney, its shuttered window faintly lit by the embers of the hearth fire, some of the well-yard. He could see no movement.

As quietly as he could, he dressed and pulled on his boots. He buckled on his sword and slipped out of the shed and around the corner of the house.

Moder Zglaria stood – tall, broad, black-gowned and white-skinned – in the clearing, her walking stick planted firmly before her, her face raised to the moon. Her turban, with its squashy knot in front, made her head look over-large and mis-shapen. She lowered her head, and Kinnan was shocked at the tenderness he saw where he was used to seeing sharpness or knowing or hooded looks. Her glance flicked to him, and the softness was covered again.

"What happened?" he asked.

"Nothing, yet. Did I wake you with my wandering about? I couldn't sleep."

"Neither could I." Kinnan crossed the yard to her, his soldier's eyes taking in the periphery of clearing, sky, and the low-sloping roof of the little stone cottage. "I'm tired of waiting."

Moder smiled. "Are you?"

"Who knows what's happened to Brady? Do you?"

"Not I."

"Who knows when he'll be back? If he'll be back? Do you?"

Moder Zglaria said nothing, then put out a hand. "He's coming now. Can't you hear him?"

Kinnan listened a little harder. He heard the nearly-inaudible rush of wings, then an over-sized owl swooped into the clearing and Brady stood with them.

"A welcoming committee!" the younger man said. He turned to Moder Zglaria and, to Kinnan's astonishment, embraced her and kissed her chalky cheek.

The old woman laughed and rubbed her face with the back of her hand.

"Kinnan!" Brady dropped to one knee. "What is it I call you?"

"Your Grace," said Moder Zglaria.

"What?" Kinnan knuckled Brady's head in a mock punch. "Stand up, boy, and make sense. What happened to you? Why this sudden respect for me and…." He trailed off, staring again at Moder, still with the back of her hand on Brady's kiss.

The varier stood. "I saw her – Sorcha – your sister."

"Sister…. She acknowledges me?"

"Yes."

Kinnan smacked his hand with his fist and stared off into glory.

"It's close to dawn," Moder said. "Let's wake the others and have a talk."

Brady led the way.

Kinnan stepped in front of him. "Where did you see her? What did she say?"

"I'll tell it all at once. She'll want to hear it fresh – Elsie will. I saw her parents."

Moder followed, leaning heavily on her stick. "You *have* been busy."

Kinnan and Salali sat on the bench against the wall and Moder sat at the table. In honor of the occasion, she lit a branch of beeswax candles to supplement the glow of the fire and the feeble light of dawn. Brady helped Elsie bring fresh milk, cheese, flatbread, and berry preserves up from the cold room, carrying on a mock flirtation with Salali all the while. At last, everyone had eaten and Moder waived the cleaning-up until later.

"Where should I start? Well, first: I went to Sorcha in the form of a dog and made friends. She was…. She looked…."

"Never mind that now." Moder Zglaria lit a pipe. "Answer the beren Ada's questions, if you have any mercy."

Brady smiled a private smile with the old woman and spoke to Kinnan. "Sorcha is willing to admit you as her brother. She doesn't want the throne – or so she says. She thinks Landry's frightened and dangerous. I helped her leave the Waystation, and she and Hayward have taken refuge at Oakwood with his grandmother. Hayward thinks they can hold it."

Kinnan leaned back against the wall. "So."

His one impediment had removed itself. He had been afraid that his half-sister Sorcha – a shadowy figure, never met, and wife of Landry's brother – would thwart him, somehow. Or would step over the debris of his revolution and claim what he had won. Or would get herself martyred in the turmoil and so set the people's hearts against his action. Now his way to the crown seemed free of these familial obstacles.

"I have news for you, too, Elsie. I saw Devona."

Elsie's face brightened. "You did?"

"I told her where you are –" Brady cast a worried glance at Moder, who relieved him with a nod. "She told me…. She told me…. Should we talk alone?"

"No." Elsie was silent a moment, staring at the table.

"They called her Tabby," said Kinnan. In two blunt sentences, he told what Elsie had remembered, including the two visits by the woman Tabby called Grace.

"You saw her, then!" Brady tapped on the table to break Elsie's reverie. "You've met her!" When Elsie looked at him bleakly, he said, "I told you about when I was a boy. When the viper almost killed me, and a Layounnan woman saved my life, and died doing it?"

Elsie nodded as Brady got up and took two things from his knapsack.

He put his blue-enameled tinderbox on the table, and the ebony knife case. "I showed you these and told you they were hers. I told you I kept them, hoping to give them and my thanks to her family if I could ever find out who she was."

"Yes."

Brady looked at Kinnan. "I gave my thanks to your sister. Now I thank you."

"Why…?" He had only been partly attending, most of his mind on tactics, strategies, and hopes.

"When I saw Sorcha beren Ada, it was like seeing the woman who saved me over again. That woman was Layounnan, on the way to Kozabir."

"How long ago, Young Master?" asked Moder Zglaria.

"Ten years."

"Ten years. Ten years ago, a needle passed through the fabric of the world. In and out, and the stitches looked like separate things, but now they draw together. Ten years ago, a woman stopped with me for some months. She made a dress of rough cloth and gave her gown to me." Moder looked at Elsie, and pointed with the stem of her pipe. "It was that gown you wore the day you came, and we washed the only set of boy's clothes you had then and waited for them to dry."

"Her gown," Elsie whispered. "Grace's gown."

"The woman was with child. She gave birth, stayed some weeks more, and left. When she left, she said the name she'd given me had been false, that she was Karol beren Ada, and that she intended to do what she could to put her brother, Kinnan, on the throne. She said she would look for him in Kozabir."

"The Emir knew her," Kinnan said. "He would have listened to her. She could have bought an army there.…. But she never came. I would have known."

The old woman touched the tinderbox, then the knife. "I gave her these things as parting gifts."

Then Kinnan heard, as an echo in his mind, what Brady had said, how he had recognized Sorcha, and why. He groaned. Ambitions and rights and arms forgotten, he mourned his sister. "Karol!" He felt stabbed to the heart, as he had when they told him the mother he hardly knew had died, as he had when his father died, and when they told him his brother was dead and his sister, Karol, was missing. He had long assumed she was dead – the certainty shouldn't have this power to hurt. "Why?" His voice was plaintive as a child's. "Why did she…." He shook his head.

Brady spread empty hands. "I've often asked myself the same question."

"I remember the first time I saw her." Kinnan looked at the door, as if she would step through again, young and alive. "I thought she was the most beautiful woman I'd ever seen. The second time she came, she brought me this –" He held up one wrist encircled by the bronze bracelet. "It went around my arm several times, back then. I've worn it ever since, for her sake."

"I'd bring her back to you, if I could." Brady's eyes were bright with pity.

"Gone." Kinnan seemed not to hear. "And her child gone, too. If there's any comfort to be taken, it's that she thought she left her baby safe."

Elsie's eyes misted with memory. "She said to call it Gosling, and I loved it as my own."

Moder Zglaria's keen gaze rested on Elsie. "That baby wasn't her first."

Salali laughed. "Blind! Are you blind?" She pointed to Kinnan, then to Elsie. "Look at the shape of their eyes. Look at their jaws, at their cheekbones. Look at the set of their mouths."

Brady drew back from Elsie, inspecting her, comparing her to Kinnan, comparing her to Sorcha.

"I see it." He looked to Moder Zglaria for confirmation. "Don't I?"

Moder grinned.

"I don't," said Kinnan.

Elsie shook her head. "Are you saying my mother…?"

Moder Zglaria finished the sentence for her, "…was Kinninger Karol beren Ada, Kinnan's half-sister, and Brady's deliverer."

"And Gosling's mother. My mother. 'Grace' was… *our* mother. And Landry killed…."

Brady touched the tinderbox and knife. "It seems a thousand years since I told you where I got these and why I carry them."

"And you said you'd pay her back if you could. And all the time, you were saving me. Her daughter. One of her daughters." She blinked, but tears rolled in large round drops to fall from her cheekbones into her lap.

"Where's the proof?" Kinnan leaned forward, hands fisted on his knees. "You can't claim a bloodline based on chance resemblance. Even if I believe it, the people would want proof, and so would the Thanes and the rulers of our neighbors. I have my sister's letter, signed by her hand and marked with her seal."

Moder chuckled. "If she legitimated her brother, why would she have left her children nameless?"

The old woman went to a chest carved with long-tailed birds. She took out a bundle wrapped in homespun cloth, and a tooled leather belt. Holding her burden close, she returned to the table and put belt and bundle in Kinnan's lap.

He spread the belt along the table. Its pattern of leaves and flowers was scored in many places.

"The Swords hunted her through the woods," the old woman said.

Kinnan unwrapped the bundle and let the homespun fall to the floor. He held Karol's gown in trembling hands. It was made of red wool, thin and light, heavily embroidered with gold and green crescents. "I've seen her wear it many times." He fingered the rents and ravels of the ruined finery.

Moder turned the skirt inside out. A pocket the size of Kinnan's hand was sewn at the waist, laced shut with white ribbon. "Open that."

He did, and drew out an oilcloth packet sealed with the remains of a sprig of dried sage pressed in wax. Inside was a letter. There were two entries, made in slightly different ink, dated four years apart.

"…the Bahari baby farm," he read, "under the name of…Tabby. …This child, if I deliver safely, I will leave under the name of Gosling."

Kinnan beamed indulgently at the young woman. "You are my little niece."

Elsie raised her head. Yes, Kinnan thought, he had seen that chin-tilt, that firming of the mouth, that spark – on both sides of Karol and Cameron's clashes of will.

"And you," she replied, "are my mother's baby brother."

A rapid wheeze began quietly and grew louder, breaking the tension and resolving itself into Salali, doing her best to keep her laughter silent.

Moder Zglaria grinned and drew on her pipe.

"You think it's funny?" Kinnan asked the trinket-woman. "You shouldn't. Your reward hinges on my fortunes. Why should you laugh?" When Salali made no reply, he realized the answer. "I wanted it to be 'if you help me gain the throne,' but you insisted Landry's overthrow was the condition. I thought it was the same thing."

Brady couldn't help a lopsided grin. "Farukh told you it wasn't a bargain he'd have made."

Salali's laughter stopped. She met Kinnan's glare with flashing pride. "You were warned, as the boy says. My terms were plain and you agreed to them. Have I tricked you? Take back your vow, then. I don't want a promise unwittingly given and unwillingly kept."

Kinnan reddened. "What do you take me for? I made the bargain. Have I asked to be released? You've done your part."

Salali turned away, disgruntled at the concession.

Moder Zglaria lifted an eyebrow. "You're counting your losses too soon, Young Master. It does seem 'Elsie' has the right of bloodline, but you have the mandate bag – had you forgotten?"

Brady put out a hand again and fiddled with the knife and tinder box on Moder's table. "Does a mandate bag have to be rich?"

Kinnan opened his mouth to say *Of course*.

"No," said Moder Zglaria. "It only has to be true. Why?"

"The woman who saved me – Karol – had a bag with her, but not like Kinnan's. It was old and torn and dirty and empty. We buried it with her."

"Buried the mandate bag of Onagros?" Kinnan thrust his jaw at Brady as if it were a fist.

Moder nodded. "That was right."

"How could it be right?"

"It was time for a renewal, maybe. He said the bag was old and worn and empty. Maybe it's time for a new bag, a new mandate, a new pledge between monarch and people. Maybe yours, Young Master."

Was it possible? It did seem hard – all the suffering and struggle, the waiting and desire – all for someone else's benefit. He had grown used to thinking of himself as rightful Kinninger of Layounna, unwilling but unquestioned. Now that the weight of duty was lifted, he found he couldn't give it up so easily. This possibility was sweet, like the last fresh apple of autumn.

Moder Zglaria stirred and stood. She blew out the candles, gripped her stick, and stumped across the room to open the door. The light of the risen sun shone in.

Then Kinnan remembered her tale of a badger who wanted to be emperor of the world. He stole a look and saw her, silhouetted against the light, remembering it, too.

chapter 2
LION'S BLOOD

Dangerous, to be without my Chief Sword, Landry thought. Whether he meant he needed Guthrie's protection or didn't trust Guthrie out of sight, he couldn't have said.

He stood at the narrow window of his mother's room, looking out over Kudasad, wishing the window faced the bridge so he could scan for the Sword's return. Behind him, flanking the fireplace, sat Oliva and Corvina. Without looking at them, he could see his mother's and sister's twin postures of confident ease, their twin expressions of smug expectancy. Since Corvina's illness and her betrothal to Guthrie, the two had become so close they all but breathed in unison.

"How long is Guthrie to be gone, Moder?"

"I told you, My Lord, I do not know. Not long, I think. We agreed, did we not, on the urgency of his errand?"

"Yes." Landry picked a crumb of mortar from the embrasure and cast it out. "I cannot have a man by me who serves another, not even if that other's goals fit conveniently with mine. If he is in thrall to some Power through his sword, he must be freed, or...."

"Dispensed with," said Guthrie's promised bride.

"Preferably freed."

Oliva inclined her head in agreement with her son. The Chief Sword might yet be of great use to her as well as to the Kinninger. "The villeins have put up a smithy for silver work against the tower wall–"

"Why there? Why not down against the bailey palisade with the other artisans?"

"Did you or did you not tell me I might do as I wished with the smith?" Oliva didn't like the querulousness in Landry's voice. That tone had always been a storm warning, signaling a burst of temper. "The smith's enchanted bit, the mandate bag, harnessing your Chief Sword's ambitions – these are all bound up together. If you're content with matters as they are, or as they're becoming, very well. I'll have the smithy dismantled and moved. All shall be just as you wish, My Lord."

"No, Moder. Let it be. I only wondered."

Oliva smiled to herself, hearing Landry scramble down from his position like a child from too high a chair. "I want the smith where I've put him. With Sorcha out of the Waystation, the people are rushing back to their old beliefs. We can use that to our advantage: It strengthens the claims of our mandate bag. But we must take care. If it should be known that we plan to kill a unicorn, that we've hired a Kozabirian smith who dabbles in Hidden Matters to help us…. The old superstitions die hard, My Lord. This one, about the so-called sanctity of Life is particularly vigorous."

Oliva's lips twisted. "These unled sheep – they're afraid of Life! Afraid to grasp it, tear it, drink it down, bend it to their wills! Sorcha might not be permitted to refuse the throne, if the people were sufficiently aroused. Better to keep the smith away from the other villeins. Besides, the new smithy is above my cellar temple. This man has power in his work, and I want that power near me. I want to influence that power, to direct it as I want it – to your good, my dear."

Landry hardly heard her, though he nodded abruptly. *Sorcha is gone.* That was what he heard as a steady hum under everything else, a refrain that was coming to haunt his dreams: *Sorcha is free and at Oakwood with Hayward.* She continued to reject the crown, but she was free and had her name again and claimed her House. His spies told him the people were in a nasty holiday mood over the business. His Midsummer Festival would siphon some of that off, and his Mandate Ceremony would squelch the rest.

"I doubt she and Hayward and Grandmoder would come here to a feast."

Corvina gave a soft abrupt laugh. "That would be too much to hope for."

"Still…." Oliva tapped delicate fingernails on the arm of her chair. "Letters of delight from you, and from Corvina and myself to your brother…. Presents might smack of tribute, but some token would look gracious."

Looking again for Guthrie, Landry spoke with his back to the women. "The Onagros silver, perhaps? With the implicit message that the castle will no longer need anything bearing that device?"

Oliva considered the suggestion. "Yes, that might be a nice touch.

You're becoming a diplomat, my dear."

When Landry didn't answer, Corvina said, "It's as well Guthrie was away when this news broke: He would have advocated bloody slaughter, or at least siege and starvation."

"His lack of squeamishness is his value to me. It's his only value. He slays my enemies, he doesn't make my policy."

"I'm glad to hear it. Does he know?"

Landry chuckled. "Perhaps not altogether. When and if we need to, we'll wake him to his real position."

Oliva regarded the two fondly. "We're agreed on our attitude toward Sorcha, then? We're overjoyed to welcome her back to the world and our united families?"

"Yes. I'll write personal letters to Sorcha and Hayward."

"And I'll write, too, and echo your 'pleasure.' I have written, in fact. Would you like to hear?"

"Yes."

Oliva took a sheet of thick vellum, edged in gold, from the mantelpiece, unfolded it, and read:

> *To my dearest child Hayward and to my other-daughter Sorcha at Oakwood, under the banner of Audre beren Oda:*
>
> *How happy I was, Sorcha, to learn you had renounced your vows to the Way and returned to us! My only sorrow is that you chose to retire to Oakwood, rather than joining us here (may the blessings of the gods shower upon my beloved mother, for sheltering you!). Of course I understand that, after the cloistered life, the court might have been too bright and busy for you. Perhaps, after a rustic interlude, you will return to your rightful place as a highborn lady, wife of Hayward of Sarpa.*
>
> *How I long to see you again, my dears, and my grandchildren! They are all grown now, all but Vevcy, may she rest in the heart of Tarkastrus – or of The Way, as you prefer. I am told that Blaine has married and set up housekeeping in a tenant's cottage. Will he bring his*

wife and children into Oakwood? Is Joia still happy as
Waymistress of her distant Station? Has Atwell ever sent
word of where he is and what he's been about?

"You have a far-seeing eye, Moder," said Landry. "Best to see if we can track them all down. If we can't have them in hand, we must have them in mind."

My fondest regards to my mother – kiss her for me
and tell her I pray our common delight in your decision
will mend an estrangement that was not of my will.
Until we meet, as we should and must, I remain
your most loving mother,
Oliva

She folded the paper again. "Will that do?"

"Moder, there is none to match you." Landry left the window and kissed his mother's silver hair. "That should put them off their guard, even Grandmoder. They might be satisfied with the possibility of seeing their young made my heirs. If not, they'll think pretending to be satisfied will lull me for a while. In the meantime, you'll get your unicorn and I'll get my mandate, and an attempt to overthrow a mandated Kinninger will not be so heartily supported. I suppose there's no doubt of Guthrie's success? Rhu failed, and Rhu was the perfect huntsman – so you said then."

"The Mystic Arts are neither obvious nor simple." Oliva exchanged another look of camaraderie with her daughter. "That's why they're called 'arts,' and not 'shopwork.'"

Corvina smiled agreement. "The Unicorn is said to herald a royal birth. Perhaps the Chamberlain was too low-born to interest it."

The Kinninger replied sharply. "Low-born, perhaps, but raised as my companion. He sat through lessons with me, took my punishments when I slacked or misbehaved, heard my confidences until my needs outgrew his nature. If Rhu was unfit for the hunt, it wasn't from ignobility."

"I had no idea you were sentimental, brother."

"Do not," Landry spoke deliberately, not expecting to be obeyed, but wanting it remembered he had said it, "underestimate the Chamberlain."

Corvina laughed. "My future husband will succeed where your old playfellow did not. The bit will be made by a wonder-working smith from Kozabir, and you know the Spirit Animal the Kozabirians most venerate." When Landry, who had more on his mind than another country's religion, looked blank, she said, "Tortoise, brother. Tortoise controls Kozabir and its magics, and our mother controls Tortoise."

The fire hissed savagely.

"My betrothed will succeed because Tortoise will see to it."

"Trust me for that." Oliva smirked.

"And I will marry," said Corvina, "and bear children."

Landry smiled sweetly. "And I think, after all, I will keep them near me. Safer." He returned to the window.

CHAPTER 3
FLOW OF THE TIDE

Andrin beren Tooli, former Royal Waymaster to the House of Onagros, scratched his chin through his short white beard and sighed in contentment. What a day this had been! He had risen with the sun, had swept the dirt floor of his wattle-and-daub cottage, had jumped into the Fiddlewood shallows for a morning wash, had dried in the sun while he exercised, had eaten what his marvelous Kozabirian kettle had provided for him....A morning like most mornings had been since Landry had exiled him from the castle bailey. He had tended his herbs and vegetables, had eaten some of them fresh for lunch, had cut some herbs and hung them to dry fragrantly in his windowless one-room home....An afternoon like most afternoons since he had taken refuge here. He had talked to Chandler, his old hen, had explored up and down the riverbank, collecting stones and shells and feathers, had caught a fish, had cooked and eaten it for supper, watched the sun set, washed again in the Fiddlewood, and retired to the cottage, now lit and warmed by a fire in the stone hearth. An evening like most evenings since he had accepted his new life.

Chandler settled into her nest in the corner, fluffing her feathers and crooning.

He slipped out of his only outer garment – a pair of ankle-length breeches – and sat, cross-legged in an unbleached cotton breechcloth, on his cot. This life suited him, he thought. He was a vigorous seventy-odd years, white hair and beard cropped haphazardly when he thought of it, white mustache drooping, because he only trimmed it where and when it tickled his lips. He looked blocky and heavy, but his exercises kept him quick and strong. His black-purple eyes were still lively – livelier, in fact, every day he spent looking at wind-blown grass and waves instead of the to-ings and fro-ings of Royalty.

It had been nice, seeing the Chamberlain the other day after so many years – could it really be ten? Rhu beren Robia had penetrated whatever barrier had shielded Andrin from all the castle folk save Biddi. He wondered if this meant something; if Rhu had been let through to remind Andrin of the life he had left behind. Was it a test, to see if he still longed for his silken robes and his shaven head, his perfumed tea and his Royal honors? Or was it a warning – a notice, rather – that his retreat was about to end?

Either way, what would happen would happen.

The fire died to embers, Chandler closed her eyes, and Andrin slept.

He dreamed of water, and of small fish. The fish were Karol's children. He was aware of having dreamed this before, years and years ago, and he knew what would happen. He clutched at the fish, trying to save them, as he had in that earlier dream. As before, they slipped through his fingers. This time, they were swirled away from him by a whirlpool; it pulled the little fish off in a wide circling, down its throat into cold darkness.

Then, instead of waking in despair, as he had before, he dreamed he stood on the grass outside his cottage, staring at a coracle: a small, tub-like boat, such as the poorer anglers used. He launched the boat and stepped in and lay down, content that he would now follow those little fish down the vortex. Instead, he floated drowsily with the current.

Then he dreamed his grandmother, in her water dragon form, perched on the edge of the coracle, not weighing it down in the slightest. Her large, blue-green face hovered above him; the feathery scales of her ruff fluttered in the soft breeze of their passage.

"Would you like to hear a story?" she asked.

"If you'd like to tell me one."

~*~

Long, long ago (the dragon said), there was only One Dragon. The earth was her body, and the moon was her pearl; the waters of heaven and earth were her lifeblood, and the sun was her heart. One day, to amuse herself, the Dragon created Time. Then she knew that she was old and she knew that she was lonely.

The One Dragon then took scales of the five colors from her body: red, green, blue, black, and yellow; scales soft, like cloth, because she had no enemies. She spun the scales into thread and knitted little dragons, using her talons as needles. She invited her three friends to come help her celebrate the end of her loneliness.

They all came: Tortoise Spirit, Phoenix Spirit, and Unicorn Spirit.

"These children of yours will live in the world," said Unicorn Spirit. "They will need protection."

Tortoise gave the little dragons armored scales. Phoenix gave them fire. Unicorn gave them back what their mother had lost – freedom from the shackles of Time.

"My children are wiser and stronger than I am," said the One Dragon.

"Then come with us," her friends begged her, and she agreed.

One Dragon left her body and became Dragon Spirit, and her children were the first dragons. They were all the dragons there were and all the dragons there would ever be. Every so often, one of them would discover Time, and would leave its body and join its mother as part of the Dragon Spirit. So, to keep dragons in the world, the first dragons created Translation. A human who learned what a dragon must know – patience, acceptance, courage, joy, and freedom from enslavement to Time – could be Translated into a dragon. And these dragons are the strongest of all because they, being partly human, can be aware of Time yet take no notice of it.

~*~

Andrin laughed and woke. Seated on the bed, facing him, was an old woman.

She was as brown and wrinkled as a walnut shell; tall and sturdy-looking, the wrinkled flesh of her face and hands dense with vigor. She wore a short-sleeved tunic of green and a long skirt of blue tied around her thick waist with a drawstring of woven black and red. Her white hair was pinned on top of her head. Around her neck was a necklace of gold in the shape of a dragon.

"Grandmoder…," said Andrin.

"Good morning, Dumpling," said the old woman, in that whispery lilt Andrin had become accustomed to hearing from a dragon's lips. She stood, and Andrin sat up.

"Thank you for the story," Andrin said.

"Aren't you going to ask me what it meant?"

"Did it mean anything?"

Andrin's grandmother laughed, the skin around her deep brown eyes crinkling, her white teeth flashing. "You do learn." She rumpled the old man's white hair. "Time to get up."

Andrin took her hand and held it next to his own.

"I'm as old as you are," he said.

"But I'm still your grandmother. Time to get up." She patted Andrin on the cheek and turned away. "I'll put breakfast on the table."

Andrin slid out of bed and carried his trousers outside with him. Chandler woke with a flurry as the door opened, and he waited for her. When he came back with the smells of sun and wind and water and crushed greenery surrounding him, the table was set for two. Plain fare: brown bread and cheese and butter and fruit.

"You haven't asked me why I'm here this morning," Verrina beren Unna said. "You haven't asked me why I appear in my old form today."

"Is there a reason?"

"There is. The time you've longed for is nearly here."

"What time?"

"The time of the fall of Sarpa. The return of Onagros to power. The return of Onagros to the true Way. Disorder has ruled long enough. Now the flood recedes, the stone settles back into the mountain. Harmony is about to shake itself; to rid itself of those who would bridle it and bend it to their wills."

"You sound as if it matters," said Andrin, surprised. "The path doesn't care who treads it, or who leaves it, either. What interest does a Spirit have in the affairs of Time?"

Verrina beren Unna chuckled. "I'm only immortal, not Spirit. The people weep, and I can taste their tears. I ride the crest of the Way, and do what I can as I pass. As you say, the path has no attachment to the travelers, nor is it to blame when those who stray from it tumble to their ruin. But I am attached to this land and these people; I wait in patience, but I rejoice when the time comes to act. You must leave this place – go back into the stream of time. Are you ready?"

Andrin felt a tingle in his blood, as if he were entering a dream that promised ventures and discoveries and nothing worse at the end but an awakening. In a far corner, he found the rest of the clothes he had worn from the castle. He put on his boots, and the tunic which had once had "Liar" painted on the back of it. Years of washing had faded the word away.

"I'm ready."

He squinted against sudden sunlight. He stood outside, in the clearing by the river. His cottage and garden were gone. In their place sat a light, two-wheeled cart; his kettle, cold and empty; an ebony box, open to show the casting stones it held; and his sleeping pallet, rolled around bundles of aromatic herbs. Blinking, he turned in a complete circle: the fruit trees that had embraced the clearing had been replaced by ten large books with leather bindings. Chandler, his hen, sat placidly near one of the books and pecked at the cover.

Here were all the things he had brought with him from the castle ten liquid years ago.

"Here are all your treasures," said his grandmother. "Take as much as you will."

Andrin walked from one item to another, caressing the surfaces, delighting in the variations of textures. Then he picked up Chandler and tucked her gently beneath his arm.

"My 'treasures' were more useful as a cottage," he said. "But a friend can't be left behind."

The books became trees again; the cart, a wattle-and daub cottage; the casting stones became a chimney. The ebony box, Andrin presumed, was once again a table, the kettle once more on the hearth.

"I'll keep your cottage for you," Andrin's grandmother said. "If the Way brings you back to it, you'll find it as you left it. If the Way leads you elsewhere, I'll know it."

"Thank you, Grandmoder," said the old Waymaster. He embraced her, one-armed, and kissed her soft cheek.

She cocked her head, as if assessing him. "What troubles you?"

"Biddi. She was always one to speak her mind. Landry has pretended tolerance for the little servants of Onagros, but if he should turn on them.... Biddi is one of the first he'd seize, I think. I'm afraid for her."

"Where would you like her to be? Here?"

He thought of the woman, her auburn hair turning to silver, her doll's-mouth set in scorn at weaker spirits. "Yes, here."

"Fetch her, then. Do you dare go into Kudasad, into the shadow of the castle tower, and fetch her?"

"I do."

"And her companion, Nerissa beren Matka? She's an old acquaintance of yours."

Andrin recalled no Nerissa beren Matka, and could tell from the twinkle in his grandmother's eye that meeting Biddi's companion would be more an unfolding than a reunion. In another life he would have protested, would have demanded to be given an answer. Now he merely put Chandler down and said, "All right."

"Your path may not lead directly to your friend, or straight from her to here."

"It goes where it goes."

Verrina smiled. "Give Nerissa a message from me. Tell her Grandmoder sends her love. Tell her the pearl was well used. Tell her to take Chandler's eggs and use whatever comes out."

"I will," said Andrin, his eyes on the hen, so intent on her he wasn't aware when his grandmother disappeared.

He carried Chandler to the road, where he stood, drinking in the sights and sounds of human traffic as a man might drink wholesome wine after a fast. He felt just as intoxicated as such a man, too. He could feel himself grinning like a simpleton.

Chandler twisted, and flapped out of his arms. He chased her across the path of a pair of horsemen bound toward the city, past a puppet show kiosk, and into a ditch. He wondered if it were the ditch into which he had thrown his razor so many years ago, if it was his fate to now retrieve it. Then he remembered the vision child whom he had, at his grandmother's insistence, directed to it. Grandmoder had sent a message to Biddi by that vision. Now she was sending a message to someone else by him.

Slight messages, both of them, masking power. They had all been like that, all the messages he had received of her these ten years. Subtle but inarguable, like the flow of the tide. Her last one, for instance, that his way to Biddi might be roundabout.

"I'm not chasing you anymore," he told the hen. "I'll follow you without snatching, but could we please walk on the road? I prefer dust to ditchwater."

Obligingly, Chandler flapped onto the highway and Andrin clambered after her, a parade of two into and through the streets of the capital.

Nothing had changed in Kudasad in the ten years he had been gone. Nothing superficial. But there was a new manner in the people, an odd manner, at once furtive and defiant, like a subterranean fire about to rupture rock into flame.

Chandler led the way to Broad Street, past the open door of a scrivener's, and through the scrivener's courtyard arch.

"We're on private property," Andrin observed, not surprised to find Chandler unimpressed. The hen crossed the cobbles and ushered herself into the garden beyond, where she settled under the shade of a stand of rhubarb. No one burst from the manor, shouting and shooing, so he entered the garden himself, his calloused soles unmindful of the gravel paths he wandered. A bee hummed, a lizard sunned on a wall, a hummingbird chitted and zizzed. A somewhat disreputable-looking tortoiseshell cat lolled on a patch of marjoram and eyed Chandler speculatively. Andrin, having seen Chandler rout a pack of stray mongrels, abandoned the cat to its fate. Bemused by this haven, Andrin explored the vegetables, the flowers, the herbs, and admired the bee-busy skeps tucked into their niches in the back wall of the manor.

A small woman, graying braids looped behind her ears, appeared at the garden's courtyard entrance. Sunlight flashed from her spectacles as she bent and spoke, inaudibly from where Andrin stood in shadow, to the resting hen. The cat mewed loudly and leaped onto the low wall between the vegetables and the flowers. The woman's regard followed his leap, and she started at the sight of a stranger deep within her garden.

"You like chickens?" Andrin asked, threading the paths back toward where she stood, straightened and dignified.

"I thought it was somebody I know." She flushed. "…I mean…. Never mind."

There was a breathless pause as Andrin felt himself on ground long lost, as he knew with the certainty of the sun's heat, the shade's relief, that this woman could be trusted.

"You are Devrina beren…. I'm sorry, I don't have your name. You came to the bailey with your husband when he was invested as Deputy Roll-Keeper of Layounna ten years ago. I was Royal Waymaster then."

"Andrin ber –" the woman stopped herself and glanced furtively around. She stepped closer, then spoke again, quietly. "Andrin beren Tooli. They say Landry had you killed. Of course, they also say you flew over the castle palisade in a cart pulled by…a chicken…."

"Her name is Chandler. And yours, again?"

"Devona. Devona beren Valda. Wife of Darcy, who is now Chief Roll-Keeper of the Realm."

"Ah. And Gilbert? The old Chief?"

Devona said nothing.

"Dead in truth, or in rumor?"

"In truth."

"Ah."

Devona absently placed a hand on the cat's head. It stiffened. They gave one another narrow looks. Devona slowly removed her hand and the cat forbore to bite her. All this was done in so practiced a manner, it was clearly what passed for affection between them. "Where have you been, all this time, Master Andrin?"

"I've been… in retreat."

"And now you're back. For a purpose?"

"So I believe. I'm not yet sure of what it is. By and by, I must go to the castle."

Devona shook her head so hard her spectacles slipped down her nose. She pushed them back with an irritated forefinger. "They're mad up there. They took my daughter as a bride for Landry. They –" She stopped.

"Your daughter is Consort?"

Devona shook her head again, slowly. "She escaped. But they claim she's still in the castle. They want me to pretend I visit her, as my husband pretends, to swear she's well and happy."

"But you will not."

The scrivener's mouth formed a thin but inflexible line. "I will say or do nothing in aid of Those People."

"Then, may a renegade beg your hospitality? Water, bread, perhaps a dollop of honey? A scattering of hay to sleep on in your stable?"

"Of course. Of course! If you aren't afraid you might be discovered."

Andrin laughed, surprising both of them. He raised a helpless open palm. "If I am, I am. Aren't you afraid you'll be discovered harboring me?"

Devona gazed across the gardens to the herbs, to the shielding wall, to the bees who listened to confessions as the sun went down. "The only thing I fear is that my husband will claim we trapped you for Landry."

The Waymaster waited for Devona to turn, for their gazes to lock. Then he said, "If I'm discovered here, let him claim my capture. I'll swear to it." Devona opened her mouth and drew breath, but Andrin shook his head. "If I'm taken, I couldn't bear for you to suffer by your charity to me. Promise?"

After a moment's obvious struggle, Devona said, "I promise."

Sunset that night was azure and golden, like a sea misted with blessing. Andrin felt filled, topped and overflowing. He had gone from Royal Waymaster of the Realm to homeless beggar, and his riches were almost more than his spirit could contain.

chapter 4
The smith of kudasad

Trahern rode with Guthrie beren Melanell, to the Chief Sword's right and a little behind. Guthrie never urged Trahern to keep even, never turned to make sure the smith was still with him. Assurance was in his posture, in the set of his head, in the one-quarter view of his expression Trahern could see.

The sun shone relentlessly; Trahern's bald pate was hot, even beneath the hat of blue cotton he wore to protect it. Guthrie's head was uncovered, the sun turning the red of his hair into glowing copper.

The smith felt a little dizzy, and not only from the heat. What was he doing, in this strange land of Layounna? In two days' riding, he was sick of the weird, folded landscape and over-lush vegetation, of the water sitting about everywhere in unguarded pools and ponds, streams of it glinting in the distance, the Fiddlewood grown to unthinkable size beside their road. The clothing here was different – slightly, just enough to be disconcerting. The food Guthrie beren Melanell had bought them along their way had been different in taste and texture – different meats, different vegetables, flavored with different herbs. He had enjoyed the novelty the first day; now, he began to long for a bit of familiar bread. It was one thing to spend a week in Granitz, surrounded by the babble and flash of a dozen countries' languages and looks. Trahern found immersion in a foreign culture much more difficult to bear.

It would be a hard thing, dying so far from home. And he supposed he would die – it seemed the most likely outcome. He could make this bit and bridle Guthrie's Lady asked for, but whether it would suit her – whether power entered into the piece – he could no more control that than he could pull a cloud between himself and the sun. If he failed, would Guthrie's Lady let him live? Would she let him live if he succeeded? Trahern doubted it, in either case.

He would die, and what would happen then? So much water about, yet these people burned their dead, he had heard, without so much as a handful of mud to float a soul to the Safe Haven. Well, perhaps Guthrie would trouble to spit on his victim's corpse, and do him a favor by chance.

Now they were nearing a large town, if increase in traffic were any guide. They passed a stand of trees, and a bridge came into view.

Guthrie led Trahern delicately through the maze of people and conveyances, across the bridge and along the winding road beyond.

Trahern was surprised at Guthrie's consideration for the simple folk; he would have expected the Chief Sword to rise in his stirrups and shout, "Kinninger's business! Move aside!" or simply ride down anyone in his way. Then the smith realized Guthrie was making no fuss because he had been ordered not to. This bringing, and the making that was to follow, were not to be noised about. Not that the Emir would care for the disappearance of so unimportant a subject as a smith…even a smith whose goods had found royal favor more than once. Whatever use Guthrie's Lady had for this bit and bridle, it was her own people who mustn't know of it

Trahern wondered if he could break away and seek shelter somewhere – lie hidden and escape, as Brady and Elsie had done. He wove a sudden fantasy of finding Elsie's mother, of telling her what he knew of her daughter's whereabouts, of her helping him escape – To what? Guthrie would find him at his forge. He would have to leave, leave the forest he loved, leave the custom he'd spent his life building.

And could he, even if he were willing? Could he escape this current that held him in its rush? He suspected he could not. Something was moving in this part of the world, for good or ill or both or neither – it was moving. He was part of it, and must move with it or be dashed to bits.

He thought again of the lantern he'd left burning when he'd left his smithy for Granitz. Who had followed it? Were they there now, waiting for him, or had whoever-it-was been meant to come to an empty house, Trahern's absence part of the baffling pattern?

The smith shrugged behind Guthrie's back. Matka Hayat knew, perhaps; her poor smith did not.

Ahead lay Kudasad. Above the rooftops fluttered the pennants of the castle, Sarpa's red and gold device, snapping like lions hunting in the sun.

Trahern birn Matka stood uneasily in the center of the Great Hall, his hat limp in his hands.

Guthrie had hailed a Sword on the palisade, ordering him to send runners to Thane Oliva and Kinninger Landry Oliva beren Ada, telling them he had returned. No word about the smith, as if word of Guthrie's return were the same as word of his success. They had stopped at the stables to leave their horses and to wash away the worst of the travel-dust. Then Guthrie had led Trahern up the motte's steep wooden walkway and within the upper palisade, up the stairs and into the tower itself.

Rushes covered the floor of the Great Hall. The wall opposite the door was hung with a banner almost as large as the wall itself bearing Sarpa's device: Red, with a golden lion on his hind feet, looking back over his shoulder, his blue claws and blue curly tongue extended. Four ornately carved chairs stood empty on a slightly raised dais before that banner.

A door opened, and a tall dark man came through and held the door wide for those behind him. Guthrie sank to one knee, motioning Trahern to follow. Grudgingly, Trahern knelt.

A man came in first. He was slim, of average height, but carried himself with arrogant grace. His black hair hung straight and long, locks on either side of his olive face bound with jeweled gold. Next came an elderly woman, small but still vigorous, judging by her walk. A younger woman came last, pretty enough, if one fancied dangerous creatures.

The man must be Landry Oliva beren Ada. From the little Kinnan had said, Trahern surmised the older woman was His Grace's mother. The younger woman would be Corvina, Landry's sister.

Landry seated himself, speaking before the women were settled. "Rise, Thane Guthrie. Join us."

The seat to Landry's right was empty. Guthrie beren Melanell took it, leaving Trahern alone on his knees.

The man who had held the door took up a position behind Landry and to his left.

"My Lord," said the older woman, "will you order the smith to rise?"

"As you wish, Moder." Landry motioned with one of his delicate hands, and Trahern stood.

Landry's mother smiled in a way Trahern sensed meant bad luck for someone. "Welcome, smith. I am Thane Oliva beren Audre, mother of the Kinninger. It was by my order you were asked to come here."

Trahern said nothing. He had picked up a smattering of Layounnan in Granitz; enough to follow this, but not enough to reply in suitable terms.

The tall man spoke in Kozabiri: "Do you know our language?"

"A little, Great Master."

The man's lips twitched. "I am no Great Master. I am Rhu beren Robia, His Grace's Chamberlain." In Layounnan, he told the others, "He understands, if you speak slowly and simply."

Thane Oliva smiled a very minor thanks, her attention still on the smith. "Have you been told what's wanted?"

"A bit and bridle, Lady." He doubted the simple title was proper, but it was the only one he knew. The tall man who spoke Kozabiri could have corrected him, he was sure, but no correction came.

"A special bit and bridle. Can you do it?"

"I can make a bit and bridle, Lady. Only the power can make it special, and I don't control that."

"You will do your best?"

"Yes, Lady."

"Very well. I'll show you to your new smithy." Oliva stood. "This way." She passed him with her head high. "Rhu, you will not be needed."

"I'll come," said the younger woman.

The smithy was small. There were shutters to the window and a door with upper and lower panels that could be connected or opened independently. There was a low bed in one corner, a washbasin on a stand, a chamber pot beneath. A small brick forge stood a little away from the other corner, a bin of charcoal beside it. In the center of the room were a worktable, a large wooden anvil, a press, and a polisher/grinder powered by footpedal. Shelves held small wooden anvils, racks of wooden tools, graphite-and-clay melting pots, and a coil of silver. Bricks of different sizes and thicknesses stood in stacks, in case he needed to make molds. An oilcloth-wrapped lump – probably clay for lining the chiseled hollows before he filled them – lay on the table.

"Where is the steel for the bit?" he asked in halting Layounnan.

"There is no steel. There must be no steel or iron of any kind in here. This bit must be dainty and highly ornamented, and it must be made of pure silver."

"I work in iron–"

"You will work in silver."

"A silver bit would be too soft. Especially pure –" He stopped protesting. The Lady's face told him she knew what she was asking.

She nodded at his silence. "If there is anything here you lack, you have only to ask. Tell the servant who brings your food you have a message for me, and I'll come to you myself. Say nothing to anyone of what you do here. Give no one a message to carry, except that you need to speak to me. Do you understand?"

Trahern nodded.

"Begin as soon as you can. Work as quickly as possible without bruising the power. Serve the crown well in this, and your reward will be great. Serve us ill, and…." Oliva didn't finish. Her eyes, and the mahogany eyes of her daughter, finished for her.

~*~

Three days passed while Trahern approached his project. He had never attempted to craft anything wondrous – it had happened, or it had not. He had no notion of how to go about it; indeed, he hardly knew whether he wanted to. Nothing could be done quickly, anyway. The unfamiliar tools, the unaccustomed material, the outlandish graphite-and-clay melting pots – they all had to be tried and mastered.

And every day, he moved more slowly. Every day, he thought with more difficulty.

Trahern had never been ill before, and his weakness would have frightened him if he had had strength enough for fright. Was it some sickness carried to him by the Layounnans? He had felt well enough until his journey here had begun. Then he had noticed a faint queasiness, then an irregular twinge of nausea, but he had blamed it on the peculiar food.

He sat up, now, fully clothed, having gone to bed that way the night before. *Waves…. Like waves, rolling through me, over my head. Foul… The stink of it sickens me….* All sound was muffled, all colors dimmed into shades of gray. Trahern was unused to thinking of spiritual matters, but now he wondered if his distress might be a response to taking this commission. He had done little toward fulfilling it; he certainly felt better not working on the silver bit than he did working on it.

"Tortoise help me." He lifted a heavy hand to the plate by his pallet and brushed the food onto the stone floor. He tipped over the wooden cup, spilling what was left of his ale. "Offering to you, Tortoise," he whispered. "Help me."

~*~

Biddi beren Anna knocked at the smithy door. Whatever secret this smith worked in silver, it was for Oliva, so Biddi wished bad luck to it. The frown on her face was less for the work, though, than from concern for the man. He was good and decent – anyone could see that – and she had taken him under her wing when she brought his first meal. Now he was ill. Three full days he had been in his forge, and every day he ate less. Every day he spoke more softly. Every day his skin had less color and less life.

She barely heard his reply to her knock.

Biddi entered and put her basket on the table. "Still ailing, Master Trahern? The shutter still up, and the door still shut, and the fire still banked? And you've spilled your food – ate none of it, looks like, just knocked it over. What's wrong?"

"I don't know. Contagion. Feel it?" He struggled to express himself in Layounnan, for Biddi knew no other language. "Smell it?"

"No." Biddi looked at the tower wall forming the fourth side of the forge. "But I know where it's coming from. You sit here and drink some of this broth, if you can. I'll see what I can do."

Trahern raised a hand. "Stop. I have something for you. Made it yesterday. Not for her. For you."

A malicious smile broke through Biddi's grim look; three days, and the man had managed to do nothing for Oliva's plan, whatever it might be.

"Here." Trahern handed Biddi a disk of silver, the back carved with crescent moons, the front polished to perfect smoothness. "The power is in that piece. I feel it. Look into it." His voice weakened and faded to a whisper as he said, "It will show you the face of a true friend."

"Andrin...." Biddi looked. It wasn't Andrin who looked back, but the Chamberlain. "Rhu! But he...."

The smith rested his head on his hand, his elbow on the table, and seemed to go to sleep.

Biddi touched his shoulder. Slowly, he opened his eyes.

"Thank you, Trahern. I'll help you. I'll do something."

Trahern nodded and Biddi left, tucking her mirror into a pocket of her skirt.

She found Rhu beren Robia in the storeroom, giving orders to a group of villeins. His rough-cut black hair had been evened by the castle barber, but it was still shockingly short. Biddi bit her lips. Her fault. She touched the mirror through her skirt. How cruel she had been that day. After that interview with Oliva, how he must have needed a kind word – how it must have cost him to ask for one! – and she had spat contempt and left him with his spirit raw and bleeding.

The villeins left. Rhu turned to Biddi, his expression as closed as the smithy's shutter.

"I'm sorry!" Biddi blurted. "I'm sorry. I wronged you. Rhu, I'm so sorry."

If Rhu had any reaction, he kept it hidden.

"I came to tell you the new silversmith is ill. He's very ill, but I don't think it's of the body. His smithy is right above Thane Oliva's temple. I think her nastiness is poisoning him, somehow. Whatever it may be, I can't tell her. She knows what I think of her precious Tarkastrian Arts; she'll think I'm inventing it. But he's ill! Dying, surely! Can you help him?"

Rhu nodded. "I'll speak to her. She doesn't want him dead, or he wouldn't have come here alive."

A word from Rhu, spoken against Sarpa! This was something Biddi had never thought to hear. Suddenly, without meaning to, she began to weep. "Please say you forgive me! Andrin keeps telling me –" She stopped with a gasp, then spoke again, deliberately. "Now you know something Thane Oliva would like to hear. I've known where Andrin is all this time. I don't believe you'll tell her."

"I haven't, and I won't. I saw Andrin, myself, the day I returned from the hunt. …Stumbled on his cottage and stayed for dinner. He told me then that you visited him."

"You could have told her…?"

Rhu nodded again.

Biddi sniffed deeply and her tears trickled to a stop. "I *am* sorry!"

One corner of Rhu's mouth twitched up and his eyes came alive again. "Forgiven," he said. "I'll see what I can do for your smith."

"What is it, Chamberlain?" Oliva had agreed to see him in a small room off the Great Hall. Now she sat, leaving him standing.

"It's the new smith, My Lady."

Oliva sat a little straighter, and lowered her lids a trifle more. "What of him?"

"He sickens, My Lady. The girl who carries his meals says he eats less by the day, and looks and sounds weaker."

Oliva looked away from the Chamberlain, pondering this news. She came to the same conclusion as Biddi, though she didn't couch her conclusion in quite the same terms. As the powers of Corvina's art and the alicorn had struggled for supremacy, so the power wielded by the smith was struggling with Oliva's, and the smith was losing. This was not what Oliva had had in mind, at all.

"Anything else?"

"No, My Lady."

She dismissed the Chamberlain with a flick of her fingers.

What to do? Move the smithy, after all? Or…. Perhaps Corvina can think of something….

~*~

"Guthrie beren Melanell would never secure the unicorn without some Artful Device," said Oliva to her daughter. "If anyone can fashion one, this smith can do it. But he can't work if he's weak or dead, nor do I want him distanced from me. Can I have what I want – all that I want? Or must I choose which I want the most?"

Corvina held up a hand, nodding to show she heard, running over her powders and syrups in her mind. She played various properties and combinations over and tried them against the feel of the problem her mother had given her. Then she smiled. "I may have an answer. If it works, you will have all as you wish it. And what will I have? Pride in having served My Lord Brother?"

"Always that, of course." Oliva smiled slyly, just mother to daughter. "And this: If Guthrie can catch or kill the unicorn, we will have the skin and horn and blood. Landry wants the horn and the blood. You've had all the alicorn you care for, I take it."

"Yes." Corvina thought of the chip now hidden in an alabaster bottle in her workroom.

"Landry has granted me the hide." Oliva sat a little forward. "Unicorn flesh decays to nothing in minutes after the creature's death. Unicorn blood turns to powder."

Corvina looked blank for two blinks of an eye, then she laughed. "Some of the powder will cling to the inside of the skin."

"I'll unroll it and scrape the powder into a jar for you – best if you don't touch it."

Corvina shuddered, remembering the nausea and pain of contact with the alicorn.

"Everything is falling into place for us – for our House," said Oliva. "Tarkastrus shows the way to glory, and Tortoise himself serves our needs." She tapped Corvina's wrist with one admonitory finger. "But it turns on this: Can you invigorate the smith long enough for him to do his work?"

"I can."

~*~

"Did you tell her?" Biddi caught the Chamberlain by the elbow as he passed in the courtyard.

He frowned down at her. "I did."

"What's wrong? What did she say? Did she… speak to you the way she did… after the hunt? Oh, Rhu, tell me I didn't send you to that!"

He shook his head, and the frown lessened. "No, she was interested – even concerned, though she tried to hide it. But…. I had thought she would give me orders to… oh, to make different arrangements for the smith's housing, or to send to Kozabir for his native foods or hire a Kozabirian cook for him –" he shrugged, "– something." He shook his head again. "She dismissed me with curt thanks. I wonder if she's deciding what to do or if she's decided; if she's given someone else her orders. I wonder what orders she might have given, and to whom."

Biddi glared at the base of the tower, as if the force of her contempt could topple it. "She's giving orders to that pet god of hers, that Tortoise. If I believed that Tarkastrian gibberish, I'd offer him a sacrifice of my own."

"What would you have him do?" Rhu asked, bemused.

"I'd have him spit in her eye, that's what."

Rhu very nearly smiled. "That's hardly likely to happen. Neither you nor I would be willing to outdo Thane Oliva's bloodletting." He put a finger beneath Biddi's chin and scrutinized the face she raised to him. "I don't think you've developed a taste for that kind of thing, have you, Biddi?"

The maid remembered the birds Thane Oliva had taken from her hands and Janet's report of their condition after Oliva's ministrations. "No. Thane Oliva is welcome to her rites, and much good may they do her."

A churl called to the Chamberlain from across the yard. Rhu waved to show he heard.

"We've done what we could," he said to Biddi. "Now we can only wait."

"As always," she muttered to his back.

~*~

He vaguely heard the door to the smithy open.

A touch on the side of his neck, like the touch of an eel – Trahern jerked upright, eyes wide.

The young woman from the tower stood before him, lit by what sun the closed shutters couldn't keep out. She held a steaming cup in one hand. She spread her full lips in what seemed to be a smile, though her dark eyes were cold.

"We were never introduced." Her voice was like oil. "I am Corvina beren Oliva, the Kinninger's sister. Can you say, 'Corvina'?"

It took Trahern some moments to translate this speech, his wits had grown so dull. "Corvina."

She held out the cup. "I've brought you something. A healthful broth. We heard you weren't well."

Trahern didn't move, but his eyes dropped from her face to her hands and the cup they held.

"Please drink it." Her voice sounded muffled. "You'll feel much better, I promise you."

Trahern mustered his thoughts as best he could. They couldn't mean to poison him with his work undone. They must want him well and useful. So this must be a healing drink. So he should drink it. He nodded as well as he could, but was unable to raise his hands to take the cup.

"I'll put it to your lips." Corvina beren Oliva tipped a little of the warm brew into Trahern's mouth.

Convulsively, he swallowed. He closed his eyes again, feeling strength ease tentatively into his muscles.

"Ready for another sip?" Her voice was a little clearer now.

Trahern nodded and took a deep drink. He opened his eyes and looked around with new interest. The world had color again. The woman before him had a delicate olive tone to her skin. Her eyes were lustrous and dark. Her hair….

Trahern took the cup from her hands, hands delicate as porcelain, the nails like translucent shells, and drank again. Her hair hung in thick black braids on either side of her face, frothing behind in a blue-black mass, glinting in the sunbeams like stars in a midnight summer sky.

"Finish it." Corvina's voice was warm, but not as warm as the look in her almond eyes. That voice – those eyes – they made his heart sing as it had never sung before.

Trahern drained the cup and handed it back, trembling as her hands lingered on his.

"Now you feel better, don't you?" his darling asked, her voice like honey.

"Yes."

"You'll make this bit and bridle for me? A lure to draw and hold a unicorn? It must be exquisite and almost fragile. Nothing else will be strong enough."

"I'll work with all my heart." He felt easy in his body again, easy in his mind. Even the barbarous Layounnan language came smoothly to his tongue. "I'll start on the bit right away. The bridle must be made of silk, dyed in five colors: red, yellow, black, green, and blue, five threads of one color twisted into a strand, five strands of each woven into a rope. Do you have such silk?"

"Yes."

"It must be made by five maidens, who must not speak as they work. If one speaks, she must be killed and another must take her place, all without a word. Can this be done?"

"Yes."

"Then you'll have what you want. The metal work must be right – I'll know when it is – and then the engraving must be just so. The bridle rope will take time."

"The maidens will work without stopping. If their fingers bleed with it, I daresay maiden's blood will increase the attraction."

Corvina left and Trahern began his task.

~*~

Still hoping to see Andrin, Biddi tucked herself into a quiet spot in one of the poultry houses and took out the mirror Trahern had given her. She polished it on her skirt and looked into it. The mirror still didn't show her the Waymaster; this time, it showed Trahern as she had seen him last; weak and ill. He looked up, as if someone had spoken to him. His lips formed the word "Corvina." His color freshened, his eyes brightened, he drew himself straight – and he faded from the shining surface, leaving it blank.

Biddi threw the mirror to the floor and growled, "Corvina! Worst of luck to you! Waste and loss to you! May your plans run foul and your hopes run dry!" She spat toward the empty mirror and bolted out, leaving it in the droppings and dirty straw.

~*~

Evening came, and the smith worked on, the glow from his small forge shining through his unshuttered window. He had eaten everything Biddi had brought him at noon and in the evening. He must be at his best and strongest and most alert – this work was for *her*, and he must not compromise it by neglecting his body. The girl who brought the food, he did neglect. He ate because it was his duty. It was not part of his duty to waste time with a kitchen maid. He ignored her chatter and shrugged off her idiotic concern. He was well and he was working. Was that cause for tears?

The open window darkened, forge-light spilling out in a red-gold fan. Trahern stretched and forced himself to rest. His body was tired; it would be best to stop for the night. As he turned to the window, a shape fluttered to a perch on the opening.

It was a bird with a tail of five long feathers. Its body was an unhealthy white, with a sheen to it like the trail of a slug. It opened its beak and poured out a vile string of noise that grated on Trahern's ears.

"Stop it!" The smith advanced on the window, hands flapping to frighten the disgusting creature. "Go! Shoo! Off!"

The bird stayed where it was until Trahern's hands actually smacked it off its perch. It caught the air as it fell, and flitted away. Trahern slammed up the shutter and fastened it in place.

CHAPTER 5
THE MASTER'S CURSE

After Elsie and Kinnan's clash, Moder sent Brady to the goat shed to catch up on lost sleep. She harnessed Layounna's heir by right of mandate to a plow and set the heir by right of birth to follow him, breaking ground for another strip of garden. None of the three objected.

Amused, Salali made a Nishian gesture of obeisance, running her right thumb from her hairline to the tip of her nose. "And I? What would you have me do?"

Moder raised an eyebrow. "Do whatever you do. You haven't come to me for help – Have you?"

"…I?" Salali's slight frown was puzzled, troubled. "I have no need of help."

"Your heart's desire is within grasping distance, isn't that right? How long have you sought it? Since before you saw Master Mandate, I think."

Salali met Moder's steady gaze. Flames of understanding flickered in the Nishite's eyes, then were gone.

"I thank you for your interest, but I have no need of help."

Moder shrugged. "And I have no need of service."

So the trinket woman left the cottage door open, and unshuttered the windows. She spread her pack on the table and, in the light of day, fashioned baubles for the market place.

When Brady rose for a midday bite of bread and cheese, Kinnan tried to talk of plans and stratagems.

Moder Zglaria tapped Kinnan on the shoulder as she passed behind him. "Not now, Young Master. We've no time for war councils today. We have seeds to plant."

"But it's nearly Midsummer!"

"If you want food in the fall, you plant in midsummer."

Kinnan and his new-found niece went back to the plow, and Moder directed Brady to pick stones from the turned earth.

For the rest of the day, Kinnan seemed under a spell of silence. He couldn't – or wouldn't – speak at all, if he couldn't speak his mind. That night, though, in the freedom of the goat shed, the spell broke. "Now do you see, Brady? Do you see the justice of my cause? Now that you know what Landry is capable of doing?"

"I'm more likely to back you now that I know what your sister Karol was capable of."

"Then you–"

"I've had all day to think. This is as far as I've gotten: My mistress, Devona, risked her life to get Elsie out of Kudasad. She trusted me to do that. Kinninger or no Kinninger, I can't take Elsie back there. Can't take her, lead her, or advise her to go. If you want to risk your life – well, I'd rather you didn't. But as far as I'm concerned, Elsie stays here or goes on to Kozabir as arranged."

"Elsie might not agree to that."

"She might not. It isn't as if she's ever listened to anything I had to say before. This time, she might."

Kinnan was not displeased. Let her stay here. Let him lead the people to freedom and then see who they wanted to rule them. "If Elsie would stay safely here, would you come with me and tell your story and Elsie's–"

"*No!*"

Kinnan looked shocked at the violence in the word. Brady controlled his anger and said, "I'm sorry. I didn't make it clear: My mistress risked her life to send Elsie away. If I tell my story and Elsie's, I expose Devona and Darcy, don't you see? Now, Darcy may deserve it, I don't say he doesn't, but I will not put my mistress in jeopardy, not for any number of Royals. I won't. If there's something I can do that doesn't threaten her, let me know, but I won't do this."

He would discuss the matter no more.

"Sleep on it," Kinnan said.

Brady turned his back and hunched a shoulder into his blanket. He didn't expect to sleep, certainly not to sleep deeply. He lay wide-eyed for some time until, without an awareness of transition, he was dreaming.

He stood on the bank of Fiddlewood River in the rain. He looked for Kinnan but he knew, as one knows in a dream, that Kinnan was out of reach. He heard thrashing at the water's edge. Although no one had been there an instant ago, now Moder Zglaria stood ankle-deep in mud, struggling to free herself, tearing out clods of muddy earth and digging at the eroding bank with her blackthorn stick.

A sense of evil and danger pulled his gaze upward. A man of unclear shape and visage crouched on a limb above Moder's head, ready to drop on her and, Brady knew, to kill her.

Why was she so desperate? In his dream, Brady was disappointed to see Moder suffering from the fear of death, just like an ordinary person. Then he saw the woman from his dreams, the hem of her embroidered tunic foul with mud, struggling at Moder's side. She showed no fear, though; she had an arm around the old woman's shoulder, wrapping her in her palla as if cloth could ward off the man's intent. Moder, Brady realized, was trying to get away because the maiden would never leave her to her fate; only her own escape would save her defender.

The young woman cried out, "There you are! Come here! Come here! Oh, help me! I don't know what to do!"

"I know!" Brady said.

Before he took two steps, a man stood between him and the women. Not the man from the tree. This man was tall and thick with muscle, from his matted black hair to his broad flat feet. He scowled, and even his tangled mustache and beard seemed to block Brady's way. He was bare from the waist up, except for a baggy vest.

Brady knew him at once. "Tartarus!" He wasn't sure if he were happy to see his old master again, angry for his desertion, or frightened at his sudden reappearance. He only knew he had to get past him.

Tartarus moved when Brady moved, throwing out a sinewy arm to stop his advance. "Leave them alone. It has nothing to do with you."

"Yes, it does! The old one took me up where you left me, and the young one haunts my dreams."

"She can't haunt you till she's dead. If you like being haunted, stay where you are. As for the old one.... Let her be."

"I have to help them!" Brady dodged, but the other man was faster.

"Stay out of it! Didn't I teach you anything?"

"Yes!" Brady's mouth filled with insults to Tartarus' teaching, but he swallowed them when he remembered his strangest lesson.

In a blink, he had transformed into a dog and ducked past Tartarus' outstretched arms. Impossibly, Tartarus was before him and, with one swipe, knocked him back to his starting point. Brady lay breathless on his back, a man once more.

Tartarus opened his mouth and uttered a hiss so loud and deep it rumbled. His leathery skin was encased in leather armor of black and red-orange plates; his head was covered by a visored black helmet. Four brass rings hung from holes along the edge of the warrior's round shield.

Brady recovered his breath. He knew the figure before him was terrible and deadly, but he wasn't afraid. He was too desperate to be afraid.

Strategy.... He could make his own size match his opponent's – but the warrior could probably grow and strengthen, too. Not bigger, then. Brady vanished.

Not quite vanished.... A bee flew straight through the black visor; its target, the warrior's left eye.

A force stronger than the blow that had felled him earlier threw him back, again a man, groaning with the impact.

Tartarus replaced the warrior, filling Brady's vision. "Look at the mighty hero! He knows no fear." His face twisted with indignation and scorn. "Not afraid of me. Not afraid of anything, eh? Is that right? Not afraid of anything?" He shoved Brady with his foot – not a kick, just a contemptuous prod.

The sounds of the women's struggles disappeared, along with Fiddlewood. Brady lay on the beach below the shack he had shared with Tartarus during his training. Surf crashed on sand, and salty breeze mixed with dead fish in a rich blend of scent.

"Somewhere," his former master said, "there's something you fear. I don't know what it is – could be *you* don't know what it is – but it's out there. Somewhere, there's an evil so loathsome you don't even dare think about it directly." His grin showed his chisel-like teeth. "Go there." He threw his hands out toward Brady in a gesture of dismissal. "Go there!"

Brady covered his face with his arms, as if Tartarus' gesture were a physical blow. He cried out and wrenched himself awake.

The sound of surf became the screech of ravens, and sand changed to rocky soil. Salt air turned rank.

Opening his eyes, Brady found he was not in Moder's goat shed, where he had gone to sleep. He was lying on bare ground between a wooden palisade and a steaming compost heap. He stood. Beyond the heap he saw a fowl yard and coop, a kitchen garden, and more of the palisade enclosing a busy courtyard. In the middle of it all rose a wooden tower. Above the tower, a banner flapped in the morning breeze: a red banner with a yellow lion standing on its hind legs and looking over its shoulder. Tartarus had blindly sent him to the upper bailey of the castle in Kudasad, the stronghold of Landry Oliva beren Ada.

For a moment, while sleep fought with shock, Brady dithered. His first thought was escape. His second thought was, *How*? What if his old master had removed his shape-shifting ability? *But that was only a dream.* Yet he had gone to sleep in one place and was now most undoubtedly in another. That dream had been no mere dream, as his bruises and aches could testify.

Flight was quickest. A Brady-raven huddled between the palisade and the compost heap. It would take only a hop and a flap to lift him to freedom.

He couldn't move. No enchantment held him; he was immobilized by memory of his dream: Moder struggling so urgently, his dream-love bound to her in terror and peril, and danger crouching above them.

He had defied the tower willingly before, for his mistress. Now he had been given the chance to defy it again. Kinnan thought he needed public outrage to conquer Sarpa, but Kinnan was wrong. What he needed was information. He needed what Brady could give him and would never have volunteered for or agreed to. He needed a spy in the enemy camp.

The raven disappeared. In its place sat an extremely fluffy black cat. *The kitchen…. That's the heart of any rumor mill.*

Brady trotted across the courtyard, following the odors of burning wood, hot metal, and food. *Down those stairs.* He stepped into the stair-well, one eye cocked for violent objectors. A young girl, all bones and dirt, all her attention on a covered tray she held in both hands, came up as he padded down. Brady stepped aside for her, feeling an unexpected desire to arch his back and rub against her ankles.

The kitchen was a bubble of organized chaos. Brady tucked himself into a corner under a stool and reconnoitered. The large, boiled-looking woman with the fierce expression was probably the chief cook. Another woman, with faded auburn hair, sat at the nearest table.

"Now, Biddi," the cook said to the seated woman, "dip those blossoms in beaten egg white and then white sugar." Biddi nodded. In a quieter voice, the cook said, "Did you ever find out what he's doing?"

"Making something out of silver for Oliva, that's all I know."

"So what does My Lady Corvina have to do with it? Arvis said he saw Corvina take something in to him yesterday and, after she came out, the smith opened his shutter and went to work."

Biddi arranged a cluster of sugared flowers on a pewter plate. Her expression was grim, her voice dark. "I don't know what she did, Janet, but I know she did something. Now he eats, but he won't talk."

"No!" Janet's exclamation held more satisfaction than alarm, Brady thought, as if a taste for drama had been gratified. "If *she's* been at him, he's a lost man. Well, let the girl take him his food, then. The less we have to do with *her* creatures, the better off we'll be."

In a rare moment of silence, Brady heard a quiet step on the half-flight descending from the Great Hall. The cook and Biddi exchanged a look and suspended their conversation.

By craning his neck, Brady could see the stairs and Rhu beren Robia descending them. Brady thought the Chamberlain looked wearier than when he had greeted Landry's supposed bride, yet somehow more at peace. His hair had been cut short; Brady wondered if he had done it himself or if it were a punishment for something. *Elsie's disappearance?*

"They're nearly done with the roast and the eel purée," Rhu said. "I've told Albertus to serve them once around again, then clear away and bring in the vegetables and the pigeons with almond cream."

The cook nodded curtly, her head bent over a dish of stewed onions she was garnishing with celery tops. "They'll be wanting fresh trenchers, too." Janet counted and stacked half-loaves of hollowed bread onto a tray. She gestured to a cloth-covered trencher on a warming shelf beside the fireplace. "There's yours."

Biddi hopped to her feet. "I'll get it. Sit, Rhu. Eat something before you go back in."

"I will, thanks. And thank you, Janet."

As Rhu ate, he watched Biddi fashion strips of lemon peel into rosettes to decorate the platter of candied flowers. "Very nice. Let us do all we can to please My Lady Oliva."

Brady, an expert in the use of wry mockery, knew it when he heard it. *Landry's man is not so fond of Landry's mother…. That might be useful information.*

The child Brady had passed coming in stole down the steps, eyes widening at the sight of the big man at the table.

"Who's this?" Rhu's voice was gentle. "I don't believe I've met you before."

The girl stood silently, one dirty foot on top of the other, hands behind her back.

Janet laughed. "Nerissa beren Moder. Kitchen maid's assistant."

A parade of villeins came down the inner stairs, each carrying a tray loaded with picked-over food.

"They want you, sir," one of the men said.

"Thank you, Albertus."

Biddi sighed irritably. "I'll keep your food warm."

Brady considered trying to slide into the dining hall after Rhu, but the earlier talk of a making in silver intrigued him. Janet's first words to Nerissa decided him.

"Did you take that smith his tray?"

Brady settled under the stool again.

"Yes, Lady."

"I'm not 'Lady,' I'm Janet. Did he say anything?"

"No...Janet. He didn't seem to see me. He just took the tray and sat down."

Biddi nodded. "You see how it is. Corvina's got to him."

The cook shook a heavy finger at her. "Don't even think of meddling."

"Just leave him to it – to whatever *she* has planned?"

Janet leaned over the table and rapped, close to Biddi, with her rocky knuckles. "Leave it."

Biddi began quartering cheeses. She flushed, her chin thrust out in mute defiance.

Janet snapped her fingers at Nerissa. "Get one of those trays for Biddi to put the cheese on. Can you handle a knife? Help her do that, then. Wait a minute – wash your hands first, cheese shows every smudge. Our fine Sarpans can't eat cheese with dirt from a poor girl's hands on it, oh no."

Nerissa did as she was told. As she took her place next to Biddi, she caught sight of Brady. "Whose cat is that?"

"Where?" The cook followed the girl's gaze. "Where did that come from? Hairs in the food – whatever next?"

Brady, in true cat fashion, blinked and stared back.

"Better than what the mice have been leaving," Biddi said.

The cook grunted, her fists on her hips, her elbows sticking out. "True, supposing he deals with the mice and doesn't just lay around eating his head off."

Brady stretched insolently.

Biddi winked at the girl. "I'll throw him out."

"I can throw him out for myself – if the time comes I want him thrown out. This is still my kitchen, and liable to stay so, for all the chance there is of your stepping into my slippers. Put that trencher on the floor for him." She pointed to a bread-bowl rich with gravy and bone.

Nerissa gave Biddi a grin. She put the bowl on the floor, brushing against the cat and drawing quickly back, as if she expected a snap. Brady found himself purring and pressing himself against the skinny ankles. Delicately, he took mouthfuls of gravy-soaked bread and picked roast from ribs. When Nerissa swept cheese crumbs into her hand and added them to his dinner, he rubbed his head against her fingers.

Later, he dozed, one ear cocked for interesting tidbits, but nothing else was let fall.

The pudding was fished out of its boiling kettle, unwrapped, garnished, and sent in, followed by the cheese, fruit, and nuts.

Janet wiped her damp red face on her apron. "That's it, then; all but the cleaning up. Nerissa, go fetch that tray back from the smith's. Nice and quick."

Brady followed the girl up the kitchen stairs and around the corner. She turned and saw him and bent to stroke his back.

"You're the second cat I've met since I ran away from Isa and Barand. I like cats. I think cats like me. The other one did, though he tried to pretend he didn't. You like me, don't you?" She scratched Brady behind the ears. "Do you have a name? I'll call you…Rady. That means 'thunder,' because you're black as a storm cloud and you purr like thunder. Do you like that name? Rady?"

Brady couldn't understand himself. He'd been a cat before, and he'd never felt as if he'd like to curl up in somebody's lap and stay there for the rest of his life. And, yes, "Rady" did mean "Thunder" in Kozabiri, but why had she settled on that particular word, so close to his true name? He was still puzzling over it when he leaped onto the windowsill to have a look at this smith and found it was Trahern.

But it was not the Trahern Kinnan and Brady had left in Vatra. This Trahern was a stranger. The eyes he now turned on the girl hardly saw her. They didn't see the cat. They saw something else – this project of Oliva's?

There was a stench of sorcery in the little smithy, a foul feeling to the very air.

SHE's been at him, they said. Corvina's done something to him – bound him to her will in some way, for some purpose. So now…what am I going to do about it?

~*~

He did nothing for two days except watch and listen and think. He ate in the kitchen and slept in the women's dormitory, curled against Nerissa, feeling both safe and protective in their shared warmth. In that time, he learned that the smith was essential to some plan originating with Oliva, but not what that plan was. He learned that peace was being sought with Hayward and Sorcha, Rhu being dispatched to carry a letter to them. He learned that Rhu was not involved with the Sarpan machinations, but the Chief Sword was. He learned that the Sarpans were insensible of how they balanced on a razor's edge, oblivious to the enemy beneath their table and taking for granted the support of Oliva's Divine Master, Tortoise.

chapter 6
deceit

Corvina beren Oliva sat in her workroom before an embroidery frame. Any woman about to be married, even for a second time, has a great deal to prepare. A woman with Corvina's imperative had very special preparations to make. A new cloth, she had decided, to cover the marriage bed, would be effective and seemingly innocuous. She would embroider silken lozenges with fish, for fertility, and stuff the lozenges with comfrey, to strengthen her for child-bearing. These, she would sew to her side of the cloth. She would embroider other lozenges with pine trees, obscure symbol of an ancient god's unmanning, and stuff them with shredded black willow bark, to decrease a man's desire. These were for Guthrie's side of the bed.

Idly, Corvina ran through a catalog of the men she knew, gaging them as child-sires. None of them appealed to her, either personally or as breeding stock. Ah, well, let Moder or Landry choose, and she would accept – if the choice didn't displease her.

She stroked her belly, where a girl-child had grown until the baby-to-be had been beaten to death, still in the womb, where she should have been secure, should have been sheltered, beaten to death by the man Corvina had chosen as both husband and child-sire.

Corvina pricked her finger on the embroidery needle. She held her hand away from the silk and watched the blood well up into a flattened bead. Slowly, she inverted her hand, and the bead turned to a drop and fell, with an inaudible splash, to the stone floor.

He had not survived his daughter by many weeks.

Now, there would be other children, and they would be safe. Safe from her husband, safe from her child-sire, safe from her brother. Around them their mother and grandmother would weave conspiracies and incantations that would baffle any attack, overt or covert.

~*~

Oliva waited while Rhu beren Robia unlocked the door to the Nursery suite. His manner was, if anything, more reserved and deferential than it had been before his fruitless quest. No doubt, Oliva thought, he suffered shame and guilt for failing his Mistress – his cutting of his hunter's braid was indication of it. She had certainly done her best to see that he would, and then had never mentioned his incompetence directly to him again. A kind word now, she judged, would be like a caress to a chastised dog – it would intensify his loyalty and love by lifting his previous disgrace.

He swung the door wide and stood back for Oliva to precede him.

"By his Grace's orders through you, My Lady, we prepared the Nursery rooms before the Bridal Day. We've kept them swept and fresh, of course, since…."

He left the sentence unfinished. They both knew but neither could speak the end: since the castle is pretending the Kinninger's bride is still in residence.

"Excellent." Oliva beamed at the Chamberlain. "You have done well. Sarpa can always depend on you for the highest degree of service."

"My Lady is too kind." Rhu bowed.

He couldn't meet her eyes. Oliva was pleased.

"You may leave me. Send someone to wait in the hall for the key."

Rhu bowed again, more deeply, and closed the door on her.

Oliva walked slowly through the large playroom, the toys now packed away in chests. Screens flanked the cold hearth, ready to dry infant garments and air bedcloths. The next room was the nursery-maid's; a small room, sparsely furnished. The maid would not be there to live her own life, after all, but to nurse and tend the royal children. The third room, Oliva knew, held two beds still there from Karol and Sorcha's childhood, but the maid's room held what she had come to contemplate: the cradle.

Slices of circles on either end let the cradle be rocked. The head and foot boards bore shields carved with the lion of Sarpa. They had, before, borne the device of Onagros, but that had been the first thing Oliva had seen to when the Nursery was reopened for Landry's now-vanished bride.

She sat on the maid's bed and lowered herself to her knees by the cradle. She touched the wood, stroking it, marking it with invisible symbols inside and out. Raising her hands, she gestured over it, whispering words of attraction and strength. This cradle would hold an heir of Sarpa before another year was out, or she was a false Adept.

Oliva felt the power flow through her and out of her. The Divine Ones must hear her call and would answer. Corvina would birth an heir – Oliva beren Corvina, perhaps. Or Landry would sire a child on a woman of his mother's choosing and claim it for the throne. Or Hayward and Sorcha would feel safe to return with their family, to fill the halls with beren Adas who were also heirs of Sarpa.

That, indeed, would be quickest and surest. The people would welcome the beren Adas' return, and the brewing trouble would end. If Landry could be persuaded to accept Sorcha or one of her heirs as co-regent, his own rule would be tolerated, even legitimized. Then, at Midsummer, when the mandate bag was given to Landry, the transfer of power would be final and peaceful. Let others decide who would sit the throne after Landry's death. So long as her own children survived and thrived, so long as the heir was of Sarpan blood, so long as she, herself, was an acknowledged power behind the throne during her lifetime, Oliva cared little who ruled when she was gone.

~*~

As he rode past Devona beren Valda's scrivenry, Rhu beren Robia looked through the open door. Not for the first time, he considered making a personal appeal to Devona to second Darcy's witness that Elsie was happily housed in the castle. Landry, Oliva, Corvina – they were growing harder to read by the day, even for him, whose position and dignity depended on his ability to anticipate their whims, wants, and intentions. If they should decide to resent, to punish, Devona's recalcitrance, could he turn them from it? If he could neither find nor aid the woman his heart had settled on, he could at least advise her mother.

His mind shuttled from Elsie's mother to his own, serving at Oakwood. He had years ago offered to request her retirement with a pension and a cottage with a patch of garden. She had preferred to continue in service. He had offered to request her removal to the castle, where she would be in his care and company, but she had chosen to stay at Oakwood. They had spoken little since his childhood move to the Kinninger's household, they had spoken less since her refusal to join him.

There was no sign of Devona now, no gleam of light off spectacles; no bright, intelligent regard.

Perhaps she was in the domestic part of the manor.

"Wait here," he told young Captain Bryan beren Basha, the Sword riding escort. He dismounted and handed the Sword Ebenos' reins. In response to the Captain's inquiring look, he said, "The crown has long charged me to take interest in this house and its inhabitants. I realize your Chief will want to know all my actions; be sure to include this one."

"If you say so, Your Honor."

Memories crowded upon him as he stepped into the courtyard. He recalled the flurry of preparation for its new tenants and of his first meeting with the Roll-Keeper, with Devona, and with the child who would grow into his beloved. He recalled visits full of hope, as he began to dare think of himself as a woman's chosen bridegroom. He recalled visits full of gloom, as Darcy's indulgence turned a charming girl into a budding harridan.

Before he could knock on the manor house door, he noticed a figure working in the garden. An old man stopped hoeing cabbages and turned to face him.

~*~

The Chamberlain had altered. When Andrin last saw him, he had been dressed for the chase, with his long black hair in a hunting braid. Now, he wore a light woolen tunic of blue over linen hose and a cape of red, fastened with a brooch shaped and painted like the shield of Sarpa. His hair was cropped to barely below his ears.

More than that: Andrin was overcome by an impression of evil. A deadly luster enveloped the Chamberlain. Rhu was steeped in wrongful death; he exuded poison.

"Andrin! How do you come to be here?"

Andrin's heart sickened. "Rhu beren Robia, what have they done? What have they done to you?"

"What do you...." Rhu touched his hair self-consciously. "I did it myself. Childish." His attempted laugh was awkward. "My Lady Oliva suggested I style it as the Swords do, but I didn't cut my hair to be mistaken for a Sword."

Andrin probed the haze that all but hid the Chamberlain and saw him through it, saw him standing clear and guiltless. The aura wasn't his; he wore that foul atmosphere as a clean man might wear a dirty suit of clothes. "You cut your hair because you would not be mistaken for a proud man of Sarpa."

"My Lady approved; she thinks I did it out of shame for failing in the quest she set me."

"You did it out of shame for *accepting* her quest."

"Ah," said Rhu, and his manner added, "yes."

"And now?"

"Now I bear letters from His Grace and his mother to Sorcha and Hayward and Audre beren Oda."

"Letters.... Of course. Full of sweet words and secret venom."

"So I believe," said Rhu. "And so I will advise."

Andrin was not surprised to hear of Sarpa's perfidy – or of Rhu's rejection of it.

"The House of Sarpa and I have parted ways," Rhu said. "I can't hide that when I deliver these letters. I can't just pass along these messages and let Oakwood make of them what they will. Honest words are the only weapons I have." Rhu was not a born warrior – his eyes showed fear, but less fear than fortitude. He held out a hand for Andrin's clasp. "You and I may never meet again, outside the heart of the Way."

"Here or there," said Andrin. "It's all the same. What matters is how we walk the path."

~*~

Devona, Andrin told him, was consulting with a client. Rhu left his regards for Andrin to pass on to her, and his hope that he could see her on his return from Oakwood.

Rhu retrieved his reins from the Sword and mounted Ebenos.

After a few paces, Captain Bryan said, "I don't ask what you did there, who you saw and what they said."

Haughtily, Rhu answered, "You are not senior enough to ask me those questions."

The Captain patted his horse's neck. "Any Sword is senior enough to ask anyone anything." After a few more paces, he said. "Yet I ask nothing."

This left Rhu to wonder why. Was he not questioned because the Sword already knew the answers? Was it because he had been ordered (by whom?) not to question the Chamberlain? In either case, why had he pointed out his reticence? Was it a warning? A threat? A taunt? Rhu glanced at him.

The young Sword's countenance was expressionless. When he saw Rhu looking at him, he gave the faintest of smiles and one brief nod.

What was one to make of that?

~*~

Rhu stopped in the doorway, but Audre beren Oda motioned him forward.

The Kinninger's grandmother sat in a low-backed chair, with Sorcha and Hayward on a bench to her right. Her youngest grandchild, Sorcha and Hayward's eighteen-year-old, Blaine, leaned against a sideboard, watching. Blaine's wife, Margaret, sat behind an embroidery-frame, turning a square of canvas into tapestry.

"Welcome to Oakwood," Audre beren Oda said. "We have all read the letters you brought from the castle. I trust you and your escort were made comfortable while you waited."

A highly-polished stool, its legs in the shape of Sarpan lions, stood empty, and Audre waved Rhu toward it. A mate to the stool was already occupied. Rhu was well-acquainted with the occupant.

"Thane Robeard Caitlin beren Regan." The Chamberlain bowed.

The Thane sat with feet flat on the stone floor, back straight, arms stiff, hands on bony knees. His waist-length white hair hung down his back; plaits, woven and bound with the spruce blue of the House of Leven, hung one on each side of his face. He nodded a wary greeting.

Audre beren Oda waited to speak until Rhu had taken his place before her. "Thane Robeard was about to tell us the news from the south."

The Southern District was Layounna's largest, by far. It had been the last annexed, and it still convened its own Council of Thanes. Layounna's rulers liked to pretend that the Southern Council was only a formality, but Layounna's rulers – and the Southern Council – knew better.

Thane Robeard stared silently at Rhu, his mouth shut but not pressed close. Rhu stared back, equally at ease in silence.

Thane Audre tapped the arm of her chair with a fingernail. "Speak freely, my friend. Our council is open. We have nothing to hide."

"Let it be said, then." Robeard's voice was low in timbre but not in volume. It was a carrying voice, a voice people listened to with respect. Rhu knew that Robeard was not the senior Thane in the Council, but had been elected its head seven years ago and had never been challenged for the position. "My Lady Audre, you've never been a fool. If you let this man into an estate preparing for a siege and propose to let him out again, I'll keep nothing from him."

"I want to keep no secrets from my elder grandson." Audre beren Oda's bearing was as haughty and erect as that of her daughter, Oliva. Rhu knew that flush of temper in the cheeks, but not the honest flash of the dark eyes, where Oliva's would have been hooded and equivocal. "I've even given the Sword who came with him free run of the place. I expect my daughter and grandchildren to learn everything he's seen here and everything he's heard. As for Rhu, I believe I could trust him to keep any confidence, and I trust him to convey every truth."

"My Lady…," Rhu was surprised into speaking, "…do you want His Grace to know…?"

"I want him to know everything. I want him to know that his words of sweet poison fail to charm us. I want him to know that this estate defies him. Let him attack us. Let him besiege us. He's had ten years and more to prove himself worthy of the throne he stole, and he hasn't done it. I won't tax my people to pay him tribute so he can hire men to threaten my peace."

Thane Robeard slapped a hand on one leather-clad knee and declared, "Well said! Well and truly said! I came to hear how you stood since Hayward and Her Grace took refuge with you."

Sorcha shook her head. "Not 'Her Grace.' My sister…."

Rhu's heart grated and thumped. Was Karol alive, then? His first thought, good steward that he was, centered on the return of the rightful ruler. His second thought was that, if Karol lived, Landry couldn't claim Elsie as his bride.

"My sister kept a secret for our mother," Sorcha finished "I have a brother. A younger brother. Kinnan beren Ada."

"I remember his claim." The Chamberlain saw again the big provincial boy, asserting his right to the throne with little more than his own word for proof. "Landry dealt harshly with him. He has fomented rebellion ever since. Some say he's dead."

"He lives. And his claim, I believe, is just. I believe strongly enough to consider it, if he places it before me. I am willing to concede to him, if he convinces me."

Thane Robeard collected acquiescent nods from Hayward, Blaine, Margaret, Audre. This had been discussed and agreed upon. "Your daughter Waymistress Joia is very like you, My Lady. When I asked her what she thought of being in line for the crown, she said, 'What crown?'"

Joia's family hid their smiles in deference to the Thane's frustration.

He held out a palm, as if begging for a crumb of surety. "Do you know where this Kinnan beren Ada is, My Lady?"

Sorcha shook her head.

Thane Robeard lifted an eyebrow at Rhu.

The Chamberlain thought with shame of the concessions he had won for Landry from the heads of other countries, the permissions for Swords to pursue the brash young man into cities where he must have felt safe. "Nor I, My Lord. I know Landry has sent Swords against him wherever he was rumored to be, and I do not believe success would have gone unheralded."

"I agree." Robeard Caitlin beren Regan gave a tight smile of satisfaction. "Good. Whether this fellow is a true successor or not, he'll help to confuse things for Landry."

"And for the people," said Thane Audre.

"Oh—" Thane Robeard waved away the suggestion. "The people will sort things out, once they're given the chance. All we need do is clear the way for them. Which brings me back to my news. Of course, we all have eyes and ears in one another's Households, and envoys have come and gone between like-minded Houses. Most of the Thanes – not surprisingly, all of the female Thaneholders and heirs apparent – agree with you. Landry has had his chance, and he has proved worse than inadequate. We've all learned better than to stand alone against him, but we're ready to speak in concert. The Southern District Council of Thanes, having heard that you—" he spoke to Sorcha, "– had taken back your name, voted unanimously to support you as Layounna's rightful ruler." He waved away Sorcha's protest. "Whether you choose to accept your place or not, the place is yours. They sent me with a petition to Landry that he should step down and vacate the castle along with his family and retainers." He cast a slightly apologetic look at Rhu.

After a stunned silence, Rhu said, "You will permit me to carry the petition to Landry for you?"

Robeard snorted. "I will not! Do you think I'm afraid to place unpleasant news before any man – even a man who styles himself as my liege?"

"My Lord, I doubt you would fear to stand before The Black Warrior himself."

Thane Audre laughed aloud.

Thane Robeard chuckled gruffly, not unflattered. "You go before me, beren Robia, and tell 'His Grace' that Oakwood defies him. I'll follow with the Southern Council's petition. Our own little contribution to the Midsummer Festival."

~*~

Rhu beren Robia paced through Oakwood's kitchen garden, the civilian preparations for siege swirling around him. Fish that were usually caught as needed and eaten fresh were being salted and smoked and pickled. Half-grown pigs and cattle were going the same way, with only a few kept within the defensive walls to be fed on what could be spared. Scents he associated with autumn – the smoke of aromatic woods, the oily smell of rendering fat, meat scraps being boiled down into gel – mingled in the air. He stooped through a low doorway into the manor's main kitchen.

An old woman snapped beans into a wooden bowl. The gnarled fingers moved with deft speed, but the efficiency was all in the flesh; her eyes followed the motion of her mind, not of her hands.

She was smaller than he remembered, though he had last seen her only months ago. With a stab of dismay, he glimpsed the pink of her scalp beneath the tightly-braided hair, the scantness of the once-plump braids. How long had her age been so obvious? And how had he tricked himself into not noticing?

"Hello, Moder."

Kitchen activity paused as the other cooks and scullions looked to see who had spoken. They saw Robia beren Dela's youngest son, the one she spoke of most proudly, the Kinninger's Chamberlain. The whole manor knew of his arrival and something of his errand – carrying messages from the castle. The whole manor knew he had been received with caution and that he was leaving as a friend. If he had returned the workers' looks, he would have seen smiles and nods but his attention was all on one pair of faded eyes brightening as they focused on his figure, on his face.

"Rhu!"

Robia beren Dela fumbled with the wooden bowl in her lap, the rhythm of her work interrupted but its remnants still lingering in her muscles, making them clumsy in a new activity.

Rhu set the bowl on a nearby table. He drew her gently out of the kitchen and into the yard, where they could speak more privately. He was preparing to return to Landry as an enemy, in company with a very cryptic Sword. This could very well be the last time he and his mother met. Her cheek was soft beneath his kiss, and pink with delight when he patted it.

"I would have come to see you yesterday," he said, "but we were in council until early this morning."

He submitted to her searching gaze.

At last she said, "I didn't know what to say to you."

"Yesterday? About what?"

"For a long time. About *them*."

She had said enough when Rhu had been chosen to serve and companion the older son of Sarpa. "Honor," she had said. "Up in the world," and, "Fit for more than working with his hands." She had prevailed against Rhu's father, dead now these many years. Since then, she had said less and less.

"I go back today," Rhu said. "I have a reply to carry."

"Will She like it?" *She*, not *His Grace*. Oliva still ruled Sarpa, though her son ruled the realm.

"If not, it's my place to take the brunt."

He saw her pain and knew the memories that caused it – not memories of her own maltreatment, but of his. Ever the diplomat, he smoothly plucked the thorn. "My place as Chamberlain. It's a place I'm glad to be in – now, more than ever."

"Stay here." His mother's plea surprised him. Once she had spoken, she clasped his sleeves. "We're all here now, all my chicks at Oakwood. Sorcha beren Ada brought Levana back with her. She was the last of you away from the estate. Now there's just…," her grasp tightened, "…my baby. Can't you stay?"

It had been a long time since they had spoken openly to one another. She had pushed him into his position, had ignored or refused to fully credit his reports of ill-treatment. Eventually, he had stopped making the reports. At first, there was no use telling one's unhappiness to someone who wouldn't believe it; later, a man kept his thoughts to himself; lately, a rebellious heart didn't speak of its mutiny to a supporter of the status quo. Now he wondered how much had changed within his mother's mind and heart while he was changing on his own side of their common barrier. Her rejection of a move to the castle no longer seemed a rejection of himself. He hadn't noticed her aging. What else had he missed, blinded as he was by the past?

Rhu kissed her forehead. "I'll see you again. Soon, I hope."

"She'll ask you for a report of our defenses. You won't tell her the truth, will you?"

Rhu blinked, startled. "If anyone had told me, when I left Sarpa Thanehold, that I would even consider…."

"You will lie, won't you?" Robia peered up into her son's stony face.

"Sarpa has not served the country." He spoke as much to himself as to his mother. "Sarpa has served Sarpa; not Landry nor his mother nor his sister care what happens to anybody but themselves." He thought he saw the faintest nod, and went on: "Layounna is diseased with their selfishness. My integrity would be a small price to pay, if it would help with the cure." He spared her a small smile from his meager store. "Besides, Hayward is Landry's brother, and Audre beren Oda is his grandmother. Hayward and Sorcha's children are part of Sarpa, too. If I lied to protect them, I would still serve Sarpa. If I wanted to throw my conscience a sop, I could throw it that. As it is, Audre beren Oda wants me to carry the truth. And so I will."

"But you're willing to lie? To His Grace? To Her?"

"If I need to."

She released him. "Loyalty works both ways. They think we're things they can use and throw into the rubbish heap. It isn't like that with Audre beren Oda. It isn't like that with Sorcha beren Ada or Hayward Oliva beren Ada. The new ways are wrong. It isn't wrong to fight wrong. You lie to her, if need be." Rhu's mother shook a finger in emphasis. "Tell her whatever Audre and the others want you to, but lie, if it comes to it. We'll pick these oath-breakers out of the castle like deboning a fish."

His mother's scowl reminded him of Biddi's, and of the time Biddi had nearly led the bailey villeins to stone a contingent of Swords. Landry thought he had the land's most ruthless fighters in his service, but he was mistaken. Thane Robeard thought he had the country's power behind him, but he was mistaken as well. If the small people, the "helpless" people, decided to rise up, could all of Landry's weapons and armor put them down? And how many would die in trying the question?

The road running between Oakwood and Kudasad was thin of traffic, so the two men rode side-by-side. Behind and between them trotted a mule, empty panniers bouncing on either flank. The covered straw baskets had carried the Onagros silver to Sorcha at Oakwood, the excuse for sending a Sword as escort.

Rhu's expression, as usual these days, was bland shading into grim. The fresh-faced Captain rode smiling and easy, controlling his mount with his knees, holding the reins loosely. He had learned in numerous border skirmishes that if people *knew* you needed your hands on the reins, they didn't even see you reaching for your sword until you already had it out and swinging.

Captain Bryan beren Basha surreptitiously contemplated the man beside him. They had ridden in almost total silence from the castle to Oakwood and had ridden silently from Oakwood this far. When he spoke, he looked ahead past the Chamberlain, catching Rhu in his wide peripheral vision, another trick that had served him well.

"My gran works in the kitchen at Oakwood."

Rhu neither replied nor altered his expression.

The Sword spoke again: "She's a friend of your mother, she tells me. They're very thick."

After a slight pause, Rhu's smooth deep voice slid into the silence, cool and apparently impersonal. "Your grandmother is fortunate in her friends. I trust my mother is, as well."

"It's a wonderful thing," said the Captain, "to be fortunate in your friends. It's a wonderful thing to know who your true friends are."

Nothing more was said for the rest of the ride, but now the surreptitious contemplation was mutual.

~*~

"Enter, young man. You may be seated." Oliva indicated a low stool near her feet. Bryan beren Basha gave a soldier's bow: quick and shallow, hand on sword-hilt, head up and face front.

He sat. "Many thanks, My Lady. I am honored beyond deserving."

She nodded. "What have you to tell me?"

"Sarpa prepares for a siege –"

"I know about Sarpa's preparations. Rhu beren Robia gave a thorough report. What have you to tell me about Rhu beren Robia?"

The Sword met her sharp gaze with guileless bewilderment. "We rode together to Oakwood. We parted in the courtyard. We met in the courtyard when his business was finished. We rode together back here."

"Is that all?"

"He stopped at a scrivenry, saying he was charged with keeping an eye on the place, but the shop was empty and he rejoined me at once."

"Did he speak to anyone?"

"He was gone only a moment."

Oliva's basilisk stare rebounded off the Sword's openness.

"What do they say of him at Oakwood?"

"That he is loyal, My Lady."

"To me? To us?"

"You should trust him, My Lady. Absolutely."

Oliva nodded. "Very good." She smiled. "You have done well. You have our thanks."

The Captain bowed and left Oliva's presence. He was extremely proud of himself.

chapter 7
SILVER AND IRON

The day came when Nerissa found the smith too abstracted to answer her call at the window. Rady was elsewhere for once, so she put the tray on the ground. She clambered through the window, unlatched the door, and retrieved the tray.

"I brought your food."

The smith started and looked blearily up at her, then returned to studying the object in his hand. It was a cylinder of silver worked into a bit – a bit sized for a pony or a goat. It was covered with delicate tracings of vines and flowers, the edges of the cuts catching the light and throwing it back.

Nerissa blinked at the glitter. "That's beautiful."

"It's…too…small…." Trahern sounded as if he were giving himself the answer to a problem which had baffled him, as if he only knew this when he heard himself say it. He spoke in Kozabiri, to himself, not caring whether the girl understood or not. "It's much too small. She isn't a delicate little beauty. This ought to be…." He dropped the bit to the table, where it rolled until it reached the edge, teetered, and fell to the floor with an insignificant *clunk*. He spread his hands. He spread them farther apart, and farther, until they measured a bit that would fit the mouth of a monster.

Or the Unicorn.

Nerissa grasped one of those huge hands and tried to tug it out of its position. "What are you doing? Do you know what you're doing?"

Trahern half-looked at Nerissa again. "I'm doing as she bids me." He smiled in delight. "And now that I know how to do it, it won't take long." He pulled his tray closer and began to eat. "It won't take long, now."

Nerissa recoiled. "No!" Trahern ignored her. She backed out of the smithy, leaving the door standing open, and ran for Biddi. Biddi would understand the horror she felt, the sense of hideous danger that rose from the smith like steam. Biddi would know what to do – where to turn.

Nerissa ran to the poultry yard. Not there. Into the castle. Not in the kitchen. She pelted down the stairs into the well-room. Not there, either. Panicked, bewildered, despairing, the girl cast herself into a corner. She huddled behind a row of barrels, wrapped herself in her arms, and sobbed aloud.

She was alone. Even her cat – She caught sight of Rady. "There you are! Come here. Come here…. Oh, help me! I don't know what to do!"

Rady stepped from between two barrels, shaking his head as if equally mystified.

Nerissa reached out for him. "That smith…. He's making a silver bit. He's making it big… to catch it. To catch the unicorn. What can I do?"

She couldn't pit herself against the Lady, her worship and her sacrifices. The Lady had the blood of animals to offer – what did Nerissa have?

The razor of Biddi's friend Andrin suddenly weighed heavy in her pocket. She had kept it, kept silent about it, treasuring it as a touchstone to the wonder of her journey from sea to tower. Not really hers, but not really anyone else's. Now, she pulled it out and opened it.

Rady *miaou*wed and came closer.

Blood. The Lady offers blood.

She had never prayed before, had never heard an offering, never witnessed a ritual. Unhesitatingly, as if speaking heart to heart, she said, "Tortoise, accept this sacrifice in place of the Lady's. Stop your ears to her prayers, and listen to mine. Protect your Kozabirian smith from her. Set him free from her power. Don't let her hurt him, and don't let her use him to hurt the unicorn. By the power of this blood, I pray."

She laid a trembling hand on Rady's head, savoring the warmth and the softness of his fur. She placed the razor's blue steel blade against the inside of her own wrist.

Brady, whose cat body was always either hungry, sleepy, or restless, was delighted to find the storeroom door open. He slipped in to scout for loose chunks of cheese or dried meat. Remembering his own near death beneath the claws and rump of Trenel, he hoped Biddi had been wrong about the mice. At any rate, he hoped no one would happen in if he came face to face with one. He couldn't control his metabolism – there, a cat was a cat – but he lacked both the skill and the will to stalk and pounce on a mouse, let alone consume it.

His cat senses caught a scent...a scent he knew. Nerissa. Upset. When he pricked up his ears, he heard her muffled sobs and followed them to her.

She had probably been wounded by some sharp word of Janet's. One look at the face she lifted, one sniff of her fear, and he knew it was more than that.

"There you are!" Nerissa reached for him. "Come here. Come here.... Oh, help me! I don't know what to do!"

Brady gave his head a hard shake. He had done this before. He had heard this before.

What was she saying? The smith was making a bit to catch the unicorn? Dreams and visions mixed in impossible ways in Brady's mind: The unicorn in the mud bank, the day Kinnan and he had seen it in the rain; Moder Zglaria in the mud bank, in his dream, and the girl who came to him only in his dreams, struggling in the mud, trying to pull the old woman free; the same girl, on the unicorn's back, saying these words, asking what to do.

I'm supposed to say, "I know," Brady thought. *But I don't know.*

He *miaouw*ed and stepped closer. The tear-streaked child rested a shaking hand on his head.

Between one blink and the next, the storeroom vanished, and he found himself on the floor under a bunk, the air filled with the smells of leather and steel, sweat and oil and men. He was in a barrack of the Swords.

~*~

A heavy body plumped down next to Nerissa with a sigh.

"That's enough of that."

She jerked, the razor opening a nick in her skin.

"You!"

Tartarus scratched his armpit and shrugged, grinning his evil grin.

"Rady?" Nerissa didn't think so – fluffy and gentlemanly were not traits proper to her old master. But Rady was gone, and Tartarus was here....

"Just put him out of the way. Thought I might need his form, in case somebody came in," he said. "Somebody played the same trick on me, once; might as well get some use out of it."

"What are you doing here?"

"I was called."

"Who called you?"

He stretched and grunted. "Who hasn't?" He took the razor from Nerissa's clutch, closed it, and dropped it back into her pocket. "But I came to you, Guttersnipe. Because of what you did."

He said this with such a surly expression, Nerissa replied with a smirk.

"I don't know what I did," she said. "But I bet it served you right."

A peculiar look came over Tartarus' face. "Did it? Do you want to know what you did?"

Nerissa nodded.

"You fed me, though I repaid you with indifference. You defended me when I bit you. You told me the truth. And you offered me your own blood, when you had another Life in your hand."

Nerissa's thoughts were a confusion of questions and certainties. She supposed she should be surprised, but felt only that she had been told something she had already known. Fed him? Defended him? Tartarus and the scruffy cat on the beach. Of course they were one and the same.

"But you told me *not* to feed him! You told me not to touch – You're even nasty to yourself!"

"Who wanted you pawing and slobbering all over me, when I was only spying to make sure you didn't run away?"

"But I *did* run away."

"Yes, you did. Disobedient, ungrateful brat." There was a touch of praise in his voice, as if he were conferring a title of esteem. "Lost your fear of Tortoise, too, did you?"

Nerissa shook her head, remembering her panic when she'd wakened in the wood-side cottage, certain that the shadow by her bed was Tortoise. It had only been....

Another certainty filled a place now ready to receive it. Offered him her own blood, he had said. She conquered an impulse to prostrate herself. This was not a Divinity who would appreciate cringing. She looked into his fierce orange eyes and said, "Tortoise, will you help me?"

"I will. And I'll tell you why: Some people think a sacrifice is a fee for service. Some people think they can make a payment and put Divinity in their pockets." His evil grin was beautiful to Nerissa in that moment. "Those people are wrong. Even my brother has been known to teach that lesson, and he's the soul of compassion. As for my sisters...." He closed his eyes and chortled.

"You will help me?"

"I said I would." He held up his admonitory finger. "Not for your sake, but for the sake of my sister, and for the sake of that man out there." He jabbed his finger toward the smithy. "Not a true relation, exactly, but close enough – a connection, at any rate."

"You're doing it for me, too," Nerissa stated firmly. "You are." It was important to her – imperative to her – that he admit it and that she hear his admission.

Tartarus glared, grinding his teeth. "Not for you."

She smiled, as if he had said the opposite.

~*~

With utmost caution, Brady flattened his cat body and eased from under the iron bed frame. It would take only a touch to any of the steel-work or ironmongery crowding this place to undo his shape. Devona had discovered him with a straight-edge ruler; Trahern, with an iron trivet. Here, disclosure lurked on every side and underfoot. Fortunately, the barrack was deserted at this time of day.

The door opened and four Swords came in, unbuckling their sweaty leather armor as they came.

The soles of their heavy boots were hobnailed; a kick might break a rib as well as an enchantment. He didn't dare try to duck back under a bed. He would just have to chance the open.

"What's this? How did that get in here?" one of the men said.

"Target practice!" said a second man, drawing a wide-bladed knife.

Brady sat in the middle of the floor, yawned, and looked beyond the man with the dagger.

The marksman stamped and shouted, "Scoot!"

Brady looked at him, then past him again.

Another Sword laughed. "No sport in a sitting target." He squatted and extended a hand. "Kitty. Here, kitty."

The man with the knife sheathed it, the impulse fading.

Brady slid past his would-be friend, and the steel on his would-be friend's clothes.

As he made his escape, he heard the fourth man say, "Cats and women, Bryan. You have the same effect."

And now I know, Brady thought. *I know what to do.*

~*~

"Don't tell anyone you saw me," Tartarus ordered, "and don't tell anyone I helped you."

"Because it would be dangerous for me, if the Lady heard."

"Because it's none of the Lady's business, or anybody else's. Your danger is your own fault. If you'd done as you were told, you'd be safe in Kozabir right now."

"I know. And the smith would make his bit, and the unicorn would be caught. And then what do you think would happen to it?"

"Nothing she couldn't handle."

As Nerissa opened her mouth to reply, Rady plunged through the door and turned into a young man.

The man staggered headlong across the room, as if unused to walking upright, windmilling his arms, shouting, "I know! I know!"

Tartarus surged up from the floor and grasped the man by the front of his shirt and tunic, pulling him straight and stable.

"What are you doing here?" the young man demanded.

"What are *you* doing here?" Tartarus growled.

"You sent me."

"*I* did?"

"Of course. Well… I dreamed you did."

"This is where you landed?"

The man nodded.

With an air of exasperated defeat, Tartarus let him go and slouched against the wall.

The man, dark of skin, black of hair and eye, knelt beside Nerissa. He rubbed the knotted loop that hung from his ear. "I'm Brady. Brady birn Ilka. You knew me as Rady, but this is who I really am."

"A thief," said Tartarus. "A thief and a varier."

"I'll bet you taught him both!" Nerissa snapped.

"I did. He's good at both, too." He spoke to Brady: "She hates thieves."

"I didn't say that!" She explained to the varier, nearly breathless with hope: "I said stealing is mean, but I meant regular stealing. You can change your shape and steal that bit!"

"That isn't good enough." Brady pulled the girl to her feet "We have to undo the spell Trahern is under, and we have to do it without hurting him. He must have been enchanted by guile; he can only be safely freed by what he asks for."

Nerissa ran to her old Master and stood before him with clasped hands. "Tortoise, you helped the Lady lay the spell. Tell us how to break it."

"Tortoise…?" Brady remembered his dream – all of it. "Tortoise?" He backed into a barrel.

Tartarus grinned wickedly. "Not so brave when you're awake, are you? You don't see the Guttersnipe backing away." He reached into the air and held Biddi's silver mirror. "Here's another one with backbone." He tossed the disk to Nerissa. "Give this to your friend, the kitchen maid. Tell her you found it in the chicken house. You haven't grown too pure to lie, I hope?" He began to fade.

"Where are you going? You said you'd help!"

"Apparently," he said sourly, "I already have." He vanished.

Nerissa clutched Biddi's mirror. "He promised! I should have known!"

"Shhh," Brady said. "We can do this. Together."

~*~

Brady, as Rady, eased through the smithy's open window and watched Trahern work a twist of silver – a large twist, forming a bit too big for a war horse.

Nerissa slipped through the door.

Trahern stopped his work and raised his head. His eyes narrowed. "Out. You get out. I don't half like you here at the best of times; today, the sight of you sickens me."

"Why?"

"You smell of…corruption. What's that in your hand? What is it?" Trahern raised his wooden hammer.

She showed him a rusted horseshoe and stepped closer.

"Get that away from me! Get it away!" Trahern struck the table a blow that left a dent.

Nerissa jumped and dropped the horseshoe closer to the smith.

"Pick it up. Get it out."

"It's closer to you than it is to me. Pick it up yourself, if you want it."

His face and bald head darkened with rage. "I'll brain you, you pestilence!"

She picked up the iron and carried it to the window.

"Out!" he roared.

Nerissa tossed the horseshoe away.

"You too," he said, more moderately.

"I have to talk to you."

"Do I have to throw you out myself?"

Trahern was at the window in two strides, hammer high.

Nerissa squealed, but stood her ground. She raised her thin arms, as if they could protect her from a mallet in the hands of fury. "Please listen! Please!"

A muffled clang turned the smith's attention. Rady had knocked the half-worked silver to the ground. He pushed it, rolled it, nosed it under a bench. He crouched, guarding it with his teeth and claws.

Trahern flung his hammer at the cat. Rady flinched and snarled as the mallet cracked into the wood above his head.

"Give me something to throw, girl! Quick, now!"

"What do you want?"

"Anything!"

"This?" *Let him say yes. Let him not look around.*

"Yes! Anything!"

No wonder the enchanted smith had hated the sight of her, hated the smell of her. She had carried this from the day she came to the castle – had never been without it. Andrin's beautiful blue-steel razor.

Trahern's right hand was out to her, his face toward the spitting cat.

She pulled the case from her pocket and put it in the smith's hand. His fingers curled around it, then clutched it until his knuckles turned white. He looked stupidly at it, then at her, then at his fist again. With a groan that seemed to start at his toes, he sat heavily on the floor.

Nerissa crept past him, wanting to reassure herself that "Rady" was unharmed. As she passed the smith, his left hand shot out and grasped her wrist. She looked at him in panic, tugging against his grip until she saw his haggard, bloodless smile.

"Mother bless you, child," he said. "I'm free."

chapter 8
faith

Biddi saw the smithy's shutters slam closed as she approached.

So – It seemed the smith enjoyed her company as little as she enjoyed his, these days. She reminded herself that he wasn't Corvina's creature by any wish of his own. Well, he would speak to her today, whether he liked it or not: Nerissa had been seeking her in a panic, and Biddi meant to ask him if he knew why. She knocked at the door.

"Who is it?" Trahern called.

"It's Biddi. Has Nerissa been here?"

The door opened wide enough for the child herself to pull the woman in.

Nerissa's wide grin alone would have reassured the kitchen maid, but the change in Trahern made her weak with relief. He leaned against the shutters, drawing deep breaths, like a man coming out of a cave filled with foul air. His face, glimpsed before the door closed them into dimness, was fatigued but peaceful – and cleansed of Corvina's pollution.

Nerissa all but danced to the smoldering brazier and transferred fire from charcoal to straw to candle.

"I couldn't find you, Biddi," the girl said, sounding delighted with the failure. "I think I wasn't supposed to."

"They told me in the kitchen you were frantic. I was afraid something had happened."

"Something has," Trahern told her. He opened his clenched fist.

Biddi recognized the object on his palm. "Andrin's razor! He told me he lost it." – *Didn't he?*

She thought back to the day, almost ten years ago, when she had carried a basket of food out of the bailey and followed a trail of gossip along the way Andrin was said to have taken. Many people had seen him leave through the city gates, but no one had seen him cross Kudasad Bridge. Even then, the day after his exile, people were saying that Landry had ordered him pursued and murdered.

Biddi might have returned to the castle, baffled and frightened, if a piercing cackle hadn't caught her attention. She had seen a very familiar black-and-white hen on a gentle rise near the plaza, and had followed her to Andrin's cottage.

Until that day, she had never seen the Waymaster other than clean-shaven. The white stubble on his normally smooth dark skin had been like extra-fine sugar on chocolate – a surprising contrast, but appealing.

You haven't shaved.

I lost my razor. – No, that wasn't right. If he had said that, she would have brought him a new one; she hadn't, for his hair and beard had continued to grow.

I threw away my razor. I don't need it. That was it. That was what he had said.

Nerissa looked at Biddi slantwise. "He *told* me to pick it up. The same time he told me to ask for you, and to tell you the hen lays well. But he didn't tell me to give you the razor."

Even after all these days of kindness, the child said this with the sullen aggression of someone daring an abuser to do her worst.

Gently, Biddi said, "Then he must not have wanted you to. He wanted you to have it."

Nerissa threw her arms around Biddi's waist. Biddi embraced the child and laid her cheek on the rust-colored hair.

Trahern folded his deliverance into his hand again. In his halting Layounnan, he said, "Your girl put it into my hand, and it broke the enchantment. I almost think the little trickster knew it would."

Indignantly, Nerissa said, "Of course I knew it would!"

He held it out to her.

The child shook her head. "It broke The Lady's spell. Maybe it can protect you – keep you from getting sick again. You can give it back to me when you go home."

"I thank you." The smith pocketed the razor and gave Biddi a wan smile that wrenched her heart. "But I'll never see home again."

There was a loud *miaouw* from beneath the bench, and Rady emerged. He stared keenly at Trahern and *miaouw*ed again.

Biddi couldn't help a chuckle. "I think he says you will."

"I wouldn't believe anything this cat says – he's a thief!"

Nerissa seemed to find that very funny.

Trahern retrieved a large silver twist from under the bench. He carried it to his work station and tossed it onto the table with a *thud*.

"Biddi, there was a bridle rope to go with this bit." He cocked his head, brows puckered in puzzlement. "There was something about it…. I gave some order…. I can't remember."

Biddi felt Nerissa squirm, and realized she was clutching the girl's thin shoulders. She released her grip. "Is that what Thane Oliva brought you here to make? A bit? For what?" But she knew. Rhu hadn't enslaved the unicorn. Now Guthrie would be sent.

The smith confirmed her fear by nodding. He sat down heavily at his work table.

Alarmed, Biddi stepped to his side. He waved away her concern. "I'm fine. Just tired. And very happy." He picked up a large pair of snips and clipped the twisted silver into lengths and lumps. "Dear me, this project is taking a long time. But it has to be just right. It has to be *special*. I'd better get to work."

Nerissa peered under the table. "What did you do with the one I saw this morning?"

"Melted it. I'll have to begin again."

Biddi gripped the edge of the table. "You can't–"

Nerissa patted her back. "Don't worry. He won't."

~*~

Nerissa stayed when Biddi left, saying she wanted to watch Trahern work.

When the door was closed and latched, the cat gave one last *miaouw*, then Brady rose from his haunches. The man was even more beautiful than Nerissa remembered. His black eyes glittered in the lamplight like the facets of Trahern's scrollwork. His hair was smooth as black silk, and hung loose around his dark face and down his back.

"Trahern, you cat-killer! You nearly brained me!" He laughed. "A fine way to treat an old friend!"

"Brady!" the smith clasped hands with the young man. "So I have you to thank, lad! You're the last answer I'd expect to a prayer."

The varier winked at Nerissa, making her heart leap. "Depends on who you pray to."

She shook her head violently and cast a warning glance at Trahern. She had promised to tell no one about Tortoise's appearing to her in the storeroom. Brady didn't know telling had been forbidden, but Tartarus wouldn't let a little thing like Brady's not knowing spare the young man from punishment for disobedience. A moment's reflection assured her that oath-breaking would not only be acceptable to that particular Divinity, it would be very nearly a sacrament. Still....

"You and I did it," she said. "Nobody else."

"All right. You and I." His hand went to the silver knot hanging from his ear. He seemed to have difficulty pulling his attention away from her and directing it toward the smith, to whom he said, "You'll be all right now. For a while, at least. I've listened under their tables and prowled in the corners of their councils. They'd like to have the unicorn before the Midsummer Festival, but they're willing to wait." He bowed with mock reverence. "A master artisan cannot be rushed."

"I'll take as long as I dare. The Kinninger and the old one may have patience, but the young one, that Corvina–"

Nerissa raised both her fists and shook them. "She won't hurt you! I won't let her!"

Trahern smiled wanly, but Brady said, "Don't underestimate this one. I leave you in safe hands."

"Leave?" She felt a shock of rage and disappointment. This was worse – much worse – than Farukh leaving her in Tartarus' hut. It was worse than her bird's disappearances or Tartarus' abandonment in the storeroom. "Where are you going? You can't leave! You live here!"

Brady tweaked her ear. "I don't, you know. I'll come back, but I have to leave, now. I have things to tell someone who needs very much to hear them."

"Kinnan?" asked Trahern.

"Kinnan and Elsie."

The smith's drawn face lit up. "You found the missing woman, then?"

A hot feeling rushed through Nerissa. "Who's Elsie?"

Trahern raised an eyebrow.

Brady ignored it, and answered, "An old friend of mine."

Oh, someone old.

When she said nothing, the varier continued his justification: "I have to let people outside the keep and the capital know about Trahern, so those reptiles in the throne room don't feel free to make him disappear."

Mollified but terribly unhappy, Nerissa nodded.

Brady touched his earring again. "I *will* come back. I promise."

"He sets great store by his promises," Trahern said. "I've seen that. I'll vouch for him."

She suspected that the smith found her fervor amusing, and she resented it. Rady – Brady – though, took her seriously. He had to leave, he gave reasons because he thought she deserved them, and he promised he would come back.

"All right," she said. "You can go."

She opened the shutters. A sleek black-and-white magpie hopped past her onto the windowsill. With a parting whistle, he plunged into the sky and was gone.

~*~

Biddi went looking for Rhu. She found him coming down the tower steps, a fold of gold silk cloth in his hand.

"I know what they want with a Kozabirian smith," she said. "He's been making a bit. A silver bit to catch the Unicorn!"

"Ah!" Rhu whispered comprehension. He lifted the slight bundle he carried. "So that's what this is. I've just released the girls who made this rope–"

From the chattering and clattering descending the staircase, Biddi would have thought he had loosed five talking horses rather than five maidens.

She leaned closer and lowered her voice. "He said something about orders he'd given for a bridle.... It seemed to worry him."

"Did it, indeed? I'm exceedingly glad to hear it. I wonder if Corvina's powers are less than she supposes."

"But that's my news! He's well! He won't do it! Nerissa broke Corvina's enchantment!"

"Nerissa? The new little maid?"

The girls drew rapidly nearer.

The Chamberlain edged past Biddi. "I'll take this to the smith."

He hastened down the stairs.

Biddi radiated displeasure. Rhu had seemed less concerned about Trahern's unicorn bait than he was about avoiding a group of rambunctious girls. Then she remembered the last time she had been disgruntled with him, and the look on his face when she had told him so, and the grace with which he had forgiven her.

The maidens clacked into sight. They were all between ten and thirteen, children of castle villeins, and notable for their nimble fingers. Biddi had known each of them from their cradles, and wasn't surprised when they swept her up into the excitement of their liberty. They were all talking at once. She was content to let it wash around her until the fragments began to make sense.

"–days without saying a word?"

"–harder for you than for me. I didn't–"

"–then Allison–"

"–didn't mean to! I cut my finger! Before I knew, I–"

"–thought–"

"–terrified–"

"–Jenna, the old harpy–"

"–killed!"

The word was whispered as the tower emptied into the Great Hall. The girls, Biddi still in their midst, tiptoed along the wall until they reached the kitchen, then poured through and out into the kitchen yard.

Before the gabbling could begin again, Biddi waved them all to silence.

"Allison, you tell me."

After some shuffling and giggling, she said, "Rhu beren Robia told my mother I was to come to the castle and make something. She was to have five gold pieces to put aside for me afterward. So I went."

The others agreed that the same thing had happened to them.

Allison went on: "So Rhu beren Robia took us to a room in the tower. And then old Jenna said the Lady Corvina said we were to weave a rope, and we weren't to speak a word before it was finished, or we'd be killed!"

Sick at heart, Biddi asked, "Did Rhu beren Robia know about the penalty?"

"Not before he brought us to the tower," said Allison. "He asked her to say it again."

The others agreed.

"He told Jenna to call him if any of us broke silence. And he told us to keep our tongues between our teeth and our heads on our shoulders. And to work well and work fast. So we did."

"And then you–"

"She–"

"I–"

Biddi flapped her hands again, as if their words were so many hens. "Allison?"

"And then I cut my finger, and I said, 'Oh, I've cut my finger!' And old Jenna said, 'You've spoken your own death warrant. No one else speak, or she'll get the same. I'm sending for the Chamberlain.' And she unlocked the door and called to a Sword – It was that Bryan beren Basha, the one who's always flirting –" The girls all giggled. "– and sent him for Rhu beren Robia. And they both came in. And old Jenna told Rhu beren Robia I'd spoken, and that Bryan was to kill me." She giggled. They all giggled.

Biddi marveled at youth, that could follow such a statement with a silly laugh! Then Allison explained.

"The Chamberlain gave her a look like this–" Allison drew herself up, narrowed her eyes, and looked down her nose. The corners of her mouth were stretched straight in a parody of Rhu's expressionlessness. When she spoke, it was with a pomposity Rhu never displayed and in speech Biddi was quite sure had never come out of his mouth. It probably held the sense of what he had said, though, even if it missed his usage.

"And he said, 'I tend to believe your ears deceived you. I certainly hope they did. You are too valued a retainer to lose. You chose these maidens. They are in your charge. If one of them has done a bad thing, you are responsible. If Bryan must kill one of them, he will then kill YOU!'"

The others howled and hooted with laughter. A harrowing experience had already become a tale that the storyteller Farukh would be proud to claim.

"Then old Jenna asked me if I had said anything, and I said I had only coughed." They all giggled again. "So she apologized for calling him, and said she must have gone to sleep and dreamed I said something."

The general consensus seemed to be that Allison was lucky the Chamberlain was even more cruel than old Jenna.

No wonder he isn't worried about Trahern's bit! He helped Allison blight the spell on the bridle! I might have known. No blame to the girls, for thinking Rhu was cruel. Some friendly faces were harder to recognize than others.

~*~

Rhu opened the smithy door, not knowing what to expect.

He, along with everyone but Biddi and Nerissa, had been forbidden to visit the smith. It had been implied and understood that the finished rope was to be taken to Corvina, but that implication and understanding had never been put in the form of an actual order. Therefore, no one would be more than irritated to find that poor Rhu, thick-witted son of Thanehold serfs, had misunderstood.

He had to see the smith for himself. No better chance had offered, and none was likely to. He had to see if Biddi's latest report could be trusted – if the smith truly meant to refuse his commission. If he did, the Chamberlain was determined to save him – somehow – from the consequence of his defiance.

At his entrance, the smith looked up from the table where he dug at a brick with a hard wooden chisel.

"I'm just starting," he said in his halting Layounnan. "Had to plan, first."

Rhu answered in Kozabiri. "I've come to deliver this." He placed the gold cloth before the smith.

Trahern unwrapped it. Without looking up, he said, "Was there… any trouble in the making?" Rhu said nothing, but waited in silence for the Kozabirian to meet his eyes.

When he did, there was more silence, as each man weighed the other.

The Chamberlain saw despair and pleading as Trahern repeated his question. "There was no… trouble?"

Satisfied, Rhu shook his head. "There was no trouble. They did their work as flawlessly as anyone – well, as you or I – could wish, and no one will suffer by it. No one." The last of Rhu's doubt dissolved at the relief on the smith's face.

"You know, Great Master—"

"Rhu."

"You know, Rhu, I haven't been paid. Not so much as a copper penny. I think the work would go better for that."

Rhu produced a handful of coins and sorted out a dull brown penny piece no bigger than his thumbnail. He placed it on the table next to the bridle rope. "But you must be careful that the copper doesn't mix with the silver you melt down for My Lady's bit. The silver must be pure."

The Kozabirian showed a very solemn face. "I see we both know the proper way to do things." He picked up the coin and revolved it, looking at the impression of a sprig of sage on one side, the profile on the other. "Whose likeness is this?"

"Karol's. New coins won't be struck until after Landry's coronation."

"If the old coins don't strike first," the smith said, cryptically.

CHAPTER 9
PLAYERS

When Kinnan woke to find himself alone in the goat-shed, he thought Brady had risen earlier and was in the cottage filching extra bits of breakfast. He didn't realize his loss until he walked in as Salali was spreading out her pack for the day's work.

Elsie looked up and into the empty space behind him. "Where's Brady?"

"He was gone when I woke. Hasn't he been in here?"

The women exchanged looks of inquiry.

"No," Elsie replied.

Kinnan snarled. "Deserted!"

"No!" Elsie said again. "He wouldn't! You should know that, as well as I."

"I frightened him, asking his help. He hadn't even the backbone to face me with his refusal, just slunk off in the night."

Salali clucked disapproval of Kinnan's inconstancy, then clenched her fists, dismayed with herself. Her shining boy, her dear delight – How could she feel his fault so deeply? No mortal was perfect, but where was the pool of devotion that should fill his flaws for her as water fills anything lower than itself? Her thoughts went to Farukh, wishing she were sitting with him, rhapsodizing about the young rebel's strengths and glossing over his weaknesses.

Moder Zglaria stuck a straw into the fire and lit her pipe with it. "Your favor changes quickly, Young Master. A friend keeps no credit with you."

Kinnan flushed.

Moder thumped the floor with her cane. "Swallow your discontent with your breakfast, Master beren Ada. We still have work to do in the garden."

"Elsie and I–"

"–Will finish what you began." Her lips twitched. "Think what a fine story it will make for your admirers: How Kinnan-in-exile worked an old woman's garden while he waited for his time to come."

"It's come now." It was more of a grumble than a battle-cry, and was ignored as such.

~*~

Days passed, while a placid Moder Zglaria found one chore after another that could not wait, Elsie obeyed her unquestioningly, a fretful Salali tied one love-knot after another without satisfaction in any of them, and Kinnan sulked at his work.

A morning came when Kinnan stated, "I leave tomorrow, with Elsie or without her." His petulant bluster held the sound of a man determined to act against good advice.

Elsie looked to Moder Zglaria for a sign.

The old woman puffed at her pipe, then said, "He's coming back."

Kinnan lifted a shoulder. "No doubt I will."

"Not you. Brady."

Elsie, the light of a sudden thought filling her face, lifted the lid of Moder's carved wooden chest. "Hah! He left his pipes and his pack. I *knew* he didn't run away."

Moder regarded her through a curl of smoke. "You spoke no blame of him, whether you doubted him or not."

Elsie closed the chest. "He's done a lot already, some without knowing, some intentionally. For all we know, he's on our business now."

Kinnan snorted. "A pretty story."

A rap at the open door took their attention.

"Not as pretty as one of mine, I hope."

"Farukh!" Salali felt a great relief, as if a window she desperately needed to see through had been wiped clean.

"Come in, and welcome." Moder poked the stem of her pipe toward the bench. "Take a seat and share what's left of the morning meal."

"I've had only one breakfast today, so I'll accept your gracious offer." He turned his brilliant smile full-force on Salali, who blinked, then handed him a bowl of cream-drenched berries and a piece of flatbread.

"What brings you here?" Kinnan was all too glad to divert attention from himself. He collected his own food and sat beside the storyteller.

Farukh, his mouth full, shrugged.

Moder answered for him. "He lost something, a long time ago. Want has become need. He's come looking for it."

"He lost something here?" Elsie held out her hands, palms down, to indicate the cottage.

"He didn't lose it here. He came looking for it here."

Farukh stared into the fire. "Stop."

Moder narrowed her eyes and spoke more softly than was her custom. "As a matter of fact, he didn't lose it at all. It was stolen from him."

The storyteller turned beseeching eyes to her. "Stop. Please."

"He could recover it in an instant, if he only remembered who stole it."

Salali stepped between Farukh and Moder Zglaria, facing the old woman. "'*Stop*,' he said. What kind of hospitality is it, that feeds the full and denies the beggar?"

"A perverse kind." Moder spoke in her usual voice. "Not my kind – though I know whose kind it is. So do you, eh, Master Storyteller?"

Farukh cocked his head to see around his defender.

Before he could answer or question, a flurry of wings in the open doorway resolved into Brady himself.

Elsie clapped her hands in triumph.

Kinnan sighed irritably. "Where did you go this time?"

Brady strolled into the room and accepted a piece of flatbread from a grinning Moder Zglaria.

"I've been to the keep." He took a nonchalant bite.

Kinnan, nonplussed, asked, "The keep?"

Brady smirked, relishing the drama of his revelation. "The keep. THE keep. The castle keep."

Elsie's face lit in delight. "Did you see My Tall Man – Is all well with... the staff? My foster father, I mean... and... everybody?"

"The tallest man I saw there was Rhu, the Chamberlain. Remember when he used to visit the scrivenry when you were little?"

Kinnan gritted his teeth. "Tell her if the staff is well, and get on with your news."

Brady fingered the bauble in his ear. "The staff is well. I was a humble cat. I've eaten scraps from Landry's dinner and picked holes in his mother's dearest plot." More seriously, he said, "They have Trahern." He couldn't repress a smirk. "And yet, they do not."

Kinnan felt off-balance, stumbling to change directions, to catch up.

"Trahern," Brady told Elsie and Moder Zglaria. "Our friend the smith.

We told you about him."

Moder grunted and said, "I'm well aware of your friend the smith."

"Yes, I thought you might be. Corvina bewitched him, but I broke the spell." He fingered his earring again. "A little kitchen maid and I."

"You had grudging help from someone else, I think." Moder's lips twisted in rather malicious amusement. "Was he very angry?"

"Furious, I'm happy to report." Brady enjoyed her rich chuckle, then reassured Kinnan. "Trahern is fine, now that he carries the steel that broke his spell. But here's my news: Oliva ordered him to make a silver bit to catch the unicorn."

Elsie shook her head. "Rhu already tried. He didn't do it," she finished with smug approval.

Moder sat and pushed at one of Salali's stray beads with a thick white finger. "Innocence came back to them still innocent. Now they'll send vanity, guile, and sorcery."

Brady took another piece of bread. "Not for a while. Trahern works very slowly."

Puzzled, Kinnan said, "No, he – Ah." He grinned.

Elsie tugged at Kinnan's sleeve. "You were right. We have to go. *I* have to go. It said they'll find it through me, remember?" She turned to Moder. "Let me go!"

The old woman shrugged. "I'm not holding you, Your Grace."

Kinnan's eyes shone. "You'll come with me, then? Into Layounra, to tell your story and raise the people?"

"NO." Brady's stance was as firm as his voice, feet spread, elbows out, fists on hips.

Elsie laughed. "You look just like Devona."

"Yes, think about her. Kinnan and I have to get Trahern out of the keep, before they decide they don't need him anymore. But Devona ordered me to take you *out* of danger –"

"She ordered you to take *her daughter* out of danger. Her daughter died ten years ago."

Brady met her cold look with a cooling one of his own. "Yes, you're a Royal." He turned his back and feigned interest in the pots on the mantle shelf.

"No, Little Master." Moder Zglaria prodded his back with her cane. "You pledged to serve Sorcha. Sorcha is of Onagros, and so is Elsie. She needs your help."

"I do not! Kinnan and I can face down Landry and anyone he fields against us!"

Moder let unopposing silence do its work.

Then Farukh said, "Some of my tales are dark, and filled with steel and death. This will be one: How the true Kinninger returned to Kudasad, her army growing around her, her Consort-father's army decimated, her horse treading pastern-high in blood—"

"Stop!" Elsie raised trembling hands to her throat. "That isn't what I want! But Landry must be defied and deposed. I can't let other people face that for me. I can't let other people run risks while I run away." She crossed to Brady and laid a gentle hand on his arm.

Astounded, he looked at her.

If she had dropped a tear, he would have shrugged her off. If she had smiled, he would have left. But her face was grave and her regard was nearly as piercing as Devona's when she said, "Please help. Help me think of a way to do this cleanly."

"You're determined to go back."

Elsie nodded.

He sighed. "So am I. I promised someone I would. But I promised Devona...." He shook his head. *Why is nothing simple anymore?* "If Devona came to harm through me...."

"Come with us. If anything happened that made you worried for her, you could go warn her, or help her get away, the way you helped me."

After a long, long moment, Brady, improbably, snickered.

Kinnan raised a reproving eyebrow. "What part of this desperate enterprise, what part of this knot at the center of so many lives do you find funny this time?"

Brady cast apologetic looks all round. "It's just.... This is the odd way the mind works: I was thinking that I have to go back to the keep, then I thought about Landry's Midsummer Festival and his Mandate Ceremony. He's hanging a lot on that. He doesn't expect a challenge. Not on the Day. Not on the spot. I was just thinking I'd love to see the look on his face if I turned up at his party looking like Kinnan."

Elsie shook Brady's arm and directed a warning frown toward her suddenly pensive uncle. "It is not to be considered! Brady cannot turn up at Landry's ceremony in the guise of Landry's only known rival."

"No, of course not," said Kinnan. "But I can."

Elsie gaped at him, then mirrored his twisted grin.

"Farukh is right," Kinnan said. "We could march on Kudasad through blood and glory – what Brady would probably call doing things the Royal Way – or we could do it Brady's way."

"My way? Underhanded? Deceptive?"

"Salali, you say the people are ready to rise and the border rebels are ready to strike."

She nodded.

"Would they be content with less than killing blows?"

"Less…?"

"We've been looking at this the wrong way. We've been thinking like Landry, thinking the only way to take back the throne was the way it was taken – over the bodies of other people. Maybe we ought to think like Karol. Like Elsie. You said it yourself, Kitten: we can't let other people die for our right to rule them. Not if we can help it."

Moder blew a smoke ring with smug satisfaction. "I always knew who you were. It's time you started to find out."

Elsie felt a rush of love for the man she had blithely called her mother's baby brother. For the first time, she realized the truth of it. The deepest meaning of her identity was not that she and Kinnan were the true heirs of Layounna, it was that they were family.

"How would we do it? What do you have in mind?"

Kinnan shook his head. "It hinges on the mandate. If we could face him down on that, with the people behind us…. But how to get there without drawing the Swords to us like iron to a lodestone, I don't know. Master Mischief, do you have any ideas?"

"We left Kudasad in disguise." He regarded Elsie in her boy's clothing. "We can go back in disguise."

"Easy for a varier and a woman dressed as a man." Kinnan wryly waved a hand to indicate himself. "I'm not so easily hidden."

"That depends on how you hide." Farukh flashed a radiant smile. "Perhaps we need some expert advice. The people who gave me a ride to Pazni are experts, and friends of mine. Friends of yours, too, Little Master. The Festival Players–"

Brady was all attention and delight. "The Festival Players? Florian? Silvin, Maida, Cristoval?"

"All there, and looking to increase their company."

The varier rubbed his hands together. "There's your answer. There's our safe passage. Who would look for the legendary Kinnan-called-beren-Ada in a party of playactors?"

Kinnan shifted uncomfortably. "I don't think—"

"Oh, yes!" Elsie beamed at her uncle. "It would be perfect! We could leave right away, travel with no suspicion, and be in Kudasad for the Midsummer Festival. We can slip in under Landry's very nose!"

Farukh agreed. "They were planning to go due south into the Istok Encroachment, then west to Kudasad for the Festival."

Kinnan broke into a smile. "Istok. I could make contact with this Anshar who calls himself my lieutenant. – He can spread the word to the other raiders, exiles, insurgents...."

"Salali and I will come along." Farukh flicked a glance at Moder Zglaria. "The Players are always glad to add us to their offering. What do you say?"

Salali rolled up her work in its cloth and tied it into a bag. "Of course I'm coming." She flushed, deliberately not looking for a reaction from Kinnan.

"Nearly time to name your reward," he said. "Are you ready to tell me what it is? Do you know, yourself?"

"I know." She took her bag to the stone bench along the wall and stored it in her pack. "And, no, I'm not ready to tell you." In fact, she was disturbingly unsure she still wanted it. How could she have been so fixed on the love of this boy for so long, have worked so tirelessly for him, and be uncertain now? The boon she planned to claim – marriage, with her total devotion accepted and appreciated by a husband free to take a heart-wife, free to sire children with another – seemed shabby, dull and dismal.

"But will the Players take us?" Elsie appealed to Brady. "Do you think they will? On your say-so?"

"A young couple on the run from unsympathetic parents, heading for her grandmother's freehold in the south? With a face and voice like yours and a back like Kinnan's? Of course they'll take you. Especially if they don't have to pay you. Or me."

Elsie pulled a face. "They'll never believe that story!"

"You missed the persuasive part. They don't have to pay us. They'll believe it."

Kinnan rubbed his hands in glee. *Movement, at last!* "Everyone pack up. Then Brady can go ahead of us and make the arrangements."

"What are our names?" Elsie spoke to Kinnan, but Brady answered.

"You're Ella beren Devra, and he's Kenneth beren Moder. He's an orphan, apprenticed at ten to a smith in the Eastern District. That's where he met you. You grew up together, but your family had a man all picked out for you, and it wasn't him. ...And so on."

Farukh rapped on the table in applause. "If you ever tire of...whatever it is you do, Little Master, you can always earn your bread inventing stories."

"That *is* what he does," said Elsie, wryly.

While they waited for Brady to bring word from the Players, Kinnan went to the goat shed to collect the gifts he and Brady had been given by the smith. Salali, now that she had Farukh to listen, took him outside where she could rattle away about her precious rebel, with sound taking the place of thought.

In the cottage, Elsie nervously rebraided her hair and pinned it up. She started when the doorway darkened, only relaxing slightly when she saw it was her hostess.

"I'm right to go, aren't I?"

"Are you asking, or telling?"

Elsie frowned. "I'm right to go." She had never needed advice more, but she would never find it here. Why couldn't the old woman answer clearly?

"I've something for you." Moder stumped to the bird-carved chest and carried back two items: Karol's scarred leather belt and the homespun bundle holding Karol's ruined gown. When the young woman had taken them, Moder drew two more items from her pocket and put them atop the bundle: a spindle the length of Elsie's little finger wrapped in dull gray thread and stuck through with a needle, and a round tin box – Moder's own mixture of saddle soap. "Spend your journey repairing the damage of your mother's flight. Wear her belt and gown when you come to Kudasad."

"But the thread doesn't match. And saddlesoap will never restore that leather."

Moder Zglaria shrugged. "Don't, then."

Elsie, face closed in irritation, curtseyed. "I thank you for your hospitality. When I hold the throne, you'll be rewarded."

Moder laughed aloud, thumping the floor with her blackthorn stick. Elsie stuffed belt, gown, thread, and tin box into her pack and left the cottage.

Brady returned with the anticipated acceptance of the new troupers.

Kinnan had herded Farukh, Salali and Elsie together in the yard, where Elsie was bidding an unexpectedly fond farewell to her refuge.

"I've changed so much since I washed up here," she told Salali. "How many people can one person be in a lifetime, when I've been so many already?"

"A wise question." The market woman toyed with the bangles on her bracelets and cast a sideways look at Kinnan and Farukh.

Elsie lounged against the well and watched Kinnan clench his teeth at her ease. "We can't leave until Brady gets his things."

As she expected, Kinnan whirled on Brady.

"Get your things, man. What are you waiting for?"

"To see how long it would take for your face to turn just that shade of red. –No, don't burst in two at this point. I'm going. See? I'm halfway in." From within the cottage, Brady called, "I'm inside, getting my things."

As he shouldered his pack, Brady experienced an unaccustomed drop in spirits. He wasn't surprised to find Moder Zglaria regarding him intently.

"Frightened, Little Master?"

"Not for me." He shifted his pack. "I don't want to take her back there. I don't want to leave you alone."

"I've always been alone. And she'll do what she chooses. You must do what *you* choose."

He nodded, fingering the love-knot in his ear.

The old woman pointed at the bauble with her pipe. "Did you find her? Your true love?"

Instead of the dream woman, he thought of the pinch-faced child who had braved both Tortoise and the force of Sarpan sorcery. There was something about the child, her courage, her conceit, her possessiveness. She had refused to "let him go" until Trahern vouched for his integrity – a new experience for the varier – and he had an odd suspicion he couldn't have left without her consent. She had certainly seemed to think so. *What an odd little duck!* He smiled. "No. But I'm on her track. I've met someone who's going to lead me to her." Just thinking about the urchin made the charm sting his ear. "I'm getting very close. I feel it."

"When you do…," Moder's expression grew surprisingly warm, "bring her for a visit."

Such unexpected sentimentality embarrassed the young man.

He grabbed his pipes, tootled a few notes, and hurried into the sun.

Kinnan clapped his hands. "We're off, then!" He honored Moder with a courtly bow. "A thousand thanks for everything. Shelter, advice, food–"

"Calluses," Brady added.

"I hope the seeds we planted for you grow and bear well."

"Time will answer your hope, Young Master. One way or the other."

Kinnan's superficial manner slipped as he said, more softly, "And thanks – more thanks than I can express – for sheltering my sister and my niece in their times of need. For that, I can never give you thanks enough."

They pressed each other's hands, then the bluff soldier was back, mustering his troops. "Say your goodbyes. People are waiting for us."

Salali and Elsie waved, Brady blew a kiss. Farukh and Moder nodded farewell, and the new Players crossed the causeway, leaving Wild Ass Island – its goats and geese and bees – behind, and its Mistress alone.

chapter 10
The waymaster's fish

Andrin slept, by choice, in the Roll-Keeper's stable, where he could keep Chandler company.

Devona hired a boy to move Brady's pallet from the house to an empty stall. She brought down the bedding, herself.

"I told them I've hired an odd-job man. Darcy complained of the expense, but I pointed out you would cost less than my absent apprentice."

"And when your apprentice returns?" Andrin asked. Devona made no reply, but he sensed her anxiety. "I'm good at listening."

The scrivener looked up into his gentle face. Genuine gratitude managed to squeeze through her small, tight smile. "I've kept silent so long, I might not stop once I got started. But thank you."

There were no messages from Verrina, no visions, no dreams. Andrin rose early, washed at the courtyard pump, did his exercises, weeded the gardens, fed and groomed and mucked out after old Jehan's successor – became the odd-job man Devona alleged him to be.

One day he turned from hoeing to find the Chamberlain in the courtyard, enroute to his own crossroads. As clearly as his body's eyes saw the details of the world, his Vision saw into the Chamberlain's heart. The thrill of that clear perception counter-balanced his compassion for the suffering he found there. And still, Verrina left him to his work.

Then he Dreamed.

Chandler and he were on a river bank deep within a forest. The hen pecked near him in the bug-rich humus. He sat, his back against a tree, and breathed deeply of the peculiar forest odors, the mix of leaf-dust and damp.

He found he could, by craning his neck a little, see a ribbon of sky between the trees above him and the trees beyond the river. A cloud scudded into view. It elongated, whorled, curled, took the shape of a…of a…. Of a dragon.

The cloud shaded to blue and green, and Verrina settled softly into the water, only her head and the end of her tail above the surface.

"I'm very pleased with you, Dumpling," said the dragon.

"It's come back, hasn't it? My Sight. You've given me back the Oneness I lost in the castle."

"I haven't given you anything." The dragon fizzed a laugh. "If your Sight has come back, it's because you opened your eyes again. – I have a question for you, Dumpling: What, in all you've done or not done, do you regret most?"

Andrin reviewed his long life, trying to judge it honestly. "I regret letting Grandfather buy my place in the Waystation, instead of working for it. I regret the time I wasted trying to be wise. The advice I've given from the book, not from the heart. But most…. Most, I regret the lie."

"The lie that lost your Sight?"

"Yes, but not…. If I hadn't lost my Sight, I might never have had my years by the river. I regret the lie because…." In his dream, the world around him lost and regained focus as he concentrated on his words. "Everything else I've done diminished no-one but myself. That lie…. I think people died because of it. Children. Their blood is on me, because I lied to save Karol's heirs." The dragon was silent, and Andrin went on. "I dream of children who turn into fish. I reach out for them, and they're swept away. I try to save them, but I lose them instead. What did I do? What did my lie do, besides to what it did to me?"

"Come."

Andrin stood at once and stepped from the bank onto the dragon's back, which undulated out of the water to meet his foot.

Did they grow minnow-small, or did the river become a current of The One Great River? They dove deep and swam fast and far. The temperature of the water shifted in ripples across Andrin's skin. The light around and above him waxed and waned.

When they stopped, he strained to see through the surrounding water, but all was dark, glassy green. A sudden undercurrent pushed at him; a muffled gurgling pressed his ear. He looked in the direction of the push and saw a barrel plunge through the water. It slowed, hung suspended, then slowly accelerated toward the surface. Now, around him, he could see other barrels. Some of them rose as the first one had risen. Some sank with terrible deliberation, bubbling as they filled.

He reached out to one of these, pushing off from the safety of Verrina's back, clutching at the wood nearest him. His fingers slid off the surface. He followed it down, clawing at it. It dissolved, leaving a fish in its place. All around him, though some of the barrels continued to rise and some continued to sink, some melted and left quite ordinary-looking fish.

Verrina rose under him and bore him up.

They surfaced. The sky was pearl-gray, with a flush of pre-dawn rose. Before them was a cliff; on either side of them, land stretched and curled away to the watery horizon.

Faintly, from above, Andrin heard a splintering sound and, after a pause, another. He waited in the growing light, watching the containers which eased back up from below and floated away in a tide he could not feel, while some took on water and slid from view.

A barrel tipped over the cliff and splashed, close enough to cover Andrin with spray. Another followed. Neither came back up.

"Do you have your answer?" asked Verrina.

"Yes, Grandmoder."

"Do you understand it?"

"No, Grandmoder."

"Is that important?"

The old man shook his head.

"Wake up," said Verrina, "and follow Chandler."

~*~

The Swords at the castle gate allowed him to pass with barely a glance, their amused interest absorbed by the unswerving hen who went before him.

There were more Swords in the bailey than there had been a decade before. His temple and garden were unrecognizable, one abandoned and the other fenced and horse-cropped. He followed Chandler up the earthen motte's boardwalk, the timbers worn rough and smooth again by Layounna's business, enjoying the warmth of the wood beneath his bare feet.

Through the keep's gate, past the wooden castle tower, where a building had been added like an inappropriate thought. It was closed and shuttered, and Chandler passed it without pause. Andrin knew where she was headed: home, to the henhouse she had left ten years ago in the arms of the kitchen maid.

Past the kitchen garden, into the poultry yard, out of sight of the tower and the stir of the bailey keep. Voices in the hen house. Biddi and someone younger.

"Look what I found," the young voice said.

"What is it? Oh...." Biddi's voice sounded thoughtful as she said, "I suppose that's mine."

Chandler hopped up to perch on the coop's worn sill.

"How did you get out of the yard? Come here—"

A lined and freckled face appeared in the doorway, illuminated by a ray of sun, then by joy.

"Andrin!" Biddi, holding a flashing mirror, tripped over the doorsill and sprawled against him. He was surprised to find his arms encircling her thick waist, one of his hands toying with her heavy braid. He was surprised to find her lingering against him, her breath sweet on his lips.

Then she pulled away and glanced around furtively. "Come in at once! Nerissa.... Nerissa, look who's here! It's Andrin. *Andrin!*"

Man and girl faced one another in the flesh. Nerissa seemed a bit uneasy. Andrin, on the other hand, felt nothing but delight in the workings of the Way. After all, he had had nearly the entire span of Nerissa's life to lose his attachment to "hard truth."

"It's all right." Biddi jogged the girl's elbow. "He's real, this time."

Nerissa smiled shyly and met Andrin's gaze.

He smiled back. "I have a message for you from my grandmother."

"For...me? I don't know her – do I?"

"She seems to think so. She sends her love, and says the pearl was well used."

Nerissa clasped her hands together, her dark blue eyes shining. "She's *your* grandmother?"

"She also said you're to take Chandler's eggs and use what comes out. Speaking from my own experience, it won't be what usually comes out of eggs."

Nerissa shook her head. "It'll be something... special," she whispered.

"So," Andrin picked up Chandler and put her in Nerissa's arms, "I suppose you'd better have her. She usually lays in the morning."

"Me? You're giving her to me? To have? For my own?"

As Andrin nodded, the girl's skinny arms wound around the hen, her thin hands stroking the speckled feathers. Chandler gave a contented croon and – the greatest miracle Andrin had yet seen – permitted this.

"For my own." Nerissa's voice was full of wonder.

Andrin said nothing. A sudden tightness in his throat silenced him.

Biddi filled the void with news of a silversmith, Trahern, how Corvina enchanted him and how Nerissa had broken Corvina's spell with Andrin's razor.

Nerissa's smile was crooked, puzzled, awed, like the one Andrin felt on his own face. "Is that why you told me to pick it up the other day?"

"It probably was. It's probably why I was told to drop it, ten years ago."

"I…I can't give it back yet. Trahern needs it, to protect him from the Lady's magic."

The Waymaster ruffled his shaggy white hair. "I have no further use for it. He's welcome to whatever it can give him."

Biddi checked outside again. When she returned, she was as smug as a bullied child whose big brother has arrived. "I knew you'd come back and clean out this nest of vipers. I'm with you – you know that, don't you? And there are plenty of others–"

"Biddi, my dear, I've come to do no such thing!"

"But you slipped right in without being challenged! Now you're going to go into the hall and finish the curse you started before you left."

"Indeed –" he didn't know whether he was more appalled or enchanted at her plans for him, "– I began no curse."

"Why else would you deliver yourself to them? If you didn't come in power, you've walked into terrible danger!"

"I came at my grandmother's bidding. I don't know her reason. I don't know how long I'm to stay, or what I'm to do, or where I'm to go when I leave. But striking people down is not, I feel quite certain, something my grandmother would sanction."

Biddi clucked like one of her own hens. "Your grandmother died when you were a student. We've talked of it before. Have you dreamed of her?"

Andrin put his tongue behind his teeth to form a No, but changed it to, "Yes." Yes was true enough, and simpler.

"You have to have a place to hide."

Nerissa bounced up and down. "Biddi, the new henhouse!"

The kitchen maid's eyes lit up. "We've just had a new one built, but the chicks aren't ready to move yet. Nobody comes back here but Nerissa and me. You'll be safe and dry. There used to be a cat who seems to have run off – but we don't have to tell Janet he's gone. We'll bring you food and say it's for him."

Andrin winked at Nerissa, seeing, as Biddi did not, that the girl knew more about the cat than she had told. Nerissa buried her face in Chandler's feathers and sneaked a wicked twinkle over a wing.

"I'll tell Rhu you're back. He'll help us keep you hidden."

"No." Andrin recalled his last sight of the Chamberlain, a man threading a dangerous path, navigating through a lightless cave filled with sleeping co-bras. "The Chamberlain has burden enough to carry. Let's not add my weight to it."

The kitchen maid nodded. "It may be he'll need *you* to keep *him* safe. Things are happening. The Swords are different. The villeins are different. The townspeople.... A change is brewing, and everybody knows it but the Kinninger and his House."

Nerissa piped up unexpectedly. "That's because they're the strong ones. They own you, and you have nothing. They have all the power, and you have no power, not even over yourself. There's nothing you can do and they know it." She grinned. "That's when you get away."

"Ah!" Andrin remembered his commission. "Yes. Get away. Grandmoder offers – I offer – the two of you shelter at the river cottage. Will you go there?"

Biddi heaped scorn on the suggestion. "Without you? And without Trahern? And Rhu? No, I'll take Nerissa to safety and come back –"

"I won't go alone! I won't leave everybody else here!" The girl lifted a stubborn chin, jaw set, eyes narrowed.

The profile wavered, as if seen through turbulent water.

Andrin felt himself swimming with his grandmother, barrels crashing into the sea around him, barrels floating, sinking, dissolving, fish swimming away, child-fish rushing through his fingers. And one child walking along a silent road and picking up a razor.

The two maids stared at him in puzzlement as he knelt and wept tears heavy with salt and happiness.

chapter 11
the dragon and her eggs

The bulge in the center of Layounna's eastern border defined what was known – in Layounna – as "the Istok Encroachment." Border skirmishes were fought over it for years, until diplomacy agreed to leave it alone. It was not territory anyone in Layounna coveted, anyway, except as a matter of pride and principle. It was marked by high, rocky ridges which thrust toward Layounna like fingers and long, narrow valleys. The valleys, too, were rocky, and supported no crops but weeds, wildflowers, tough grasses, and spindly trees. The local name for the ridge-and-valley pattern was "The Dragon's Claws."

Few cared to climb between the stony talons to the thick forest above – few by day, and next to none by night.

Safer to go north or south and cross the border by road, where the Primarch's official lookouts – the Dragon's Eyes – could note your presence and send word ahead. It was somewhat eerie to realize there were people far incountry who knew your movements, but it was also comforting, in a way. You were accounted for. No one would dare interfere with you except by order of the Primarch and the Council of the Wise.

The Encroachment was wilderness, a labyrinth of woods and marsh and greensward. It was thick with predators and populated by hunters and trappers, outlaws and outcasts. It was the stronghold of the Istok Raiders.

On a moonless night, a man carrying a tin lantern strode up one of the uneven valleys as confidently as if he walked his own halls by the light of day, though his lantern gave forth no light – none to eyes other than his own. He slipped into the forest. He threaded the trackless ways with sure but stealthy ease.

The Raider who watched for infiltration barely sensed him before the man's dagger was at his throat.

"Sorry, Ranulf," the man said. "I couldn't have you gutting me before you knew who I was." He withdrew his bloodless knife. His lantern glowed as if just kindled.

"K-Kinnan?" The Raider put a hand to the spot the knife had touched. "Where did you spring from? Does that bracelet of yours help you see in the dark like a cat?" The men clasped hands. "You must have a cat's nine lives. We heard at least that many eye-witnesses to your death in at least that many different places."

Kinnan's chuckle touched the night with chill. "I'm alive. Alive and moving. I'm traveling with the Festival Players, under the name of Kenneth. We'll be in Kudasad by Midsummer Day."

"The Players?" Chaffing, one soldier to another: "You plan to take the throne with wooden swords? With an army of clowns and jugglers?"

Bemused, Kinnan said, "With less blood than a wooden sword would draw, I hope. With clowns and jugglers... may be. An army is raised and bodies fall.... I hear one of your leaders, who calls himself Anshar, claims to be my chief lieutenant."

Ranulf nodded.

"Well, tell Anshar we'll count our victory by the number of lives *not* taken. They're all our people, even the ones who arm against us. If he doesn't understand that, he has no place with me. That's the call to action I want him to spread."

The lookout's face showed that he, at least, did not understand.

Tension made Kinnan's voice gruff and abrupt. "Will you tell him?"

"I'll *tell* him...."

Kinnan nodded. His lantern went dark and he slipped away, surefooted and clear-sighted.

~*~

Ranulf stood, in the dawn, before Anshar and his sub-commanders, feeling his excitement transmute to anxiety. He was acutely aware of the armed men and women who drifted up behind him, drawn by his agitated demand to speak to Anshar immediately. It had never occurred to him his report might not be believed. It occurred to him now, but he had already spoken. Now he stood between his leader and his comrades, with a highly unlikely story coloring the morning air.

"Kinnan-called-beren-Ada popped out of nowhere and then disappeared," Anshar summarized.

"Like in a story," said the woman to Anshar's right.

"Or…a dream," said the man to his left.

"And," the woman leaned forward to exchange glances with Anshar and the other sub-commander, "he wanted you to tell us not to hurt anybody."

Ranulf raised a hand in nervous correction. "Not *kill* anybody. If we could help it. He didn't say we couldn't *hurt* them."

Anshar folded his arms. "Ah. Well, that's something, anyway, isn't it?"

The mockery sparked a touch of defiance in the lookout. "I wasn't dreaming. I didn't make this up. I didn't." He felt sweat ooze up through his scalp.

Anshar was staring at him, watching apprehension dribble out of his hairline and down his neck.

"I believe you."

Ranulf huffed his relief.

"However…."

Another trickle traced the other side of his face.

"I can't afford to simply take your word for this. You see that, don't you?"

Grudgingly, the lookout nodded. False information was far more plentiful than the true, and one misjudgment could mean death for them all.

Anshar spoke to the man beside him. "You know Kinnan-called-beren-Ada, don't you? Ride out and see if you can find the Festival Players. See if one of them is called Kenneth. See who he is."

"Without seeming to look, of course."

"Of course."

"If I find them and Kinnan's with them, what do I do?"

"Come back and save this man's life."

Ranulf's head jerked in a convulsive nod.

The scout affected not to notice. "And if I don't find them, or if he isn't among them?"

Ranulf blinked rapidly.

Anshar, too, drew no attention to the lookout's anxiety. "Look longer. Look carefully. Take your time. Be completely sure. I'm inclined to think this wasn't a dream."

"It wasn't." Ranulf wiped his face with his sleeve. "It happened."

"I know. But everybody else has to know, too."

"They do," said the man at the lookout's left elbow. "This is Ranulf.

He doesn't lie."

"Not *well*," said another man, and a little tension blew away in laughter.

"Dragon and her Eggs," said a woman.

Ranulf winced as heavy hands came down hard on his shoulders, but he wasn't being seized. It was friendly thumping, and he was led away to breakfast, not to imprisonment. He was, however, kept within arm's length and under watch. Old Raiders, as they said, are careful Raiders.

They had "Dragon's Eggs" for breakfast, which was too great a coincidence to let pass without hearing the story, as well. The praitier – Istok's version of the storytellers of Sule – was put first in line and urged to eat quickly. The old man, in his distinctive beaded headband, lit a long-stemmed clay pipe and began.

Long, long, ago (he said), back in the days when there wasn't much yet to tell, there was a Primarch who was afraid to die. He asked each member of his Council of the Wise how he could cheat death. The very last one, an old woman, bent and nearly hairless, told him that the remedy was known by only one person: Alith Mayros, the Cook Who Couldn't Lie.

This was greeted by sounds of satisfaction. Alith Mayros was a great favorite in the Istok pantheon.

So Alith Mayros was sent for, and the Primarch put his question. Alith Mayros said, "Only a fool fears death. Death loves us tenderly and embraces us all, sooner or later. Life is joy, but life is pain, and it often wounds us worst in taking leave."

If anyone else had spoken so to the Primarch, he would have thrown him in prison, for the Primarch was, indeed, a fool. Alith Mayros, though, had leave to say what he pleased. After all, what is the good of someone who cannot lie if his tongue is tied?

Again, the Primarch asked for freedom from death, and Alith Mayros could not help but reply, "I have heard that one who sits down to a meal of a dragon roasted with her own eggs will never die thereafter."

The Primarch said, "Cook me that meal."

Now, at that time, dragons were easier to find. Every settlement had at least one guardian dragon. Every path, every stream, every bog, every woodland, every inch of Istok rested under a dragon's wing. To harm one, even accidentally, was a disgrace. To kill one was a crime and a sin. To eat one was an abomination, as – of course – is eating a mother in a dish with her young. Yet the Primarch insisted.

"And you, Alith Mayros, are granted the honor of preparing and serving this wonderful meal. Who else would be worthy? Go, then, and return tomorrow evening with my immortality."

"So soon? I need more time!"

"Every day you fail me brings me another day closer to death. Every day which brings me closer to death, ten people will die. Any ten – it's all the same to me."

Alith Mayros left the audience lodge and stumbled across the clearing to the cookhouse, where he sat by the cold hearth and wept. "Truth is a curse!" he cried up the smoke hole.

~*~

The praitier's audience shouted the next line along with him, a line which appeared in every Alith Mayros story: "Oh, what I wouldn't give for one little lie!" When the laughter had died down, he continued.

~*~

Then there was a scurrying in the thatch, a scraping, a dusting of straw, then a *plonk*, and a blue-tailed lizard no longer than my hand dropped to the floor. It gleamed in the sunlight that poured straight down the smoke hole.

"What are you weeping for?" the lizard asked. "I know what you want, and I bring it to you. Where is the roasting dish?"

Alith Mayros brought the red clay dish and placed it on the floor near the lizard.

"Go fire the oven."

The Cook Who Couldn't Lie went out and lit charcoal in the fire holes of the big clay oven. When he came back in, the lizard had lined the dish with bright blue and green scales and gold-yellow thatching straw. There came the sound of wings. A kingfisher dropped through the smoke hole as if plunging into water, swooped over the roasting pan, and dove back into the sky. He left one kingfisher's egg behind. Another rush of wings, and a hawk passed in and over and out, leaving one hawk's egg. One after another, ten different birds each left one egg, ten eggs for ten innocents who would die without them. Then the lizard crawled into the roasting dish and made itself comfortable.

"Now, Alith Mayros, put on the lid and seal it. When the charcoal is ash, put the dish into the oven and seal the door. When the Primarch sits down to dinner, break the seal on the oven but not on the roaster. Place it before him and tell him this: If he sends the dish away unopened, he will have a long and blessed life. His people will prosper and he will die gently. If he opens the dish, he will never again have cause to fear death."

All was done as the lizard instructed, and at last Alith Mayros and the Council waited for the Primarch's decision.

"The truth," he said. "What is in this dish?"

"A lizard and ten different eggs."

The Primarch – who really was a fool – picked up his knife. "I will eat, and then I will cut ten throats with this very blade." He broke the seal around the roaster and lifted the lid. Out of the dish rose a dragon, smelling of rosemary and cloves, growing as it rose until it filled the air over the table and its wings spanned the roofbeams. Each egg cracked and hatched, and ten more dragons unfurled themselves and surrounded the Primarch, covering him with their glimmering wings.

The dragons faded away without a sound. The Primarch's body slumped in his chair. He would never fear death again, for he had found peace in its fellowship.

The Council wrapped the body in purple silk embroidered with silver thread and placed it on the table. When they had done this – behold! – the body moved in its wrappings. In the blink of an eye, it vanished, and a lavender dove stood upon the table.

From that day to this, lavender doves are called Dragon's Eyes, and are used to send messages, information, truth to the Primarch. From that day to this, we eat dishes made with the eggs of more than one kind of bird and call them Dragon's Eggs. And from that day to this, a wise man knows the truth when he is told it… and a clever man knows when to tell the truth.

~*~

The story was well-told. It was still in the Raiders' hearts and minds when, that evening, Anshar's scout returned. Ranulf had neither dreamed nor lied. Kinnan-called-beren-Ada was traveling to Kudasad with a pack of clowns and jugglers. Anshar sat far into the night with his sub-commanders, plotting a cataclysm that would make their leader proud.

chapter 12
the kinninger's sword

Oliva dreamed. Corvina provided powders and syrups, small animals bled and died, and Oliva dreamed. She dreamed of a unicorn, graceful as a horse, agile as a goat, slender as a sword. She dreamed of Guthrie, holding his sword before him, shaving a straight path through a dense wood. The path stopped at the edge of a river. In the center of the river was a wooded island. An old woman stood on it, towered over it, shielding it with her wide black skirt. Guthrie crossed, using Deya as a bridge. He shoved the old woman aside and found Elsie. "Kinnan!" Elsie cried in Oliva's dream, and a man with dark blond curls came running. Oliva felt herself controlling Guthrie's body. She waved his arms, and Elsie, Kinnan, and the old woman all became one with the unicorn. Guthrie grasped it by the base of its ivory horn, and struck off its head.

Oliva, Landry Oliva beren Ada, and Guthrie beren Melanell stood in a small chamber off the Great Hall. Oliva had been offered a seat but she preferred to stand with the men, the better to read their faces.

Guthrie's was easy to understand: hope, banked like a fire, shone through his skin. Landry's was more guarded, or perhaps the expression was clear but the feelings behind it weren't.

"Such an island does exist," she said. "In Fiddlewood."

"And the old woman who guards it?"

"Someone of power, by my dream. No wonder Rhu was hidden from my sight on his quest. He told me he had lodged in the Wood in the hut of an old woman."

Unease stirred in Oliva's breast. She had never doubted her dreams – her visions – before, but there was something disquietingly logical about this one. This one contained too many echoes of her waking goals and desires, together with the reproduction of Rhu's report. It held no hint of danger to herself or her agent, no smallest threat of thwarting. An adept grew to expect cautionary portents along with hope and information. Still, perhaps this was good. Perhaps this only meant that victory was now assured, that Tortoise was firmly bound to her intentions.

She would keep her doubts to herself. "The old woman on the island exists. Ask your Roll-Keeper."

Landry protested with a small laugh. "He might know that much. But if his daughter's hiding there – that, he doesn't know. He hasn't the nerve to come into the bailey, day after day, with that secret in his heart. Would you think so, Guthrie?"

"I would not. But it's easily determined. May I? Men speak very clearly and very thoroughly, when they speak to me."

Oliva raised a cautionary hand. "No violence. That will come later. If you suspect him, arrest him. Otherwise, raise no alarm."

Landry nodded, and Guthrie left.

The Chief Sword hooked his thumbs over his belt to keep his hand from Deya's hilt. Oliva's dream had excited him almost beyond bearing. His release was so near.... And when he was released, what would he do with Deya? Why, begin again. Wouldn't the Kinninger have the blood of the unicorn? When the souls taken in the Kinninger's name began to sing in Deya, Guthrie would silence her with the unicorn's blood, and be free again.

Darcy stood when Guthrie entered, assuming he had come to inform him of another outspoken citizen to be removed from the books

The Chief Sword spoke without preamble. "In the Fiddlewood, there's an island. Someone lives there?"

"Wild Ass Island in the Fiddlewood...." Darcy felt his palms grow damp and chill. "Yes, someone lives there."

Guthrie wondered if he had misread the official: Darcy did look like a man with a secret, and that secret did involve the island.

"Who?" Guthrie asked. "Are you sure? Without even checking your records?"

"I'm sure. I've been there. I've seen her." The Roll-Keeper laughed uncomfortably. "She's an impressive object."

"Who is?"

"The old woman who lives there. Salvia Zglaria, she claims her name is, but everybody calls her Moder. Moder Zglaria. She's a healer of sorts."

"Anyone else?"

"No-one else registered. Why? Is she harboring somebody off the census?"

Guthrie examined the Roll-Keeper's floury face carefully. No, this was not a man to hold a serious secret from authority. If Darcy knew his daughter lived on Wild Ass Island, he'd betray it, willfully or not. He had met the old woman and she had shamed him, somehow; that was his secret.

"What does this woman look like? Describe her."

Hesitantly, Darcy said, "Old, but not frail. She's tall, for a woman. Big – not fat – solid. White skin, red hair, blue-green eyes…."

Guthrie broke into Darcy's silence. "How does she dress?"

"Dress? I've only seen her twice. She wore black, and a black-and-white…." Darcy twirled a hand over his head to indicate the headpiece he couldn't name. "Turban," he finally said. "Black-and-white turban. Walks with a cane. Smokes a pipe. That's all I know."

"That's enough. Many thanks."

~*~

When the Sword had left their presence, Oliva drew her son to a chair and urged him to sit. She sat near him.

"What will you do with your bride, when you have her back?"

"I don't know. Tarkastrus knows how little I want her."

"Still, her discovery and return would give the lie to the rumors – the rumors that have her starving in a dungeon, or worse."

"And to my claim that she's happy and unharmed."

"But you had to lie, My Lord, to keep her safe."

His mother was weaving a scheme, Landry thought, as he had seen her do so many times before, in disputes with other Thanes over water rights and boundary markers. She had seldom lost her arguments – only in the face of overwhelming evidence and a magistrate strongly predisposed to the other side.

"To keep her safe," he repeated, making himself comfortable.

"That Sword you postulated, the one Guthrie found and executed, the one who helped Elsie disappear…."

"What about him?"

"He was working for the rebel Kinnan-called-beren-Ada. She didn't escape, she was stolen. He's holding her hostage on this island, planning to use her as a shield or a bargaining chip. You told the people she was here, even though it drew ugly rumors from the mean-spirited, so Kinnan wouldn't realize you had Swords searching for her. Now Tarkastrus has found her, and Guthrie will ride to her rescue. If she dies, it will have been by Kinnan's hand."

Landry considered this offering. "That may even be true – part of it. She may have left against her will. But, in the event she did not, she must die. As must Kinnan, and all witnesses."

"Unfortunately, yes. But how are we to know her heart, from this distance? I could ask Tortoise for a Sending, if you like. Or, once the 'rescue' starts, she might prefer a willing return, even if she left you willingly. It shall be as you wish, My Lord."

"Less chance of another change of heart if she dies." Landry produced an enigmatic smile.

He wondered why he bothered altering his face, disguising his feelings, hiding his thoughts. His mother usually knew what was in his mind in spite of his efforts. What a pitiful, petty triumph – to see her guess wrong, sometimes!

Elsie, now. His mother persisted in supposing there was some passion in him toward the girl, whether love or lust or hatred. In truth, he had no more feeling for or against her now than he had ever had. He had never wanted her, he had never felt her loss, he would feel no pleasure at her return or at her death. The people would rumble less, if she were proven free of Oliva's domination, which was the rumor that had the widest credence and raised the loudest protest.

This scheme of Oliva's would serve his cause, disarm his detractors, gain public sympathy, and eliminate Kinnan's recurrent threat. If it made Oliva consider her son more ruthless than he actually was, that was also in the plan's favor.

The Chief Sword returned.

"The Roll-Keeper says there is such an old woman on Wild Ass Island. He's seen her twice; both times she wore black. She goes by the name of Moder Zglaria."

"She lives alone?" asked Landry. "So far as anyone knows?"

"She did, at the last census."

"She has one thick-witted churl to serve her if she's the same woman Rhu boarded with when he hunted," Oliva said. "Though, if my dream is true this far, she has others boarding with her now. We can do this easily if we do it quickly. I saw only one man – Kinnan – and I saw you win without a battle. Go alone. Slaughter all you find on the island, except the old woman. When the others are dead, question her at your leisure. Use whatever persuasion you find necessary, but learn all she knows about the unicorn. Do your work skillfully; be sure you draw everything from her. If she lives after that, kill her."

Landry's gorge rose. He grunted with the effort of keeping it down, and turned the grunt into a harsh laugh. This plan, despite all in its favor, was a mistake – he could feel it was a mistake, but he couldn't see what else was to be done. Kinnan must die, and so must Elsie; therefore, so must the old woman. If she suffered or if she passed swiftly, she would die all the same; why should he jib at making her death count for something?

More strongly than he felt the wrongness and the inevitability of this step, he felt the approach of the struggle's end. Perhaps he wasn't his mother's son for nothing; finality swirled in the air, like the last streamers of a heavy mist or the tail of a running horse.

In the middle of that finality stood his mother, directing it. The ruin or establishment of Sarpa on the throne of Layounna would be Oliva's doing; a product of her desire for power enough for both of them, not of his own comparatively modest ambition. He should never have brought her to the castle. But if he hadn't, where would he be now? As always, young man or monarch, he was his mother's steward.

"Go to the smith," Oliva told Guthrie. "See if that bit is finished. If not, go without it. If it is, bring it to me. And the bridle rope. Rhu placed it with him instead of Corvina. A happy mistake: One piece of power can only enhance the making of its companion. – Well, what are you waiting for?"

Landry answered. "Possibly for dismissal from his Lord, Moder."

With a diplomatic look of apology at Thane Oliva, Guthrie nodded.

"Go," said Landry.

~*~

When Guthrie opened the smithy door, Trahern looked up from his work table. In his hands was a bit, small enough to fit the mouth of a deer.

"Is it finished?"

"Oh, no, not nearly. I still need to–"

"It looks finished. Give it to me." It was flimsy and fussy, with sketchy flowers etched into it. Its tracery caught the lamp-light and shattered it into gleams. "And the bridle rope." Trahern handed him the gold cloth. Guthrie turned back the folds and laid the bit across the woven silk. "Pretty. I hope, for your sake, My Lady is pleased."

"If she is, I can go home?"

"You go when My Lady gives you leave. You haven't had your pay, yet. Your reward depends on the value of your work. She won't know that until I return."

Guthrie left the smith with that thought.

"Yes," Oliva breathed. "This will do."

Landry stroked the silver and the silk. "Can you feel power in it, Moder?"

"No, I feel nothing, but it must be right. Look at the size of it – so small – that wasn't made out of habit. This rein – Corvina said the smith gave the specifications for that, himself, under her influence. I don't feel the power because the power wasn't put in it for me. The unicorn will feel it."

Still the Kinninger disguised his unease as eager restlessness. "How soon can you leave?"

"Right away, Your Grace."

"Good. Good fortune guide you." Landry grasped his Chief Sword's hand and held his eyes. "When you return, we two have other matters, gentler matters, to speak of."

It took Guthrie a moment to realize the Kinninger was referring to Corvina.

"Yes, My Lord."

"Go with this blessing," said Oliva. "Tarkastrus guide you and protect you. Tortoise confound our enemies; let their eyes be blind and their ears be stopped; come you on them in their darkness, and work our will."

Work their will. Work Deya's will. – And my own. My own. So thought the Kinninger's Sword.

chapter 13
phoenix

The Festival Players moved south. Most afternoons, they unhitched the horse from their boxy traveling cart and set up for a show.

Salali's companionship was uncharacteristically flat, as was Farukh's. They each seemed preoccupied and ill at ease. Farukh's stories lacked sparkle, as did Salali's gossip.

Fortunately, the remaining additions to the ensemble made up for them. Brady already knew how to play the pipes and to juggle, Kinnan/Kenneth's active life suited him for tumbling as well as for heavy lifting, and Elsie/Ella quickly mastered the simple dance steps Maida taught her. Florian had promised – or threatened – to give them parts in a play someday soon.

Trahern's wonderful cooking pot, fire-starting loggerhead and fog-piercing lantern won the hearts of the Players more completely than the tale of forbidden love Brady had concocted. Everywhere they went, they spread the news of the captive smith and his enforced undertaking. The news outstripped their pace, and they heard it told back to them – with additions and "improvements." He was held in a dungeon. He was housed in mouth-watering luxury. He had defied Oliva and she had cut off his hands. He had thrown himself into his own forge-fire to escape Oliva's commission. He was a demon, who was trading the unicorn's life for Corvina's hand in unholy wedlock.

Kinnan despaired. "Such contradictory tales work against each other."

"You listen to the verses," said Brady, "but you walk out before the chorus. 'Just a story, most likely,' it goes, 'but you know there's no smoke without fire. There's something to it, mark my words.' Think I'll put it in rhyme and set it to music." And he did.

Kinnan dropped instructions in a willing ear in Istok; Anshar and his raiders would begin their advance, gathering force and distracting any possible official attention from this little troupe.

The wagon turned west – west, toward Kudasad.

Now "Ella" and "Kenneth" walked together, trying to maintain the invention of romantic runaways – difficult, when her conversation turned so often to reminiscences of a tall man with a cold face and warm eyes.

"Ella" had been delighted to get back into women's clothes, courtesy of the costume box, but had quickly tired of Florian's mother-hennish concern for the state of his hems, and she had changed back to her male disguise.

"Kenneth" rubbed his wrist, missing his bronze bracelet, his gift from Karol, the token he had worn nearly all his life. He was known by it – It figured in the tales the people told of him, according to Farukh. "I am here when you need me," the inscription inside it ran, and he would soon need all the help he could muster.

He looked up to find Salali staring at him from her seat in the back door of the wagon. As usual these days, her stare was both at him and through him, and it took a moment for her to register his attention and turn away. He looked around for Farukh and saw the storyteller walking more briskly than he had since their theatrical apprenticeship had started. He was glad to see it – Farukh had looked rather bedraggled lately, and Kinnan had more than once thought of asking Elsie if she thought he was sickening for something.

Brady played snatches of melody on his bird-tail pipes, then settled on a tune and embroidered it. Every night, he dreamed of the woman in the embroidered palla or of the scrawny little girl who would lead him to her or both. Every day, he woke happily. He was in a country on the brink of becoming a bonfire, heading for a pile of dead wood in company with the flint and the steel. And he felt like a man of high birth, great gifts, and a dowry of coin and livestock on his way to a bridal fair.

"LUNCH!" Florian's baritone rang across the fields to either side of the road.

Brady chuckled, imagining field workers all over the district sitting down to eat at that order.

Florian guided the cart deep into the shelter of a copse and brought Lumpkin, the huge and plodding horse, water and oats.

Salali clambered down, pulling her pack and a basket of bread after her. The troupe ate light for early breakfast and late lunch, often only stopping long enough to rest the horse. Trahern's pot served them for after-show feasting.

Farukh helped pass out the provisions, then cornered Florian, pulling a sheet of paper from inside his blue wool tunic.

Elsie bolted her bread standing and washed it down with a pull from her waterbag.

"Elegant." Brady lounged against a tree and ate at a more leisurely pace.

Elsie gave him a filthy look and sat near him, taking Karol's gown from her pack and spreading it across her lap. She threaded her needle and continued her repairs, resentment in every motion.

Brady, gleeful source of so much annoyance, managed to say the right thing. "You do fine work. Devona taught you well."

The young woman sighed heavily and shook her head. "The more I mend it, the worse it looks." Elsie's stitches were tiny, fine, and tight, but Moder's gray thread stood out against the gown's red wool and gold-and-green embroidery like veins in autumn leaves. "The belt looks even shabbier. I've rubbed Moder's saddle soap into it until my fingers are sore, but the wax only fills the scratches, and nothing can help the gouges but a patch. She wants me to wear the gown and belt in Kudasad."

"I suppose you realize she has her reasons."

"Oh, yes. Probably wants me to learn humility. Facing down Sarpa, rough-shod and badly mended."

Brady laughed. "She would enjoy that. I'll go back when this is over and tell her about it."

Elsie tied off her darning, snapped the thread, and folded the raveling up with Karol's now twice-ruined gown. "You don't seem to have much doubt of the outcome."

"I can't begin to predict the outcome, but she'll enjoy it, whatever it is."

Florian, who had been chatting with Farukh, clapped the storyteller on the shoulder and said, "Now, that's more like it!" He unharnessed Lumpkin and drew a deep breath.

"REHEARSAL!"

As usual, Farukh's play existed as one cleanly-written copy held by Florian. It consisted of a story line, character identifications, and a set speech or two. Florian, as company director, would cast the parts and take each player aside to explain any necessary background and the general flow of the plot. The players improvised pantomime and dialog, and the play grew around them.

"Silvin, you're the boy. Maida, you're the girl. I'll be the villain."

"A tale of young lovers, torn apart?" Cristoval practiced his juggling, which was still so poor he used it as part of his clown routine.

Farukh sat near Salali where she, like Elsie, worked during the travel respite.

"Something like that."

While Florian held brief conferences with his cast, Farukh separated Salali's beads for her, glass with glass, wood with wood, ceramics all together. A handclap like sudden thunder retrieved any wandering interest.

"Brady, set the mood. Jolly music. We'll begin with dancing – No, sit, Ella, this is just a run-through. Brady…. Good. Just right. Silvin and Maida, you two dance together…. Happy…. Do a little bit of the mirror routine, and the twin thing. You're very much *together*. Good." He stepped forward and announced, "Phoenix Divided."

Salali stopped working.

In his ordinary voice, Florian said, "We'll dig out those 'Dance of the Falling Leaves' costumes, the red and yellow ones with all the scarves. What do you think, Farukh?"

"That would be perfect." The storyteller watched as beads rolled from the market-woman's fingers onto her spread work-cloth.

"Now I come in – I'm Tortoise – sudden stop, Brady – and we start to speak. I go first."

Florian seemed to swell as he stepped into the action. His brow seemed to beetle, his black beard to bristle with hostility, even as his white teeth gleamed in a ferocious grin.

Brady wondered, not for the first time, if there might not be a little varier in all the best players.

Florian's voice was harsh and laced with mockery. "The One-in-Two, the Two-as-One! How sweet!"

"Brother." – "Brother." Silvin and Maida spoke almost in unison.

In his own voice, looking at his paper, Florian said, "Blah, blah, blah, I make fun of your virtues, you make fun of my vices, you come off well, I come off ill, the audience laughs."

He looked up and resumed his persona. "How easy it is for you. How easy it is for all of you. Unicorn prefers solitude, Dragon has family, you have each other. What about me?" A whining note gradually crept into Florian's voice, and he managed to hold himself in a way that both invoked pity and derided it. "How virtuous would you be if you had to wander the world alone?"

The varier wished he could tell Florian how excellent a job he was doing. No one who had ever met Tartarus would mistake the actor for him, but Florian had the manner – at once wheedling and belligerent – down pat. Come to think of it, Florian might not need someone else to tell him how good his impression was. Tartarus, as Brady could witness, got around.

Silvin stepped away from Maida and opened his arms to emptiness. "Virtue is the same, alone or in tandem. What's right is right, Brother, and what's wrong is wrong."

Maida stepped further away from Silvin. "Our spirit is one, but we have two minds. Even apart, we would each know how to behave."

Florian laughed. "Spend a year apart, and you won't know each other."

Maida and Silvin protested.

Salali's brown face paled. She leaned into the performance, as one half-frozen will lean toward a fire.

"Is it a bet, then? Do you accept the dare? Part for a year, live as others do, then meet again. If you recognize each other, never part again. Otherwise…. We'll see if your principles can stand alone."

Salali whispered, "No." Louder, she said, "No!"

Florian gave Farukh an approving nod, wiggling the paper. He pushed a quieting palm toward Salali. "This is just the beginning."

Silvin and Maida moved to opposite ends of the little clearing. Each mimed pain and loss.

The director waved a hand. "We'll come up with parting speeches that'll have the audience up to their knees in their own tears." He stepped back into character with an evil grin. "A lot can happen in a year, alone and open to life. She will die and be reborn. Will he know her, when he sees her as an infant? Will she know him when they next meet, and he comes from another country and greets her in a foreign tongue? Or the next time, when she's his grandmother; or the next, when he's her Master's page?"

Salali rose to her feet, head forward, trembling. Farukh stood at her side, not watching the play, looking only at her.

"How will you feel, dear Sibling – Siblings, now, the two divided – How will you feel, cut in half? Each half longing, and wondering what you long for? Each half searching, but searching after what?" He laughed again.

Salali glanced at Kinnan, but the glance was blunt, now, rejecting what she saw.

"If it happens that recognition comes to both in the same lifetime –"

Florian shrugged. "My fun is over." Another evil grin. "To make things interesting, let's say…. If only *one* of you knows the other –" Florian waggled a hand, "– I grant that one a *little* of your true nature. But –" he raised an admonitory finger, "– he – or she – is bound to silence. Neither can speak of this. Neither can tell the other, or let anyone else tell it."

Salali turned to Farukh.

He reached out for her, saying, "I've been thinking since we left Wild Ass Island. Thinking about who stole our hearts' desire from us. He always believes he's thought of everything, but he's always wrong about that. He didn't say a word about writing a play, or about watching one."

Salali's hands met Farukh's. They looked into each other's eyes and their smiles were blindingly bright.

Kinnan, Elsie, and Brady, all riveted by the off-stage drama, cringed in the sudden light, the flash of heat. The grass around Farukh and Salali blackened. Her work-bag joined the flame as the two became the Two-as-One again.

In the midst of the roaring fire, a beautiful young woman turned in the arms of a beautiful young man. Then, they were gone. The grass was green, unscorched, vacant.

Rehearsal continued, as if the other Players had seen nothing. As if Phoenix itself had not traveled with them in the forms of a storyteller from Sule and a woman from Nishi who made trinkets out of feathers and string.

chapter 14
thane's gambit

Rhu beren Robia took his accustomed place behind Landry's throne in the Great Hall. The chair to the Kinninger's right was empty. Guthrie's chair. If he were a man who exposed his feelings, he might have smiled. Guthrie beren Melanell on a fool's errand was the right man for the right job.

As it was, he betrayed neither his full knowledge of Guthrie's mission (which had not been confided to him officially), nor his hope for its doomed outcome, nor his concern for the still-imprisoned smith, nor the qualms he felt about the audience he was about to witness.

Thane Robeard Caitlin beren Regan had arrived in Kudasad and would shortly be received.

From the set of Landry's shoulders and the looks on Oliva's and Corvina's faces, they expected only another duty visit, like so many in the past two days, from a Thane here for the Midsummer Festival, the Mandate Ceremony, and Landry's official coronation.

The door opened and one of the Swords nodded to Rhu.

"Thane Robeard Caitlin beren Regan." The Chamberlain's voice expressed no more than his face.

The visitor, for his part, did not hint by sign or look that he saw Rhu as anything more than a serviceable tool, invisible when not in use. If his mission brought disaster on himself, his attitude told the Chamberlain, he would take no ally down with him. Rhu thought of Bryan beren Basha, the Sword who had ridden with him to and from Oakwood, and of the covert affiliation they had formed that day.

"Welcome, Thane Robeard." Landry motioned to one of the villeins stationed around the Hall. "A seat for our honored guest."

Robeard waved away the heavy, low stool. "I'll stand, thank you. This is no courtesy call, Landry Oliva beren Ada. I bring you this from the Southern District."

Protocol dictated that the Chamberlain take the scroll. The Thane handed it to him without meeting his eyes and stepped back. Rhu held the petition, willing Robeard to leave before it was unrolled and read, but the Thane of the House of Leven was clearly willing to risk whatever might betide.

Landry's sister stirred, as if about to speak, but the Kinninger silenced her with a gesture. "Should we hear it now?" His voice was perilously smooth.

"Yes."

Rhu doubted he was the only one in the room who noticed that the Southern District Thane had not once used the terms "Your Grace" or "My Lord."

Landry raised a graceful hand toward Rhu. "Proceed."

The petition was as Robeard Caitlin had promised: Landry held the throne against the will of the people and in spite of authentic heirs of the beren Ada line. He was to abdicate in favor of Sorcha beren Ada or her acknowledged heir and to vacate the castle with his entire Household. The document was signed by nearly all the Southern Thanes, and by many Thanes of other districts. One of the names was Audre beren Oda.

The Chamberlain's impenetrable manner wavered as he read the name of the Kinninger's grandmother. Even Oliva's shuttered façade flew open, and she gasped. Landry half-turned, his gaze searching his Chamberlain's face, as if asking for reassurance that the name had been mis-read, that it was some other name. Rhu repeated it.

Corvina laughed. "The old dogs growl at the young, and show their blunt teeth."

Landry cast her a quelling look. She closed her lips and swallowed hard.

The expression His Grace turned toward Thane Robeard was one of faintly wounded puzzlement. "My sister speaks from her surprise. This document has taken all of us unaware."

Thane Robeard ignored Corvina and Oliva as thoroughly as he did the Chamberlain. Rhu suspected the Southerner was as conscious of everyone in the room as he was of the man he ostensibly addressed.

"Unaware? You were unaware that the throne devolves from Ada to

Karol to her heirs, or Ada to Sorcha to her heirs, or Ada to any other of her offspring to her – or his – heirs?"

"I hold the throne in trust. I've always said so."

"You hold the throne out of trust." The white-haired man nodded at the scroll. "*We* say so."

Oliva drew a hissing breath. The sneer on her face was clear in her voice as she began, "My Lord–"

"Thank you, Moder." The Kinninger's tone was as dismissive as a slap. He favored Thane Robeard with one of his sweetest smiles. "Of course we know we have no mandate. Not as yet. But Sorcha rejects the throne; her children have long rejected it. Karol has no heirs, and who is left? A rabble-rouser who was offered a place in the keep and refused it? Ran away in a fit of temper because I didn't pass Layounna into his unproven hands?" Landry shook his beautiful head. "On Midsummer's Day, I'll present a mandate bag from my House to the people. If another claimant presents another bag, let the people decide between us." He flicked a hand over his shoulder at the paper Rhu held. "We have heard your petition, but it's rather pointless, after all, isn't it? Still, we're always pleased to know our people's minds."

The Thane of Leven was shown the door.

~*~

The Sarpans closeted themselves in Oliva's rooms by Landry's peremptory request. To the dismay of Oliva and Corvina, he began by giving them the option of absenting themselves during his audiences or remaining silent unless he invited them to speak.

In her own chambers, the Kinninger's mother accepted no such repression – not with Guthrie fetching power beyond reckoning.

"Why did you let him go? You should have put him in irons and paraded him through the streets. You should have hung him by the wrists from the top of the palisade, with his petition on a brass chain around his neck."

"A Thane, on Thanes' business?"

"This rumor of disaffection is demoralizing for the Swords – it's treasonous!"

"Rumor? You've seen the petition – It's no rumor!"

Corvina watched silently as her mother and brother crossed wills.

Oliva's eyes shone in that particular way they had when she was turning the truth inside out. "We have only his word he speaks for anyone but himself. He could have forged–"

"Every day brings word of uprisings and upheaval."

"A few isolated–"

"The people know about your pet silversmith, Moder, and the Swords tell me the news of him is coming from the northeast, not from the castle servants. My faithful Chief Sword apparently does not number discretion among his virtues. He must have said more in hunting the smith and the unicorn than he should have."

"Yes, he's a fool," said Corvina. "We knew that."

"And am I a fool, too? When I'm so close to the mandate, so close to legitimacy, am I fool enough to antagonize the Thanes? The Istok Raiders are no longer in Istok. Reports say Kinnan is in the country again. If the passing of the mandate to me – to *me* – doesn't set things right, I'll need the Thanes to help restore order – or to escort us to safety!"

Oliva traded looks with her daughter, looks that spoke of contempt for the frailty of their so-called Liege Lord. "We have nothing to fear, my dear. You may trust me–"

With a roughness that thrilled him even as it shamed him, Landry pulled his mother to her window and pointed into the distance. "Do you see that smoke?"

Corvina scoffed. "They burn houses and businesses. The Raiders offer a bounty for every one of our supporters taken *alive!* A revolution should swim upstream in blood. Such people are no match for us."

Oliva smiled at her daughter and glared up at her elder son. This is what came of putting a *man* on the throne. "Why do you cry 'done' so soon? Guthrie will destroy the unicorn for us. He may have done it, already. He may be on his way back, victorious! You have your mandate bag ready to present and receive again. Midsummer Day–"

Landry turned from woman and window with a sound of disgust.

Oliva closed on him. "Give it to me, then, or to Corvina, if you haven't the will to stand by your claim."

"Will? You accuse me of lack of will? After the things I've done –"
Because of your goading, he added to himself, then denied the accusation. He had done nothing because of his mother. What he had done, he had done of his own desire. All her goading had done was irritate him, half-madden him at times, as a flea will half-madden a dangerous dog.

He had had enough of her constant prodding, her twisting, her pushing, her machinations.

"Corvina, leave the room."

Corvina rose and slipped to the door, her widened eyes on her mother.

"Landry!" Oliva cried out, weakly, but he left, too, without a word.

"Swords!" he called, as he closed her door. "Guard this room. No one is to enter, and my mother is not to come out. Is that clear? A servant with my sealed permission will bring her food. No one else should be in this corridor at all."

"May her maidservant come to her?"

"She must do without her maidservant, for now. Do you understand?"

"Yes... Your Grace."

Oliva heard the hesitation, but she doubted Landry did.

It was over then – over for her. Let Landry win or lose, she had lost. Landry had shown himself her master, and Corvina and the Swords had seen him do it. With the turn of a key, she had become one of the "old dogs," part of the past, to be humored, perhaps, but not to be obeyed.

She would not have it. She would not slip into nonentity, settle for kindness from the servants. She would be remembered.

Oliva sat at her writing desk and pulled a sheet of parchment into place. She picked up a sharp bone stylus with the Sarpan lion carved into its handle, dipped it into the inkwell, and wrote:

> *All that was done evil, was done by my order. My children have been in no way at fault. I freely admit my guilt in committing crimes against Onagros and the Layounnan people, of giving my son false counsel, of using my children to advance my own ambition. Let my death serve to instruct others.*

She closed the inkwell, wiped the stylus, placed the parchment carefully in the center of her desk. Then she took out the chip of alicorn Corvina had given her... and swallowed it.

~*~

Eyes red, face pinched, lips thin with fury, Landry reached again for the parchment Corvina carried. She stood above him on the steps and held it beyond his reach.

Pettishly, he struck the wall with the side of his fisted hand. "Must I continue to dance to my mother's tune, even when she's dead? 'Done by her orders…gave me false counsel….' And I was a catspaw? A puppet?"

"We could do worse than be guided by her. You never appreciated her wisdom, her knowledge. You always resented her strength and worked against it, and look at the result!"

"Don't say that!" Landry whispered savagely, shaking Corvina nearly off-balance.

Even as they bickered, they held one-handed to one another, as if to let go would be to die.

"This is her last gift to us." Corvina rattled the parchment. "This is her final plan… and this." She turned her hand to show Landry the small, empty box of unfinished wood in her palm.

"A box?"

"She gave you a piece of alicorn for your mandate bag. I gave her *two* pieces in this box. She swallowed one and left this message: 'Let my death serve to instruct others.' By 'others,' she meant me. *I* kept one piece. We can still win."

Landry laughed, a loud laugh that rang against the bare plaster walls of the tower. "It's over for us, Corry. We'll be lucky if they don't burn us alive."

"It isn't over!"

"You're as bad as she was! Don't you think I'd take whatever chance I could? Make no more mischief."

"The Swords are rallying to you from all over the country! They're raising the citizen militia—"

"The ones who don't join the Raiders against us!"

"The stronger we are, the stronger we'll become! The people are curs: they fight on the winning side. We'll win, Lan. We'll win! Then we'll use my alicorn. We'll take the Onagrans and starve them, then dust their food with powdered poison."

"What Onagrans? Sorcha?"

"And her children. And their chief supporters."

"Who would that be? Thane Robeard?" Into Corvina's silence, Landry whispered in disbelief: "*Hayward?*" Then: "*Grandmoder?*"

"Moder gave us this opportunity that nothing else would provide. They'll have to leave Oakwood. They'll have to walk right into the keep, walk right to us. They'll have to come for Moder's cremation and my ascension to the Sarpan Thanehood."

"No, Corry."

"In three generations, no one will remember another ruler, except in tales. Hold fast."

"I will. Believe me, Corry. Doubt me not: I will."

Corvina received Rhu beren Robia in her workroom. Her mother had been wise in all things but, if Landry had failed to appreciate Oliva's wisdom, Oliva had also failed to appreciate Landry's canniness. Landry had warned against underestimating the Chamberlain. Corvina meant to take that advice.

The new Thane of Sarpa had arranged herself carefully: She sat on a low stool, to increase the distance she would have to look up at him. She took her embroidery hoop from its floor stand and held it in her lap as she had seen the humble women do. At his knock, she called permission to enter, raising the hoop before the door opened so she could lower it attentively at his entrance.

"Ah, Lord Chamberlain. Thank you for coming." With a smile meant to match her brother's sweetness and her mother's gracious condescension, she extended a hand to be kissed.

Rhu bowed over the offering but did not touch it with his lips. "Your servant, My Lady."

"Are you?" She thrust her needle through a knot of embroidery and put the work on the table by her side. "Are you Sarpa's servant, my servant, Landry's servant, or servant of the crown?"

Impassive as always, Rhu said, "They are all the same, are they not?"

A simpleminded answer – or a slippery one? "They are the same, of course. And now your service is needed in a very special way. No one else can be trusted, not even my future husband." *Oh, my Lord Chamberlain! Was that a flicker of gratification I glimpsed on your wooden face?*

"I hope you will always trust me," he said.

"The people have heard of the silversmith my mother called from Kozabir. Rumors are gathering around his presence. He must leave, and must be seen to leave. Yet we dislike the thought of his telling Layounna's business to anyone he meets on his way home, let alone to the Emir."

"What could he have to tell, My Lady? He's been well-housed, well-used, and will be well-paid. He made, I believe, an ornamental bit for My Lady Oliva."

"Which, the people tell each other, Thane Guthrie took to hunt the

Unicorn. It's a most outrageous rumor – inflammatory! ...In fact –" Corvina looked at her embroidery and cast an artfully apologetic glance up at the Chamberlain, "– he did."

"Under orders, My Lady? Or did he set himself a quest in a mistaken excess of zeal, and steal the ornament, believing it to have some kind of power?"

Corvina laughed appreciatively. "Ohhh! Ohhh, My Lord Chamberlain!" She shook a finger in mock admonishment. "This is my promised bridegroom you malign so glibly!"

Rhu bowed. "I meant no dishonor to him, My Lady. I merely asked. I know how devoted Thane Guthrie is to Sarpa. If he had done such a thing, it would be with the purest motives."

Landry was right. Moder and I both have underestimated this man. In fact, I wonder if my brother realizes the richness of this resource.

"Are you also devoted? Purely, zealously, unthinkingly?"

"Not unthinkingly, I hope, My Lady. Thinking on Sarpa's behalf has been my life."

"But would you act, if it were needed?"

"I would."

Now for the test.

"The smith, as I said, must leave, and must be seen to leave. But he must not speak to anyone. Ever. Do we understand one another?"

Without hesitation, the Chamberlain answered, "Yes, My Lady."

"You will do it?"

"If you wish, but it would be better if I arrange for someone else to do it. The best time for the smith to take his leave would be during the Mandate Ceremony, when the city is crowded with witnesses who have something more important on their minds than a foreign artisan. An escort of citizens – castle villeins under my orders and a Sword or two in civilian cloaks – can make sure his exit is remarked by a great many people, but that he has no chance to speak to anyone. Once out of Kudasad, the Swords can decide how far their escort should extend."

The Thane applauded. "Did you devise that on the spot?"

"I confess I formulated the plan in advance, My Lady, in case it should be required. As I said, thinking on behalf of Sarpa has been my life."

"Excellent! Thank you, Rhu beren Robia. As always, your service is invaluable."

She dismissed him with a nod.

A clever plan. She had, in reality, intended to send the smith away safely and richly rewarded, whatever the result of Guthrie's hunt – why not? She didn't fear the outrage of churls, villeins, and serfs, or even of freeholders and townsfolk. *Especially when beren Robia has provided such a simple way to turn my intended into a scapegoat, should one be needed. And perhaps, given my groom's dislike for the Chamberlain, I could persuade my brother to replace beren Robia after the Mandate Ceremony. Reduce him to Steward of Sarpa Thanehold. Where I would have his devotion and plans all at my own disposal....*

~*~

"This was *Rhu's* plan?"

Landry was again watching for Guthrie's return, this time with his sister only. The Kinninger had been only half-attending to Corvina's crooning intrigues, but this last item caught his ear.

Corvina, seeing that he had turned and was sharply focused on her, nodded.

"He actually agreed to arrange for the Kozabirian's murder? *Rhu?*" He tried to imagine hearing such a plot from the Chamberlain, but failed.

"You seem shocked, brother. Your old playfellow has hidden depths."

"No. He does not. Not from me." *Or does he?*

"It disturbs you. I can see how it might. The husband you've chosen for me is a strong man. It might be unwise to have two such strong men behind the throne. And, since my husband will be... my husband, the one to be dispensed with should be the Chamberlain. I quite agree with you, My Lord."

Agree with me? Did I say that? He supposed he had, in a way. But Rhu.... Could he have misjudged Rhu? Would it have been better to have turned to him, a man he knew and trusted, rather than his Chief Sword all these years? No, he had needed a brute, and Rhu was not a brute. Neither was he the "old playfellow" Corvina persisted in calling him. *If I no longer know his capabilities, then Corvina – I – was right: It's time for a new Chamberlain.*

But that was a concern for another day. For now, let Rhu plan the Mandate Ceremony. When Guthrie returned, with or without that fiend-cursed unicorn, they would all decide what best to do with a Chamberlain who betrayed hidden depths.

~*~

Corvina and Landry faced each other across another letter, both faces chalk-white. Corvina, unlike her brother, was livid with rage. Her voice dripped contempt for everyone and everything that conspired against her purpose.

"You should have sent Rhu. Someone else could have carried on with the Festival plans while he worked his diplomatic magic on Grandmoder. 'Decline to attend'…! Decline to attend the cremation of her only child, and a daughter, at that! And, if *she* won't come, of course Hayward and that drab he's married to and their witless descendants won't come. I should have steeped the parchment in poison. I should have written the invitation in toxic ink."

"The invitation itself was deadly enough, and they knew it. I told you Grandmoder was too crafty to be taken in by such a trap."

"You told me, you told me…," Corvina mocked. "All you tell me is why nothing will work." Before he could answer, she snapped, "Never mind. When the mandate is yours, let Oakwood remain rebellious. We'll lay siege to it with our loyal Thanes' warriors and our Swords and our armed citizens. We'll level the ramparts and pull down the walls. We'll overrun it and leave no soul alive."

"Leave no soul alive *there*. We'll bring them here." Landry's brow was clouded, a sign Corvina had learned to read.

"Of course, My Lord brother. The servants can't help but do as they're told. Our taking Oakwood will liberate the poor creatures. Our family, we'll bring here, where they belong. And the trouble will be over."

She smiled and patted his hand, but Landry was not reassured. He was far from reassured.

CHAPTER 15
BLOOD OF THE UNICORN

Guthrie had become accustomed to being respected – being shown respect, at any rate. As a man who loves wine knows one vintage from another, Guthrie knew admiration from envy, wariness from fear, good cheer from mockery. The farther he rode from Kudasad, the more the respect he met was imitation. Ordinarily, it amused him to watch people bite back their true feelings, but this fell into a pattern, and patterns bore watching.

Then he came to Pazni, where he had planned to leave his horse.

The head ostler at the livery stable looked at him with that slightly unfocused stare and spoke with that faintly flattened tone that signaled home-spun humor at another's expense.

"Heard you was after a Unicorn, Master."

Guthrie didn't honor him with a reply. In fact, he didn't honor him with his custom. The man looked like the kind of slack-jawed jokester who would spit in his betters' beer or stick a burr under a superior's saddle. Practice had made it easy for him to forget his own japes along those lines. He had been another person then. He had not been a Thane, Consort to Sarpa's heir.

He led his horse into Fiddlewood and tied her to a tree within sight of the island. There was a causeway, damp. Wavelets washed further over it with every pulse.

Slowly, noiselessly, he crossed.

The island was quiet – utterly silent. No sound from the sheds or the cottage, the woods or the flanking shores, no movement in the clearing. He drew Deya, but even she was silent. Even the blood in his ears was hushed. He couldn't hear his heart. He couldn't hear himself breathe.

His presence was unheralded, undetected.

He searched the outbuildings first. Geese and goats looked up, but did not stir nor make a sound. It was as if the entire island were a helpless animal, and he the serpent that held it in fascinated immobility.

The cottage, then. He pushed at the door. It opened. He walked in.

An old woman in black rose from a stool by the fire, face placid, as if she'd been waiting for him. She was just as Darcy had described her. A strand of red hair strayed from beneath a black and white turban. One hand held a pipe, the other rested on the head of a blackthorn stick. She raised her head and he looked into eyes like seawater turned to heat. Guthrie saw clarity there; he saw reason, and purity that had nothing to do with ignorance. He saw no fear. No respect.

Deya shook in his hand. She vibrated; she would have leaped across the room, but for his iron grip.

"Where are they?"

"There is no one here but you."

Deya trembled and tried to thrust, eager to bury herself in the old woman's heart. Guthrie had never felt such a pull, such a thirst in the sword.

Suddenly, he understood.

He held out Trahern's bit, its silken rein crushed against the metal. "I know you. I know what you are."

The old woman nodded.

He stretched his arm, extending the bait. "My Lady sent this to you. It's a gift. For you. Come get it."

She laughed. "Bring it to me. You've come so far, already."

Deya jerked. It was a strain, holding her back. Made it hard to think… to remember his instructions…. He was to kill everyone. No, everyone *except* the old woman. He was to question her first about… about the unicorn. But she *was* the unicorn! That being so, no questioning was needed. Oliva's dream of Kinnan and Elsie must have meant that killing this creature would end their threat. Of course. Of course. The Unicorn had enchanted itself to appear as an old woman. He would kill it, it would regain its true form, and he would bring Oliva the skin, the horn, the hooves, the bones, the powdered blood.

Guthrie looked into those terrible eyes again, those eyes that saw the lives he had taken with Deya, saw them coating him like a second skin, saw the sword inside that skin with him. He looked into those eyes and saw himself.

Deya struck.

The old woman shouted defiance as the blade descended, cutting her open from shoulder to waist. She fell across the table and then to the floor, pipe flying, blackthorn cane clattering and rolling against a carved wooden chest. Her blood pumped out, poured out, streamed out, spattering Guthrie and washing against his boots in a tide of spent life. The dreadful eyes reflected nothing.

The bit fell, chiming against the flagstones, its silken rope streaming behind it like a tail. He dropped Deya. She splintered like glass on the reddened floor. He tried to wipe the blood from his face, from his hands, but it would only smear.

The old woman's black-and-white turban fell off, spilling black-red hair. He snatched up the cloth. He worked his hands in it, but still the blood clung.

The enchantment didn't break. The body was still that of an old woman, solid and dead. There was no transformation. No skin, no hooves, no horn, no deadly red powder, no occult bones. There was nothing to take his Lady.

He had failed. Failed. He had disobeyed his orders. Deya had taken over. This bloodbath was his punishment, the mark of his miscarriage.

The turban's knot unraveled under his twisting fingers. Out of the cloth fell a jewel.

It splashed and almost disappeared into the red pool, but light glinted off a facet. Guthrie hesitated, then bent and retrieved it.

It was a ruby the size of a hen's egg. *This* would be something to take Thane Oliva!

And Deya was shattered. He had his freedom, at least.

He laced the ruby into a pocket and backed into the soundless yard. He plunged into the river and swam to the forest bank. Water cascaded from his hair, skin, clothes. The blood did not.

~*~

The old woman's body, so pale in life, turned faintly gray. A red sun sank below the belt of trees. The moon herded the hours before it across the sky, and the blood on the flagstones dried and powdered, dusted and disappeared.

Then the insects, the night-birds, the hunters and their prey resumed their quiet striving. And in all this and under all came the intake of a breath and the beating of a heart.

chapter 16
the divine spear

The Players' wagon crested the hill and turned. When the company afoot topped the rise, they saw the cart had pulled aside; Florian was working it between trees into one of his many unofficial campgrounds –"privacies," as he called them. Empty road dipped ahead, and the walls of Kudasad rose beyond. Red and yellow pennants flapped above the wooden keep at the crest of the castle's earthen motte.

Elsie's stomach lurched at the sight and she staggered to a halt. In that castle lived the man who had killed her father and would have killed her, who had given the order that sent Gosling and the other children – how many other children? – to death by Darcy's unknowing obedience. In that castle lived the man who had driven her birth mother from the throne and her adopted mother to desperation. At this close reach, at this last stop, Elsie finally fully shared Brady's fear for the woman who had risked her life to save another's. Not to save the heir to the throne – for Devona didn't know then, and didn't know now, who she had fostered those ten years – but to save another human being.

Brady moved to her side. "It isn't too late to turn back."

Face pale, she shook her head. "Too many people have died by that man's hand. More will die if I turn back – more than will die if I go on. It *is* too late. But Devona…. My mother, Devona…." And what of Rhu? Where would he stand? As a loyal servant, or as an upright man? Could she save him from his choice, whatever it turned out to be?

Kinnan threw an arm around her shoulder, in comfort or in capture. "Keep heart, niece."

Elsie shrugged him off. "I am in heart. I'm no longer a child or a thoughtless girl. That Man won't find me defenseless, this time."

Silvin and Cristoval were vitalized by the sight of the capital. They tried in vain to interest their new comrades in anecdotes of past visits and past plays, and ended by telling the stories over to each other.

Florian, having unharnessed Lumpkin and put him to grass near a small tributary of the Fiddlewood, squatted before his three glum novices.

"Here we are. Can we count on any of you for any performances here? We're liable to do well, with the Midsummer Festival crowds in a spending mood."

Kinnan focused an incredulous look at the manager/director. "The country is in turmoil. The government is in question. There's a revolution."

Florian rubbed his hands together. "People spend money like water in times like these! I know you only agreed to work this far, but I'll give equal shares of our take to anyone who stays."

Elsie laughed a little wildly. After a moment, Brady joined with more amusement and less disquiet. His reaction calmed her.

She thanked Florian for his offer, but refused for herself and her "sweetheart" saying, "We have business to attend to."

Florian raised a questioning eyebrow at Brady.

"I'm afraid their business is my business. And I think it would be better for you if we leave you before we get to the city."

"Ah." The big man stood. "We'll rest here and rehearse, and go in later this morning. You know the procedure: set-up and crying the bill, performance in the afternoon."

Brady's mouth twinged. "I'll be sorry to miss it. Maybe we'll travel together again."

Elsie grasped Kinnan's shoulder with a shaking hand and pushed herself to her feet.

"Time for me to dress."

"The Ceremony isn't for days–"

"She told me to."

There was no answer to that.

It was dim in the wagon when she first closed the door behind her, though light came from the shuttered window in the front. Off again came the boy's disguise and down came her hair. A little water from her waterbag on the tail of her discarded shirt rubbed off the worst of the road dust – though she'd pick up more on the way, she was sure. She opened her pack and dressed in Karol's gown and belt, and re-donned her boy's stockings and boots, the only footwear she owned. She plaited her amber hair into braids and tied them off with twists of Moder's gray mending thread.

She sank to the floor, her legs suddenly too tremulous to hold her. Here was a double circle: Carried from the castle to the Bahari baby farm by Karol beren Ada, from the baby farm to the sea by Landry's agents. and from the sea back to the castle by Darcy; carried again from the castle to Wild Ass Island – or near enough – by a man who only lived thanks to Karol's sacrifice, and now back to the castle with Kinnan beren Ada, Karol's brother. Even if she wanted to resign her position in favor of her uncle, could she? Would the Way allow her to, or would it turn and turn and always bring her back to her beginning? She rather thought it possible. Could she refuse? Something within her said that ignorance or submission, either one, would keep her in the Way; arrogance and willfulness would free her from its direction. Escape from destiny would be that simple. Escape from destiny into a cramped and airless box called "Me." The very thought half-suffocated her.

She stood and smoothed her gown. She was ready.

So it was that Elsie was in the wagon when the thirteen riders cantered up.

The leader was dark-complected, with black hair pulled into a knot at the base of his skull. A few shorter strands curled glossily around his face. His features were strong but well-formed and well-proportioned, and his smile was open and sweet, though his eyes were canny.

The riders – male and female – were all in civilian clothing, but all were armed.

Kinnan assessed them warily. *Not just random travelers, fallen in together on the way to the Midsummer Festival.*

At the same time, they were as jolly and relaxed as holiday-makers. The combination of ease and readiness set Kinnan's nerve jangling. His gaze met that of the front rider with a clash almost strong enough to hear and feel.

The dark man's smile widened slightly.

"The Festival Players at last! Is there a 'Kenneth' with you?"

Kinnan rose as to a challenge. He hoped his companions would have the sense to pile into the wagon and bolt the door if a fight began. He would certainly lose at one against thirteen, but there wouldn't be thirteen anymore, either.

The questioner swung to the ground, sword hand empty and extended in greeting.

"Well met! I had a message from you in Istok."

So this is Anshar – Anshar, "the Divine Spear," who calls himself my lieutenant. Kinnan took the offered handshake and cut a look toward Florian. "We should speak in private."

Florian crossed his arms. "Too late. I hope you don't run me through for saying this, but I'm not an actor for nothing. I look and I listen and I pick everything apart. To begin with, you and the lady inside are no more sweethearts than you and Brady are."

The riders laughed.

Florian continued: "And we've played in Istok many times. We've played for the Raiders, if you want to know the truth. We've played for that threat to the peace, Anshar Redhand." To more laughter, he clasped hands with the dark-haired newcomer. "'Divine Spear,' my arse."

"As long as it's in Landry's arse, never mind yours. – Dismount!"

"Now…." Florian glared unconvincingly from Anshar to Kinnan and back. "If no one minds too very much, could we be told who's been traveling with us and why?"

Kinnan had not survived his years in exile by mistaking foe for friend, or the reverse.

"I am Kinnan beren Ada. And 'Ella' is known as Elsie beren Devona, but her true matronym is beren Karol. She's come to claim her birthright."

Into the resultant clamor, Brady said, "And I–" Silence fell, as everyone turned to hear his disclosure. "And I – am nobody but myself."

Kinnan snorted. "Only under compulsion."

The black-haired Raider measured his fellow rebel. "I heard Kinnan-called-beren-Ada wore a certain bracelet."

Kinnan drew the spiral from his pocket and showed it.

Anshar nodded. "It has magical properties, did you know?"

Startled by the statement, Kinnan was still more startled by the chuckles of the other Raiders.

Holding out his hands for attention, Anshar intoned: "He has a bracelet forged by a wonder-working smith." He stabbed the air with a forefinger. "The very same smith now held prisoner in the castle! Its metal was stolen from a dragon's hoard and tempered in phoenix fire. He can never be killed while he wears it, and he can never strike an unfair blow. Once, in the dark, he challenged a boy who had sneaked into camp to steal food for his widowed mother. Kinnan couldn't see him, and thought he was a scout for the Swords. He drew and lunged at the farm-boy's heart. He couldn't miss – and yet he did. Instead of her son's dead body, the widow opened her door to her living child and a pack loaded with bread and meat." Prosaically, he said, "This is where we all start shouting, 'beren Ada! beren Ada! beren Ada!' But we'll dispense with that for the time being."

The Players applauded, Florian loudest of all. "Mind if we work that into a play? I haven't heard that one before."

"It isn't true," Kinnan protested.

Brady shook his head reprovingly. "You keep insisting on the truth. And you call yourself a Royal."

"He does!" said Anshar. "So do we all." He bowed low to Kinnan. "I am your humble lieutenant, and I bring you these pathetic underlings to use as you will."

Anshar's broad grin and the catcalls of the "pathetic underlings" would have misled some into thinking a buffoon had come trailing a band of mocking ruffians. Kinnan, having spent many years in the camps of such egalitarian discipline, was not deceived.

He nodded approvingly at Anshar and his twelve companions.

"There are more underlings where these came from, I hope?"

"Oh, yes, and even more pathetic than these are. These are the cream." Anshar grew serious, his banter becoming a report. "We've fanned out. Makes us harder to stop. The Swords are easy to evade. They want to stand where they're visible and rattle their weapons on their armor so everybody will run away. So everybody runs away, and we're hiding in the places they run to. Most of them are happy to see us. Those who aren't... well, that's why doors have locks. There are always more folks happy to turn jailer in your name than there are folks happy to turn prisoner for Landry."

In my name. Not Elsie's – mine! Of course, no one knew about Elsie. He hadn't even dared hint about an heir of Karol's body until now. *And now that they know, what next?*

The back door of the caravan opened and Elsie, in her mended gown and disfigured belt, blinked into the light.

When Elsie could see again, she was surrounded by Players and thirteen unknown warriors, all on their knees before her. Only Brady remained standing, but even he dipped his head in the sketch of a bow.

So it's begun. "Please stand. Please."

Solemnly, one of the strangers approached. "I am called Anshar Redhand. We offer ourselves as your honor guard, Your Grace."

"Why do you call me that? Why do you bow?"

"Your mother often wore that gown. She was painted wearing it – I've seen the miniature. And you are very like her, in it. Very like her."

"I could be a look-alike pretender."

Anshar shook his head. "If a pretender had used that dress, she would have produced a much better copy. You are Karol's daughter, or I'm a fool. And I am not a fool."

"She is Karol's daughter," Kinnan assured him. "She carries proof."

"She is her own proof. – Are you ready to enter your city, My Lady?"

"I am."

"Do you carry the mandate bag of Onagros, as well as the bearing and features of the line?"

A quick look at Kinnan found him with his hand on his pocket.

"My uncle carries the mandate bag he's fashioned and filled. The one my mother carried is gone."

"We just took word from riders sent out of Kudasad that Landry dares anyone to present a mandate to oppose his." To Kinnan, Anshar said, "You present yours in Her Grace's name, I presume. Or do the two of you come as rivals, not as a united challenge?"

Well, Uncle? Elsie wondered if he meant not to answer. She would never know, for she found herself answering for both of them.

"That will be as the Way leads. I, for one, will not divide the land by contending against my own blood. However it falls out, Landry's claim of sovereignty will be outfaced, and Onagros will rule again."

"Well said! In that case–"

"But these Players must go first. I would not have them found in such a dangerous band. When they're safely distanced, I'll go on."

Florian rounded up Silvin, Cristoval, and Maida, and put them to readying Lumpkin for the final stage of their journey to the capital.

Then he returned to Elsie's side. "We've talked it over," he told her, though she had seen nothing one could call a conversation. "We've cloaked you all this way. Why throw off your disguise when you need it most? Do you really think Landry would let challengers past the gate guards?"

Elsie shook her head. "If I were discovered in your company.... I would do my best to protect you, but I doubt my best would serve."

"That's understood. Well?"

Kinnan tried to explain. "Landry strikes with a broad sweep. As long as he takes his target, he doesn't care who falls with them. We'll find a way in."

Florian stood silent a moment. Then he turned to Elsie. "Hop in the wagon, Your Grace. Lumpkin's getting restless."

Take these kind performers into peril, just to lessen my own? How could she do such a thing? But how could she refuse them, when they had their own path to walk, and it was this?

"I thank you. All of you. May the Way lead us safely through wherever it takes us."

"Hear, hear!" said Brady, with more urgency than enthusiasm.

With a grin, Anshar returned to his horse. He waved a hand at his warriors. "Mount!"

Brady joined Elsie by the wagon. "This is it, then, Little Mistress. When we pass those city gates, we go into the darkest danger."

She shook her head. "No. There's danger there, but we bring the darkest with us."

He stepped back, raising his arms like wings. "Devona," he said.

CHAPTER 17
REPROOF

The day after his return to the castle, Andrin woke to the now-familiar scent of clean straw, to Chandler's soft clucks and the fall of light through imperfectly fitted boards. Another moment, and he remembered he was no longer in the manor house stable, but in Biddi's little kingdom behind the kitchen garden. The thought warmed him.

He washed in the basin Biddi had smuggled out to him. He did his exercises as best he could in the cramped quarters of the chicken coop while the black-and-white hen watched, feathers fluffed, and beady eyes half-shut.

Nerissa had wanted Chandler to sleep with her in the women's dormitory, but Biddi had doubted the other female servants would accept that. Then the child had wanted to join Andrin in the hen-house, but Biddi had pointed out that such a change of quarters might draw attention, might be reported as high as Thane Oliva herself. Her compromise was a day that started extra-early with a visit to the new coop. They would be here soon, Andrin was sure.

He spoke between exercises. "You've usually laid by the time the sun is this high." Chandler blinked slowly. "Do you think you're entitled to a homecoming holiday?" The hen nestled more snugly into her box. "Surely you aren't going to disappoint the child?"

Chandler turned her head toward the door.

He heard two female voices, one shushing the other.

"Knock first, you shocking girl!" he heard Biddi say with laughter in her voice.

Andrin knocked on his side of the door, sending the child outside into a cackle echoed by the hen behind him.

One of the maids unlatched the door and pulled it wide.

Nerissa slid past him, throwing "Good morning" over her shoulder.

"Good morning to you, too." Andrin exchanged indulgent smiles with Biddi as he took the bread, cheese, and ale she brought for his breakfast. To Nerissa, he said, "There's usually an egg by now. I'm sorry–"

Chandler hopped to the floor, pecking the straw around the Waymaster's feet for crumbs from the cut of brown bread in his hand.

"Oh!" said Nerissa. She stared, enraptured, into Chandler's nest, her hands clasped under her chin.

Andrin beamed approvingly at his feathered companion. "I should never have doubted you." He gave Nerissa a bit of bread. "Here, crumble this for her while you think about what you want to come out of the shell."

"I don't care what comes out of it. Anything will be wonderful."

"Anything but raw egg," said Biddi, sharing another smile with Andrin.

He remembered the joy on the dear woman's face when she had seen him yesterday. He remembered the feel of her, resting comfortably in his arms. *Comfortably, because they were the arms of a trusted friend. A trusted, elderly, shabby, agreeable friend.*

Nerissa watched Chandler eat as if she hadn't spent her recent life among chickens. She pointed out missed morsels with the tip of a bare toe. Unable to wait any longer, she scooped up the egg and, with a beatific smile of anticipation, cracked it open.

A single feather uncurled and drifted to the floor; a long, curved, iridescent blue feather, and nothing else.

Andrin was nearly speechless. "N-next time…." He took the empty shell apologetically. "I always decided on something before I cracked the egg. That might make a difference."

The child retrieved the feather and held it in a sunbeam. It glittered as if coated with powder-fine diamonds. She laughed and swooped it through strips of light.

"It's from my bird! He sent me a feather!"

She waved her treasure before Andrin and Biddi. "I never told you about my bird. He –" She stopped. Then, clearly having come to a decision, she said, "I come from Kozabir. I'm a runaway slave. A bird with long tail-feathers like this helped me get away. Some people would think I was making it up. You believe me." It wasn't a question, it was a sure statement.

Andrin's eyes danced with afterimages of the feather's sparks. "That's a history I'd like to hear."

Biddi tucked a stray strand of roan hair behind the girl's ear. "Tell us, Little One."

Nerissa pushed the feather into her pocket. "When – When my black cat comes back. He'll want to hear it, too. He'll be back soon – he promised."

Biddi smiled. "I'll believe in a cat that talks before I'll believe in one that keeps its word." She held up a hand to stop Nerissa's protest. "But yours is different."

A stirring in Andrin's spirit told him Biddi had no idea just how different Nerissa's cat might be.

It was a strange life he led, now. Up at dawn, exercise, a brief visit with Nerissa. –After the first day, he had suggested Biddi let the child, alone, bring him his food. It had surprised the maid, and wounded her a little. He was sorry for that, but his feelings for her were too deep and too tender to suit their long-time friendship.

Biddi, Nerissa told him, had resumed taking the smith his meals, which made Andrin loathe to listen to chatter about the Kozabirian's doings and increasing good health.

He tried to meditate. He thought about Biddi. He talked to Chandler. He talked to his absent grandmother.

Is this a test? A lesson? I learned serenity by the river. I learned how quickly ten years pass in freedom and activity. Now must I learn how to pass time imprisoned, longing for something I can't have and didn't know I wanted? I certainly hope this is not a foretaste of my future.

At night, he roamed the poultry yards and gardens, becoming the basis of several stories about a benevolent spirit that weeded and hoed while you slept, if you left him a dish of milk or a lump of brown sugar.

His fourth day in the keep, he heard someone coming almost at a run, shrieking and bellowing. The coop door flapped open, and Biddi, face red and hair disordered, thrust a roaring Nerissa inside.

"Hold her. Calm her. I'll come for her later."

Nerissa went rigid and silent between his gentle hands, except for her enraged trembling and her ragged, heaving breaths. When the door was closed and latched, she pulled away, picked up Chandler, and cuddled her so tightly the hen squawked and had to be released.

"I thought they were coming for me," Andrin said. "I thought you were fighting off the Swords. I felt sorry for them."

She was not diverted. "Biddi – Biddi is letting her take him!"

"Take who?"

"Gruffian. The little ginger billy-kid. The Lady is going to sacrifice him, down in her temple. And Biddi is letting her!"

He chided her mildly: "Kids and fowl have gone into the kitchen every day, and come out in your belly. You never protested before."

"That's different. That's for food. This is for hatefulness! Janet's man, Brannon, thanks them first, and kills them so they don't hurt. Who knows what *she* does? And she wanted *me* to bring him to her!"

"You?"

She nodded. "Janet said The Lady wanted the youngest maid in the kitchen to bring the best billy-kid to the top of the dungeon stairs when the sun was highest." Her fists knotted and she shook them toward the wall closest to the castle. "That was me! *Me!*"

"You refused Thane Oliva?" Fear for the child left him hardly enough breath to speak.

"I told Janet. I told Biddi. They said I had to. I said I wouldn't! I said I'd take Gruffian and run away! Janet dragged me into the yard and shouted that I wasn't wanted any more. Then she told Biddi to hide me, if she wanted to keep me, and I could slip back to the kitchen in a day or two. She said she'd have Maia deliver the kid. I said nobody would take Gruffian to *her*! That was when Biddi made me come here."

She would say no more. His defense of Biddi might have been made to the nesting boxes. She spoke only to Chandler, repeating her grievance, venting her rage, mourning the kid, muttering dark wishes against The Lady and her designs. When Biddi brought their lunch, Nerissa dourly ignored her, and only ate when she had gone. She was no more reconciled at supper.

Biddi was equally taciturn, her doll's mouth turned down in sympathy with the child's unhappiness. Andrin longed to hold her, as he had when they were simple friends, as he felt no right to do now.

After a night spent curled around the crooning hen, Nerissa woke merely glum. Chandler, who no longer laid every day, graced her with an egg, which gave forth a water-rounded pebble. Nerissa's delight lasted to breakfast, and she grudgingly accepted bread spread with soft cheese from Biddi's hand.

The next day, she grumbled thanks.

"For what it's worth," the older maid told the younger, "you're a bit of a heroine in the kitchen. Even Janet says you haven't got the sense of a goose, but you've got more grit than anybody in the castle!"

Andrin thought he caught a shadow of gratification pass over the girl's face.

Another sort of shadow was on Biddi's. "She calls for sacrificial animals twice a day. Nerissa, you'd better stay here, as long as she insists on the youngest maid, or until we get one younger. The Lady won't be defied, and I don't think your life means any more to her than that goose you don't have the sense of."

When Biddi brought lunch, she also brought news and Nerissa's freedom. She threw her arms around the girl and lifted her, laughing.

"The sacrifices are over – for a while, at least. Guthrie is gone on his hunt, with his useless bit and his unenchanted bridle. You can come back to the kitchen. Or do you like this life of idleness, with nothing to do but collect pretties from your pet?"

At this, Nerissa returned Biddi's embrace, mumbling, "I missed you!" into the woman's apron.

I miss you, too.

Biddi looked up into his eyes, as if she had heard him. Discomfited, he turned away.

"Nerissa will bring your meals, again," his old friend said, coolly.

Once more, he was condemned to solitary, confined from the light and alone in the darkness.

"Now I know what the inside of an egg feels like," he told Chandler.

~*~

Then came the afternoon when Biddi fumbled open the latch. She clutched the sides of the doorway with trembling hands – big-eyed, white-faced.

"She's dead."

He felt as though his heart had frozen. "Nerissa?"

"No! *Her.* Thane Oliva. Thane Oliva is dead."

Andrin was ashamed at the relief that burned through his veins like acid, the relief that a life he loved would continue, that an irretrievable loss would crush someone other than himself.

"How? What happened?"

Biddi still stood in the open doorway.

"You know."

He waved a hand at the close walls, the low ceiling. "How would I know?"

"You did it."

"No…. No, Biddi. I told you, I don't have the power to strike death. I wouldn't want it. I wouldn't use it." *I wouldn't – would I?* "Please… tell me what happened."

"Her body servant found her an hour ago." Distress muddled Biddi's pronouns, but Andrin was able to sort out which "she" and "her" was which: "She was forbidden to go in to her last night. He locked her in and told the Swords not to let anyone pass. But this morning she asked him if she could tend her Lady, and he said she could. And she found her dead. She was still dressed from yesterday, on top of her coverlet. She said the covers were half off, and Thane Oliva's body looked like… looked like it had tried to tie itself into knots. She said her face…." Biddi swayed.

Andrin reached to support her, but she drew back, turning an accusatory and tear-filled glare on him, saying,

"Not even Oliva deserved a death like that."

"Biddi, I swear to you, on whatever you like, with whatever oath you choose –," he spoke firmly and slowly, hoping to break down her conviction with the force of his truth, "– I did not compass Thane Oliva's death. I did not incite it, I did not cause it, I did not call it to her."

Impossibly, Biddi turned even whiter. "O –!" She bunched her apron to her mouth, to stifle her keening. "It wasn't you," she gasped. "It wasn't *you!*"

She turned and ran, leaving the door open behind her. Andrin saw her stop and pull something from her pocket. She dropped it and stamped it into the earth with her heavy wooden pattens.

Nerissa came not long after, bringing him a wedge of cheese and bowl of parsnip soup. She looked neither shocked nor shaken. She looked, in fact, rather pleased. The child lingered while Andrin ate. Sitting on the floor, where Chandler could scratch and peck around her, she played with the small tortoiseshell comb from that morning's egg.

"They won't miss you in the kitchen?"

Nerissa shook her head happily. "Everything's all upset. Nothing is like normal, and nobody knows where anybody is or what anybody's doing. The Lady is dead."

"Yes, so Biddi told me. It doesn't seem to bother you."

Surprised, Nerissa said, "Why should it? *She* killed things all the time.

She wants to kill the Unicorn. She almost killed Trahern."

"She suffered greatly."

"She made other people suffer."

"I fear you lack compassion, child."

Truculently, Nerissa said, "If you mean I don't care that… that… that somebody put a knife away so it can't cut me, you're right. Is that bad?"

After a moments' consideration, Andrin smiled wryly. "It's neither good nor bad, Little One. It just… is."

She gathered his bowl and spoon and opened the door.

Andrin realized he didn't have to wait till after dark to satisfy his curiosity. "When Biddi left, she threw something away, just inside the gate. Could you find it for me?"

"Of course!"

"I think it got shoved a little underground."

"I'll find it."

She brought it to him, regarding it thoughtfully.

He turned it over. It was a silver disk, highly polished on one side to mirror brightness, the other etched with crescents. Though he had seen it crushed between gravelly mud and a wooden shoe, it was unscratched, unbent, and pristine.

Nerissa ran a finger across the new-moon pattern. "Trahern made it for her. She threw it away once before, and… I found it. I gave it back to her the other day, just before you walked in." She touched it again. "I wonder what she wants, this time?"

With that puzzling remark, Nerissa left him.

~*~

Biddi returned with Nerissa the next morning, looking red-eyed and resentful.

"They're going to burn her here – where the royal family is cremated! That isn't right!"

Nerissa said sending a soul through fire instead of water wasn't right, to begin with – not the proper way to see anyone to the Safe Haven. She approved of it, in The Lady's case.

Biddi wavered between elation and guilt. "Trahern claims *he* killed her – that he prayed to Tortoise for help and that Tortoise unbalanced her mind." She shook her head. "But I did it. I cursed her. I called on Tortoise against her."

"They've been arguing about it." Nerissa stroked Chandler's back. "They argue very quietly, but they argue."

Andrin's Sight spoke through him: "They are each innocent of the fact, though they could both claim intent. And not they, alone, I think."

Nerissa's attention remained fixed on her hen.

Biddi laughed uncertainly. "I think I would like to believe I didn't cause it —" her little chin thrust belligerently forward, "— though I can't say I'm sorry it happened. Trahern is back to full health. Her power died with her."

Gently, he said, "Rest easy. And tell the smith to rest easy, too. I won't say Tortoise didn't involve himself, but neither of you summoned him or directed him."

"Nobody summons or directs him." Nerissa bit her lip, as if she had said too much.

After a heartbeat of surprise, Biddi said, "Oh, of course... you come from Kozabir – you know all about Tortoise."

Andrin nodded. This child walked closer to the Divine Ones – those he had once thought mere superstition – than most. She had met Grandmoder, she was possessively protective of Unicorn, she had been delivered from slavery by a bird with fiery feathers.... "Yes, she knows all about Tortoise."

The girl flashed him a suspicious glance, but met only a benign gleam.

Biddi's eyebrows lowered in a scowl. "Tortoise might as well have saved himself the trouble. Corvina's to be Thane of Sarpa now, and she may be worse than her mother. One of the table servants said Corvina told Landry he should find a new Chamberlain." She gave a derisive laugh. "As if he could do better than Rhu."

Andrin drank the last of his ale. "I doubt she wants a *better*."

Biddi snorted. Then she sighed and said, "Come, Little One. See if there's an egg and back to work."

Andrin tapped Chandler gently on the head. "Nothing this morning. I'm sorry."

Nerissa caressed the spot his finger had touched, as if to smooth away even so soft a rebuke.

"She doesn't have to give me anything else. See what I've had already." She dug into her pocket and laid its contents on her skirt: a tortoiseshell comb... a set of four hair beads in different colors of clay: black, white, red, and blue... an iridescent feather... a river pebble.

Andrin cast a reproachful glance at the black-and-white hen. He felt embarrassed, almost dishonored, by Chandler's illiberality. Even when she gave the child something, it was only a pretty trifle. These rubbishy things were unworthy of Nerissa's gratitude.

For the first time since his dream at Devona's, his grandmother's voice whispered in his ear: *Anything accepted with gratitude is not rubbish, Little Plum.* She said no more but, once again, he felt his burden lift, and he determined to face these days of denial with as much courage and appreciation as the child at his side.

chapter 18
the reluctant disciple

Dusk. Guthrie bypassed Pazni and picked up the Bahari-Kudasad highroad below it. Not for the first time since leaving the island, he had to stop while his stomach heaved. He had long since emptied it, yet nausea cramped and pushed. It was the blood. The old woman's blood, still fresh and hot and clinging to his armor, to his skin, smelling of flesh, tasting of salt and iron. He fought light-headedness. Sweat beaded his body, matted his hair, dripped from his ears and elbows, pink from the blood it never washed away.

Deya was gone, destroyed. His scabbard hung empty at his side, his body felt weightless in his saddle.

He neither saw nor heard the Sword thundering from Bahari until the other man, having drawn rein, shouted, "You're wounded, Brother!"

Guthrie shook his head, gathering strength to speak normally. "It's not my blood."

The other Sword laughed wildly. "I've killed today, myself. They've taken the Bahari armory. The citizen militia turned on the guard. We're all dead or taken but me. They sent me to report – and to help guard the Kinninger."

"Guard the Kinninger? From what?"

The other Sword's mount seemed to sense his master's agitation. The man calmed his skittering horse with difficulty.

"Reports have been flying the past two days. The Raiders are riding west. The Southern Thanes are demanding Sarpa's abdication. The rebel, Kinnan-called-beren-Ada, is supposed to be back in Layounna. There's a Kozabirian smith doing something mystic up in the keep, and the people want to know about it. The Swords have been called to Kudasad, just a few guarding the armories and arming the militia. But the militia—"

Guthrie seized the Baharin by the top of his armor and let the man's alarmed horse ride out from under him. As the soldier fell from his grasp, Guthrie drew his fellow Sword's weapon and slew him with it.

The blade was voiceless, soulless. Deya would have pumped her joy into his blood, her song into his ears. This was only steel – cold… barren. And yet, looking down at the cooling clay that had lately greeted him as "Brother", Guthrie felt the stirrings of that familiar rapture. It was his, a gift of nothing outside himself, but a product of his own strength, his own will, his own spirit. His shout of triumph echoed from the nearby treeline.

The riderless mount, confused and anxious, danced along the road. Guthrie sheathed his stolen weapon and swept across the way, grasping the loose reins and looping them around his pommel. Both horses were ready to run, and Guthrie ran them.

South, toward the capital. When one horse stumbled under him, he stopped and changed, walking them until their breathing steadied. Then he pushed on, cursing their heaving sides, their foaming mouths. All night they galloped, crossing Fiddlewood River at a ford just below the southern tip of the Wood. The dead man's horse went first, collapsing with a sigh when Guthrie dismounted.

Just after dawn, within sight of Kudasad, his horse's heart stopped in mid-stride, throwing him over her head to tumble in the dirt. Rising, he caught sight of himself in a mill-pond: filthy, wild-eyed. As he raised his hands to the light, the dust-caked blood renewed itself, brightened, as wet and red as when he had spilled it, pristine as the ruby he carried, hot as the heart of a bee-hive.

He heard a horse whinny. A door in the ground floor of the mill opened, and a sleepy-eyed boy came out, heading for the stable. Guthrie drew his sword.

The boy saw a vision of horror sprinting toward him. Against all probability, the lad did not stand gawping, but dodged back into the mill and barred the door.

Faces, frightened and furious, watched as Guthrie took the best horse the miller owned, transferred his saddle from his own dead mount, and rode away. They watched, and the miller cursed, but no one attempted to interfere with him.

~*~

Darcy Aminta berer. Valda had just settled to work when the lower bailey erupted in confusion. His Deputy rushed to the door, gabbled to someone outside, and rushed back in to tell the news before anyone else could.

Darcy, hearing it, sank back into his chair. This chair – it was the one old Gilbert had sat in when he, Darcy, as Gilbert's Deputy, had first heard of the old woman in Fiddlewood. Why had he told Guthrie about her? He felt weak – sickened with himself. Yet what had he done wrong? Why should he not answer simple, straightforward questions put by another of his master's men? How could he know Guthrie would ride away and return covered in blood?

His Deputy peered at him. "What is it? You don't look well."

He certainly felt ill: hot and cold at once, with a tightness in his stomach, dry lips, weak knees. "Yes. Strange…. I felt well enough this morning. Perhaps I'd better go home."

"Shall I fetch a chair and bearers for you?"

"No, thanks. I'll walk. Fresh air…."

The fresh air did feel good on Darcy's face, stirring his lank blond hair. He shivered and hurried home, feeling an almost physical need for Devona's comforting presence.

~*~

Dead?

Guthrie heard none of his future bride's artfully rendered scorn, her biting commentary on his failure.

My Lady would have understood.

And now his Lady lay cold in her cellar temple, where they were to have presided together. There she lay, stretched upon her own altar, wrapped in fine linen soaked in oil, sewn into oilcloth, waiting her cremation. At least he had not missed that.

"You might have washed before you presented yourself to your Kinninger and your betrothed," Corvina harried. "You might have shown that much respect –"

"Enough!" Landry broke into her tirade and into Guthrie's thoughts. "Our mother chose Guthrie for this errand, and he has not failed. He didn't find Elsie or Kinnan because they were *not there!* And of *course* he brought back nothing of the unicorn. Without Moder, who could we trust to deal with such potent items?"

"He didn't know—"

"Tortoise knew! Tortoise knows all. Tortoise knew our mother killed herself in his service, and blessed us accordingly: Guthrie has broken his own enchantment. I count that no failure."

The Sword looked at his liege, then, and saw the sweet smile for which he had done so much. Landry understood.

"I have not quite nothing, My Lord." He stuck two wet, red fingers into a pocket and drew out the ruby. "This was tied in the old woman's turban."

Landry drew a sharp breath and reached out.

Guthrie had never been religious, but the words seemed to anchor his lightness, to press him firmly to the ground again: "In My Lady's name... all my service for you, I do also for Tortoise, to honor her memory." Guthrie put the ruby into Landry Oliva's hand.

Landry's slender fingers closed on the jewel. The gaze he lifted to the Sword was narrow-eyed, thin-lipped. Guthrie had seen such a look on Oliva's face, many times. "As for my reluctant and elusive bride.... At last, I find myself eager to know where she is. She's led us a chase through my mother's dreams and the peasants' stories and it's time for the chase to end. We agreed that the father lacks the nerve to shield her from us, but the mother has proven tediously recalcitrant. You're weary, my friend, but tomorrow—"

Guthrie gripped the pommel of his sword. "I'll go now, My Lord. The woman's a pea-brain and her husband's a weakling." *A weakling with at least one secret too many.* "They will be much happier in the keep, where they ... can and will speak freely."

~*~

Darcy found his wife in her scrivenry.

"Devona... please... I need to talk with you. Privately." Darcy removed the quill sign from in front of the shop and closed the door, a signal to even the illiterate that business was suspended.

Devona came from behind the counter and took Darcy's icy hands. "Tell me."

"I've done something terrible." *Again.* "I didn't know it." *Again.* "Guthrie beren Melanell came asking questions about an island in the Fiddlewood near Pazni. I told him I'd been there. Told him about an old woman who lives there – what she looks like, that she lives alone. He rode away. Today he came back.... He had killed. Killed or wounded—"

Devona dropped Darcy's hands, her round brown face bloodless as dust.

The Roll-Keeper felt his own face drain white. "What have I done?"

"Elsie," Devona whispered. Then she shouted, "*Elsie!* You didn't drown her, you didn't marry her to Landry, so you sent the Chief Sword after her! *Elsie... on that island... with that old woman...!*" Devona's cry sank, smothered by horror.

Elsie! Is it the will of the Way, that she should die by my hand?

"Devona! I never meant—"

There was a thump at the door. Out of habit, Darcy had dropped the latch, but no bar could withstand the battering that shuddered the wooden planks. The latch sprang free and clattered into a corner. The door crashed wide. The Chief Sword stood, matted with gore, in the opening.

Darcy felt his knees buckle, and stiffened them. Softly, he said, "The Wall Street gate."

Guthrie stepped inside. "Come with me. Both of you."

"Of course." Darcy astonished himself with the coolness of his voice. "I was just telling my wife she's played stubborn long enough. – Pack our things, my dear."

Guthrie put hand to hilt. "No! Now!"

Darcy shoved Devona through the door to their living quarters and closed it behind her. He turned the key and dodged behind the counter with it. As Guthrie advanced, Darcy grabbed the nearest thing to hand – an inkpot – and threw it at him. He threw a pen, a straight-edge, a roll of parchment, a box of nibs – anything, everything.

~*~

Shaking with terror, Devona found she couldn't turn from the door, couldn't run as she knew she must. She shuffled backward, and met a living obstacle. She whirled.

"I'm here, Mistress. Do you want to run away?"

Brady! But what was wrong with his eyes? His eyes were orange – Brady's eyes were dark....

"Do you want to run away?" And Brady never spoke so harshly....

She nodded. She owed it to Darcy to save what he thought worth his death.

Brady grinned. "Desertion. Good! I didn't think you had it in you."

The hallway disappeared. She was in the open; a garish box on wheels stood where Brady had been. Kudasad lay not far ahead. She stumbled around the wagon toward the sound of voices. All faces turned to her. There was Brady again, his eyes their own bright black. And... and Elsie! Her darling girl, in a patched-together gown. And armed men and women on horses!

~*~

Guthrie leaned into the street to deputize some of the Swords now swarming Kudasad. "Into the courtyard! Enter the house another way! Search it! Search the garden! Let no one escape!"

Darcy stood panting behind the counter, hands and clothes ink-stained. Elsie's tortoiseshell cat, Trenel, chose that moment to saunter in from somewhere and leap onto the counter.

"Faithful pet." Darcy wiped his face with his sleeve, staining half his blond mustache black. "Come to see your master off?"

The Chief Sword turned again.

"Faithful pet," Darcy repeated, picked up the cat, and threw him.

The cat vanished, replaced by a massive warrior in black and scarlet armor, roaring – roaring with laughter.

The warrior drew a sword longer than Darcy's arm, saluting Guthrie with his blade.

"Defend yourself, killer of children and old women."

Guthrie wavered.

The warrior's laugh grated. "Cross swords with me. You gave yourself to me, not an hour ago. I've come to accept you. – FIGHT!"

He swung. The Chief Sword met the onslaught. The warrior struck, blocked, dodged, maneuvered Guthrie into the room, putting himself between the Sword and the door.

"Out, little man!"

The warrior snapped the words to Darcy, who scrambled to obey. Guthrie lunged over the warrior's guard. Darcy, too shocked at the blow to make a noise, slid to the floor, his back against the counter, pressing a hand to the flowing gash in his shoulder.

The warrior hissed in fury. His weapon arced around with a low whistle and severed the Chief Sword's neck. Blood pulsed, splashing the walls, staining paper and parchment. The head, red hair streaming, bounced off a wall and rolled through its own blood. Still hissing, the warrior kicked Guthrie's head into the street. Rage still unspent, he kicked the body after it.

He returned and leaned over Darcy.

"Don't look so pleading, Little Man. I can't save you, though I hate to see you go. I always liked the way you thought."

The light reflecting off the warrior's hooked nose was the last thing Darcy saw before his vision darkened.

chapter 19
the roll-keeper's daughter

Devona threw herself between Elsie and the mounted fighters.

"You can't have her!" she shouted. "I've lost everything – you can't have her, too!"

"It's all right, Moder." Elsie tried to edge around her, but Devona backed up, pinning her against the wagon.

Devona's tightly-coifed hair had come unwound and hung in brown tatters around her face. Her spectacles sat askew her nose, her normally placid face was drawn into a savage grimace.

The Raiders stared at her in awed stupefaction.

Brady approached her quietly, spoke softly to her. "It's all right, Mistress. These are friends to us."

The scrivener turned her rage on her apprentice. "You were to take her to safety! Why is she here?"

Elsie grasped Devona's shoulders. "He's been heroic, Moder."

Brady goggled a bit at that.

"Moder, I made him bring me. I had to. It's all right. Believe me."

Devona shuddered and covered her face with her hands.

Elsie embraced her. "What's happened, Moder? How do you come to be here?"

"Darcy!" Devona breathed deeply and let it out in an involuntary sob. "Guthrie came for me. Darcy saved me. He's dead. He must be dead."

Years rushed over Elsie – years of indulgence, private jokes, camaraderie, of flaws forgiven, arguments made up. She tried to retain perspective, to remember who she was by birth, but knew herself to be a daughter who had just heard of her father's death.

Devona raised a glare to Brady. "You accused me of desertion–"

"When? I didn't! How could I?"

"It was some *other* varier, then, in your shape?" Her sarcasm was acid enough to etch glass.

Baffled, he nodded helplessly.

Devona wiped her eyes with the tail of her gown. "I have to go back. I have to...see to him." She gritted her teeth in defiance. "Let the Swords take me!"

"I'm going, too, Moder. – Don't say no." It wasn't a request, it was a command.

Before Devona could speak, Brady explained: "I overheard Master Darcy tell you a story, the night Elsie's cat almost ate me. Elsie knows the story that comes before it. She knows who she is."

Elsie, Kinnan, and Devona, who might be recognized by friend or Sword, rode in the closed wagon. Florian drove, with Maida beside him. Brady, now blond and weedy, walked behind with Silvin and Cristoval. Anshar and his people spread around them and pretended they were not together.

Karol's daughter held Elsie's mother to her heart. Devona, mourning her husband, anxious to return to him, to sit watch by his remains as she had sat by her birth daughter's the night of Elsie's coming, rested there fitfully. She had hardly seemed to understand Elsie's story.

They passed through the city gates.

"Halt!"

The wagon, moving slowly already, juddered to a halt.

They heard Florian's jovial baritone ask what was wrong. He was told all conveyances had to be inspected.

Kinnan drew his sword.

"Put it away, Uncle." Elsie touched his wrist, still bare of the bracelet her mother had given him. "If there were hope in fighting, the Raiders would already be drawing blood. We'll have to trust our disguises – and our luck."

Glowering, Kinnan sheathed his weapon while Elsie wrapped herself in a cloak.

The back door opened. A Sword unfolded the steps and climbed into the doorway.

Elsie's mind flew to that dreadful night at the baby farm ten years ago, to the men in silver and black, to the Moder's hideous cry and her own

abduction. She could smell the sweetish liquid dabbed with fortunate inad-
equacy on the cloth tied over her face, could taste and feel the fabric on her
lips. This man was not the one, but the threat of his nearness brought it
horribly back.

Devona felt Elsie tremble, and sat up. One hand went into the props
box for something that would serve as a weapon, but everything she touched
was flimsy and useless. Veils, disguises, wooden swords....

The Sword spread his shoulders, resting his forearms on the door
frame, blocking anyone else's view of the wagon's interior. "Morning." He
canted his head back to squint at the sun. "Afternoon, I should say." When
no one replied, he shrugged and continued as if in leisurely conversation.
"We're supposed to be looking for the Kinninger's vanished bride. You
know about that, I expect. Everybody knows about that." He still got no
more response than if his three listeners had been nothing but props, themselves. "I had just joined the Swords the day the Roll-Keeper brought his
daughter to her bridal. I was as near to the maid as...well, as I am to you."
He looked at each of the three in turn.

Elsie shrank as far as she could into the shadows.

The Sword didn't seem to notice. He went on: "When perdition broke
loose today and my Chief ordered all gates closed but this one, I made sure
I got put in charge of gate duty. You see, I thought the lady might still be in
Kudasad – might try to use the upset to slip out. If she did, I wanted to be
the one who spotted her. I never thought of her trying to get *in* but, either
way, I wanted to be on duty." He smiled at Devona. "I've kept an eye on
her mother's shop, as well, though I hardly needed to, with the Chamberlain around."

Devona drew her hand out of the props box.

The Sword still lounged against the light. "I'm told there was some
kind of row at the scrivenry a bit ago. Very sad thing: The Chief Roll-
Keeper was wounded. Our Chief Sword was killed by some rogue in black
armor, who struck and vanished. The scrivener's missing, too."

Elsie and Devona slipped their arms around one another and held tight.

"The Chamberlain came and took over there, so all the Swords could
get on with the Kinninger's business." He turned his attention to Kinnan. "I
was in the Great Hall back when Kinnan beren Ada came to claim the
crown. I thought *he* might try to take advantage of all the trouble today, too.
Be funny, if he and the bride and her mother turned up together, wouldn't

it?" He backed down a step. "Well, welcome to Kudasad. Always glad to see new faces. Enjoy your stay." Down another step. "The name is Bryan beren Basha, should you strangers need anything." He folded the steps into the wagon and shut the door. "*You, driver*," they heard him shout. "I've seen you lot perform before. Follow me to the Chamberlain. I think he may want you for the Mandate Ceremony."

~*~

The Festival Players' wagon barely squeezed through the arch into the scrivenry's courtyard.

"One more coat of paint, and she wouldn't have made it," Florian said.

Devona was out of the wagon before it had come to a standstill.

"Stop! This is private pr –" It was Rhu, in the manor's side doorway. "Devona!"

Captain Bryan dismounted and supported the distraught woman. "I brought 'em to you. Couldn't think what else to do with 'em, and you know this one. She would have crawled over glass to get to her man, wherever I took 'em."

"Thank you, Captain. Very well done–"

Devona clutched the front of Rhu's tunic. "Darcy is hurt? How badly?"

The Chamberlain's face was more closed than it had ever been. "You're in time. Not by many minutes, I think. I bound his wound and had him moved into the parlor. Your shop… will have to be cleaned."

"I'll burn it." Devona pushed past him.

"Be right back. She's a bit shaky." Bryan followed her.

While the Players clustered near the garden wall, the Raiders unobtrusively patrolled the street outside the courtyard. Brady, returned to his own form, had just blended into the shadow of the entry arch when Elsie descended from the wagon.

Rhu stood staring at the woman in Karol's dress. Ten years ago, he had seen her lifted down from a cart – here, in this very yard – and his heart had seen her not as she had looked then, but as she looked now.

Elsie found a smile for him, from within her worry and sorrow. "Do you still not know me, My Lord Chamberlain? My Tall Man? My huntsman, who hoped not to find me in Fiddlewood?"

"Elsie…." The master diplomat could find no words.

She reached up and touched his face, toyed with the ends of his butchered hair.

"We'll renew our old acquaintance later. My parents need me now."
She entered the manor.

Brady found himself privy to something extremely rare: the
Chamberlain's face betraying the Chamberlain's heart. Rhu's tenderness
for the Roll-Keeper's daughter had amused the varier on the day of Elsie's
bridal. Now, he was not disposed to laugh at a man's romantic yearning.

Rhu saw him and regained his self-possession. "Ah. The missing
apprentice. Brady, isn't it?"

"Yes."

Haltingly, as if the answer were whispering itself into his ear, but in a
language he did not speak fluently, Rhu said, "Why does she wear Karol's
gown? When did her features find their shape... take on the likeness....
Who is she? I think you know."

"I think you should ask her."

The Chamberlain opened his mouth to speak, but broke off when he
and Brady were joined by Kinnan.

"My Lord Chamberlain." The soldier grinned, flush with the wine
of danger.

Rhu looked into the eyes of the smiling rebel and wondered how he
had missed so many resemblances for so many years. "I have done you
much wrong, in the name of my duty. I know now what I suspected all
along: that your claim is valid. Kinnan beren Ada." The Chamberlain focused his mind on how to move Sorcha's heir designate to Sorcha's side.
He would learn exactly how Elsie-called-beren-Devona was placed in
Onagros' family line when time permitted. For now, it was enough to know
she was of the Royal House and forever beyond his reach. That dream was
finished.

Kinnan was speaking: "I have heard *much* of you, and remember you
as a man of honor. Take my hand. We're friends."

Hesitantly, Rhu put his smooth palm against Kinnan's calloused one.
He spoke with more than a trace of bitterness: "But... I'm only a servant—"

Kinnan clapped his other hand onto the back of Rhu's, holding it in the
clasp of comradeship. "And I'm a silversmith, the son of a silversmith and
the brother of one."

"You're Sorcha and Karol's brother. You should be at Oakwood.
You and... your kinswoman, Elsie."

"I should be here. I've come for the Ceremony. I've brought my mandate to challenge Landry's. Brought *ours*, I mean. The mandate bag of Onagros."

Bryan trotted out of the manor. "I left them with him. He wasn't gone, yet, though that might have been easier than watching it happen."

Kinnan released Rhu and shook hands with the Captain. "Well met. Our thanks for the escort. Are there many of your fellow Swords who would stand with us?"

"I couldn't say. I know there are some. There may be more, with Guthrie beren Melanell dispatched."

"Enough for our plan to save the smith," Rhu said, with guarded hope.

"Oh, yes, plenty—"

Brady and Kinnan broke in, together. "Trahern?"

Rhu raised an eyebrow. "The story is widespread, but it never includes his name. I take it you know him. Captain Bryan and I—"

Lumpkin, that most placid of beasts, snorted and sidestepped in his traces. Florian clutched the harness, but the big horse clomped skittishly on the paving stones. There were footsteps – uneven footsteps – as someone trod the gravel path from the back garden.

Devona sat by the bench, holding Darcy's hand in both of hers. He was even paler than usual, waxen and yellow. His clothes and fair hair were stained with ink and blood. Elsie joined her and knelt at his head, listening for dreaded silence, weeping when she heard his faint, shallow breathing.

His eyes fluttered open.

Elsie claimed his hand from Devona.

He drew breath slowly. "What have I done? What... to you?"

"You saved my life."

"I—"

"You saved my life. I love you."

A voice rasped from the doorway. "I've come to return your visit, My Lord Roll-Keeper."

Elsie sprang to her feet. "Moder Zglaria!"

"Bring me a clean cloth and a binding strip and a bowl of fresh water."

Devona ran for what the old woman asked for.

Elsie still held Darcy's hand and reached for Moder's, as if she could connect one's weakness to the other's strength. "How did you know to come?"

Moder Zglaria stumped into the room, her blackthorn stick before her. "A little bird told me. A turtledove."

Darcy's eyelids fluttered. "The bees…," he murmured. "The bees…."

Devona returned. "He's lost a great deal of blood. Rhu thinks…."

Even as she spoke, Darcy let out a rattling wheeze. He drew no further breath.

"Darcy?" Devona whispered.

She found herself sitting in one of the room's heavy chairs while Elsie assisted the woman from Wild Ass Island. Together, they unbound Darcy's wound. It bled very little, now. Moder took a knife from her skirt and cut the cloth away from his shoulder.

"You've hurt yourself!" Elsie reached for the old woman's arm.

"Just a nick. Clumsy." She dunked her wrist into the water bowl. Red swirled and tinted the clear liquid. "Clean his wound."

Elsie did as she was told, wetting a cloth in the stained water and sponging the rent in her father's cooling flesh. She refused to register his utter stillness, but worked as if time were important.

"Now bind it."

She did.

"Now rest. We've done what we could."

Devona whimpered, knowing her husband was lifeless, yet – like Elsie – pushing the knowledge away.

Elsie stared at the floor. "His death isn't the first in this affair, and it won't be the last."

Moder folded her hands on the knob of her cane. "No."

"I don't want what I came for. I don't want it at this price. If I could bring back the lives by giving up my place, I would."

The old woman gave a huff of approval. "That's what makes you worthy of it."

When Elsie looked at her, Moder said, "Have you ever lost your balance and stumbled, and twisted your ankle steadying yourself? Have you ever fallen and hurt yourself – even drawn blood – before you could regain your feet?"

"Yes," Elsie murmured.

"That's sometimes the way it is. A fall can't be entirely controlled, of a body or of a land. It can only be taken and recovered from."

"Or not recovered from."

"Or not recovered from."

Devona cried out. She leaped from her chair and pushed between the women. Weeping, she threw herself on Darcy.

He drew another breath.

CHAPTER 20
CLAIM AND COUNTERCLAIM

Bryan beren Basha rode in silence as he led the Players' wagon out of the courtyard. Rhu beren Robia was accompanying the Festival Players to the Hall of Burgesses, where they would give a special performance for the city officials. After that, they would be free to set up where they pleased, with the privilege of calling themselves The Lady Mayoress' Company.

It was Florian, again driving the cart, who started the conversation. "There's something sticking in your craw. Cough it up, Captain. It'll do you good."

Rhu, next to Florian on the driver's seat, said, "A problem? Reservations? We agreed this was the safest course."

After a moment, Bryan said, "Oh, yes, they'll be safe, this way. But.... I know a dead man when I see one. The scrivener's husband was as near dead as any living man I've seen. Yet we're moving him, alive and speaking."

Darcy had been carried to the wagon on an improvised stretcher, joined there by Kinnan, Devona, and Elsie, who had changed into what Brady called her "Mistress Elsie" clothes. Karol's gown, she had stuffed into a sack along with her walking boots, and carried with her.

The other Players were strolling behind, juggling and singing. The Raiders, their number growing by the hour, rode discreet guard. Brady had scrambled to the wagon's roof, where he lounged and listened.

Bryan hadn't finished his questioning. "And where did that old woman come from? And where did she go? There's nothing at the rear of the house but garden and beehives. The door in the back wall was latched from inside. I checked before we left."

Brady peered over Florian's shoulder. "I can answer that. I'm the scrivener's apprentice, you know. I usually put a string on that latch. I might want to get in by that way. The old woman's a healer, in town for the Festival. She heard about the Master being hurt and found the gate on the latchstring and let herself in. When she closed the door on her way out, the latch fell down and fastened itself. It does that, sometimes."

"There was no string. I checked."

"I took it off. I have it in my pocket – Well, curse it! I've lost the blessed thing. Now I'll have to make another one."

The apprentice's face was far too fresh and innocent to doubt. Rhu and Florian glanced at him, then quickly away. Neither dared meet the other's eye.

~*~

Corvina all but crowed in victory. "They've delivered themselves to us!"

Landry slapped the paper she held. "Did you read the same words I did?"

"Kinnan is in Kudasad! Our loyal Chamberlain has him under guard at the Hall of Burgesses."

"Did you read what the people say? They say I sent Guthrie and a troop of Swords to murder the Mayoress and Burgesses. Kinnan leaped from a tapestry – from inside it, not from behind it – and killed Guthrie with one blow. The Swords don't have him under arrest – they want to take him, but they're afraid to attack again. – Oh, yes, and they say Karol has returned with Kinnan. She nursed the wounded – Swords included – bandaging them with strips torn from her own gown. The wounded were healed instantly. The dead took an hour or so."

"Children's tales. Plays done in the squares by mountebanks–"

"They are the stories the people are telling each other about themselves! About us! Can't you understand that? Do you not hear? My Chief Sword – your husband who was to have been – is dead. That's not a children's tale. They found his body in a midden by the tannery and his head in a basket in the lower bailey. Revolution boils around us –"

Corvina faced her brother. "Give up, give up, give up! That's all I hear from you! Have you forgotten your mandate? Rhu will bring the rebel to the Midsummer ceremony. Let him watch you present your mandate bag. Let Kinnan-who-calls-himself-beren-Ada see the Mayoress and Burgesses return it to you–"

"Will they?"

"Surrounded by Swords? They will. Put him on the palisade to proclaim you the mandated Kinninger. Let the people tell their stories, but they'll live by hard truth."

She greeted Rhu's entrance to the Great Hall by rising and extending her fingers for his kiss. "Ah, Rhu beren Robia! Once again, you prove your merit."

He bent over the hand and warmed her knuckles with his breath but not with his lips.

Landry sat, silent and observant, while his sister showed honor to the Chamberlain. Rich currency, to an inferior, and easily counterfeited.

"You've done what my would-be husband could not, Rhu beren Robia. And just in time for my mother's incremation and my investment as Thane of Sarpa."

Landry commanded attention by leaning forward, though he did not stand. "Name your reward, old friend." His sweet smile contended with Corvina's graceful praise.

"I am a vassal, My Lord… My Lady. It's my place to serve." With a deep bow, the Chamberlain took his humble leave.

~*~

The late Thane Oliva was placed on a traditional construction of spice-and-oil-coated wood. Landry and Corvina, now the keep's chief Tarkastrian devotees, called the Divine Ones to witness Their handmaiden's passing and to show her Their favor. Flaming torches were thrust into the kindling at the base of the pyre. An inferno flared at the edges. The small wood caught, then the larger pieces…. Then the flames died back to flickers too high to stop, not high enough for efficiency. All afternoon, the funeral pile burned sullenly, and the spice-coated wood smelled of mold and rot.

Corvina's investment, too, was plagued by misfortune. The company was thin, to begin with. The number of Thanes pledging fidelity to their new peer only increased awareness of the number who did not. Ghastly smoke from Oliva beren Audre's sluggish cremation infiltrated the Great Hall, fouling the air and tainting the delicacies Janet and her subordinates had prepared for the tributary feast.

The new Thane of Sarpa seemed not to notice. She took her mother's place one seat nearer the throne and fluttered with triumph far into this shortest night of the year. She urged her guests to drink and feast while she sipped and nibbled and watched.

Landry watched, too – watched his sister increase in their mother's absence, as one tree thrives when another, which overshades it, dies.

That night, he dreamed the castle was flying apart. Every stone, every stick of wood shot off in another direction, yet every piece struck him. Every strike brought blood and, with every drop of blood, the people cheered. He called for Guthrie; the Chief Sword didn't come. He called for Corvina; she laughed scornfully as she reached out to him, then dissipated in the troubled air. He called for Rhu, but saw only a shadowy figure with indistinct features and a wavering silhouette.

He dreamed he was alone, adrift on a river, the castle tower back where it belonged, receding in the distance as the current carried him away.

He woke with a gasp and lay, panting and perspiring, clutching his coverlet with both hands until a gray dawn drizzled at the casement and it was Midsummer Morning.

There had not been a Mandate Ceremony in living memory – or in any written record short of myth. Rhu had pieced together a ritual out of scraps of writing, oral tradition, Landry's instructions, and his own sense of fitness. It would take place in mid-morning on the longest day of the year. It would include the Lady Mayoress and the entire Council of Burgesses, representing the capital, and the Thanes, representing the rest of the people – providing those Thanes swore to abide by the proclamation of the city's representatives. Thane Robeard had, predictably, objected, but Rhu had brought him around.

Rhu was good at bringing people around to his way of thinking, Elsie had found. He had persuaded the Mayoress and Council of Burgesses to declare their allegiance – like most of the town, firmly against Landry – without revealing his own. He had convinced them to shelter the most dangerous man in Layounna until the Mandate Ceremony – and to give him up then without a fight. He had arranged for Landry to *order* Kinnan to come challenge him!

The one thing he hadn't managed was a private interview with Elsie. Instead, he had offered plans for Kinnan's consideration, conferred with the city officials, given orders, and treated her with distant respect.

Brady, although she had always credited him with the sensitivity of a hitching post, noticed. "You don't like it, do you? Kinnan playing the role of heir apparent, when we all know better? Rhu being all subservient? It's safer for everybody, you know: for Rhu and Kinnan, not just for you. Landry expects Kinnan. Rhu will present him with Kinnan. Landry and Kinnan will offer their mandates. Landry expects the Council to choose his, but they'll choose Kinnan's. As soon as that's all sorted out, Kinnan will announce your existence, they'll fetch you from the Hall of Burgesses, you'll be pronounced Kinninger of Layounna, and you can order Rhu to give you a big sloppy smooch."

Elsie felt herself redden. She gave Brady's chest a backhanded slap. "Fool!"

Let him jest, if it pleases him, but neither of us thinks it will be so easy. Well, Rhu and Kinnan aren't the only ones who know how to plot. Leave me behind, while my future is decided and others take the risk for me? I, child of Karol beren Ada? I, a woman? Moder Zglaria had sent her to Kudasad with the clothes Karol had worn in leaving it. That had not been done in order for someone else to face death in her stead. Karol had left her own hard work to others, and innocents had paid the price. Karol's daughter would not make the same mistake, commit the same sacrilege.

~*~

As the time approached, the drizzle stopped, but the day remained dim and damp and oppressive. The streets were lined with people in a high state of excitement. Swords on foot and horseback patrolled High Street and scoured the byways in twos and threes. No one offered them any violence, but no one met their eyes. The whole country seemed to be in a breathless truce that would surely hold until the Ceremony. Afterwards....

At last the People's Procession descended the Hall of Burgesses' cedar steps. A great *huzzah!* went up.

First came the Lady Mayoress. Her cote was green embroidered with gold lozenges, her surcote a simple green. The gorget swathing her ears and neck and the wimple on her head and down her back were yellow. Her chain of office was softly gleaming gold. The twelve Burgesses followed, two by two, in dark green cotes and paler surcotes, wearing gorgets and wimples, or hats like acorn caps. Behind these marched twenty town runners in full-length hooded sepia all-weather capes, extending the parade to suit the importance of the occasion. Two of the capes, it was whispered, concealed Kinnan beren Ada and the True Kinninger, Karol.

An escort of Swords walked between the procession and the crowd. They stopped at pre-determined cross streets, where Thanes, each in his or her House colors, joined the column.

A raven flew above it all and landed somewhere in the upper bailey. Many spectators viewed the flight and the cloudy weather as ill omens for Sarpa. They did not trouble to conceal their satisfaction.

Up High Street and into the lower bailey the Procession walked with swift dignity. When all were inside, the drawbridge gate was raised and barred. The closing of the bailey generated protests from the citizens left outside, but a few crossbowmen displayed on the palisade kept that to a minimum.

Corvina had wanted the throne brought down from the Great Hall and a dais built for it in the yard, but Landry had refused.

"I will meet my people at their level. I'm supposed to be giving them the chance to reject me, and they're supposed to be insisting I remain. If we're going to play out this fiction, let's at least play it out consistently."

So Landry stood, with his sister at his side, the Chamberlain behind them. The new Chief Sword and a half-dozen picked men formed a semi-circle at their backs.

The Lady Mayoress stopped a double arms-length from Landry. The Burgesses made a half-circle behind her, two deep, the Thanes a double-line behind them. The hooded followers formed a single line at the rear, ringed by a guard of Swords.

One sepia-cloaked figure walked forward to stand to the right of the Lady Mayoress. He pushed back his hood and folded his cape behind his shoulders.

Corvina clapped her hands together once in pure joy. "The pretender! We've searched for you from Sule to Kozabir, and now we have you!"

"I am not the pretender here. I am Kinnan, born of Ada."

"You are—"

Landry snapped, "We would speak for ourself, Sister. Hold your tongue."

Astonishment clear on her face, Corvina fell silent.

Landry spoke so all in the lower bailey could hear him. "Your false claims have troubled this land for long enough. I welcome your challenge. Let us put an end to your dissension. From this day onward, let Layounna be at peace with itself."

He motioned Rhu forward. The Chamberlain carried a golden plate on a red velvet cushion. On the plate lay a bag brocaded with red silk and gold cord. The plate was taken by two Burgesses and held between them before the Lady Mayoress. Rhu stepped back into place.

Kinnan plucked his own bag of mirrored cloth from his pocket and put it next to Landry's.

The Mayoress opened both bags. Gems gleamed in the clouded sunlight.

Steel whispered from sheaths as the Swords drew their weapons.

Another whisper. Eighteen of the brown-capes drew swords.

Kinnan grinned unpleasantly. "No doubt you've heard of Anshar of Istok. . . .My lieutenant."

And so it stood, arms against arms, and two ornamental sacks of jewels as rich as the treasuries of each claimant could buy.

chapter 21
reclamation

Andrin dreamed he was in his temple again, head shaved, body cased in silk, lungs filled with aromatic steam. He cast his divining pebbles and painted a pattern: Trembling on the Brink. It was a pattern of danger and turmoil, of potential and shift. From this point, events could slide into stability or chaos.

He woke to Chandler's cackle.

A brief drizzle pattered on the roof. It was the morning of Landry's Mandate Ceremony. Nerissa, Biddi, he and Trahern could wait no longer. Today, while all minds and eyes were focused on the lower bailey, they would slip down the motte and out the gate. They would, at any rate, make the attempt.

It had been a long time since he had given any thought to his appearance, but he ran self-conscious fingers through his ragged hair and beard. He could imagine his grandmother's gentle laughter, if she could see his attempt at grooming. At his age! For a woman no longer young, but still his junior by many years! – He had almost forgotten. He dug into one of the nesting boxes and retrieved Biddi's silver mirror, then tied the mirror into the tail of his tunic. When they were all safe, he would see if she wanted it back, ask where it had come from, why she had rejected it.

He had barely risen when Nerissa knocked perfunctorily and stuck her head in the door.

"I heard her!"

The old man chuckled. "Come in and see what you have, then."

Chandler obligingly hopped from the nesting box. Face shining, Nerissa cracked the eggshell.

Andrin stifled his own protest. *This is the worst ever! A wad of brown paper!*

Carefully, the girl uncrumpled it. She looked at both sides. Both were blank. Then, with workmanlike deliberation, she folded it into a cornet – a cone-shaped twist like those used in the marketplace for holding sweets or roasted chestnuts. She placed her prizes in it, twisted it shut, and put it in her pocket. With a contented sigh, she scratched the hen between her speckled shoulder blades.

Biddi squeezed through the barely opened door and pulled it tight shut behind her.

"Today is the day," Andrin greeted her. "Today holds us in its palm."

Biddi gave him his bread and cheese. "And holds another hand over our heads, ready to smack. Rhu just told me: It's true – Kinnan beren Ada is in Kudasad, and Landry wants him at the Mandate Ceremony. Landry is sure he can force the Mayoress and Burgesses to reject Kinnan's claim, but Rhu is afraid there'll be bloodshed over it." She gave Andrin a waterskin in place of his usual ale.

Well done. This is a day for a clear head, if ever there was one.

Biddi fidgeted with her braid. "Rhu's going to help us escape. He just told me this morning."

"It's a trick," said Nerissa.

"No." Biddi and Andrin spoke in chorus, then smiled at one another. Andrin felt a sweetness in his bones that he had never felt before. *So many years alone. How did I bear it?*

"I know you told me not to let Rhu know you were here. He came to me. He said I could leave with Trahern, and bring anybody else I wanted to. The Swords will meet us at the smithy and we'll skirt the edge of the crowd and get out." Biddi laughed a bit wildly. "It's just like our plan, only we'll have an armed escort! Rhu told Corvina it was so people will see Trahern leave and then the Swords will kill him – and any witnesses – but these Swords will protect us and take us to Oakwood."

Nerissa was unconvinced. "Maybe Rhu is all right, but I don't trust those Swords."

"Neither do I, all in all. But some are friends." She stroked Nerissa's face. "You wait here, Little One. I'll take Trahern his breakfast and tell him what to expect. I told Janet I gave you leave to go out into the town and see the Festival." She smiled sadly. "I wish you could."

Even in the center of the castle's tower hill, Andrin had heard the sounds of celebration far into the night. Fireworks had been forbidden, given the explosive nature of the times, but there had been music and singing, drums and shouts and laughter.

Biddi pushed open the door. She glanced back, and the strain on her face pained her old friend.

When the door had closed on the light, Nerissa took Chandler and sat in the farthest corner, where she could watch Andrin exercise without getting in his way. She said nothing until he had finished.

"You trust Rhu beren Robia?"

"Absolutely. He's a good man."

"So is Trahern, but That One got to him."

"You're a grim little duck! Or are you a chicken, like your friend, here? Is this a bill or a beak?" He pinched Nerissa's nose with gentle fingers, and she laughed. "The Chamberlain is sound. Corvina would only enthrall him if she thought she needed to. He'll see to it that she doesn't think she needs to."

Biddi returned, carrying a basket larger than the one she had used to bring breakfast. She pulled out a lightweight hooded cloak of deep green and handed it to Andrin. "Someone might recognize you, and we don't need that."

There was still a rough linen cloth in the basket, ridges and lumps beneath it. Biddi slipped her hand under the cloth. Andrin could see her knuckles as she fisted her hand around something. Something either very sharp or very hard, he had no doubt.

She cocked her head. "It must be nearly time. Listen."

Andrin heard a fanfare, then the throb of a drumbeat and the loudest notes of a processional march. "Landry and Corvina, Rhu and the new Chief Sword will be going down the tower steps… across the upper bailey… down the motte…."

They heard footsteps on the hard-packed earth just outside. Knuckles rapped on the door planks: short, long, long, long.

Biddi whispered, "That's the signal."

Andrin put on his cloak and pulled up the hood as Biddi opened the door.

Nerissa squeaked with delight. *He came back!* She had thought she missed Rady but, seeing the man Rady had turned out to be, she knew it was the man she missed. He was beautiful – perfect! And he had come back for her, as he had promised he would. The joy of not having been abandoned bubbled in her, made it hard to realize the danger they all were in.

The man smiled at her, though she thought he looked puzzled. He touched his ear, a habit she remembered from their prior meetings.

"You know him?" Biddi asked.

Nerissa picked up Chandler to mask the extent of her happiness. "Yes."

Rady – *Brady* – winked at her. She felt herself blush.

The beautiful young man stepped back outside, looked around the corner of the henhouse, and motioned them to follow.

As they came in sight of the smithy, a villein in a deep blue cloak called in at the window. "Come on, smith! You say you're homesick – Let's get you home."

Trahern came out. He flashed smiles at Nerissa, Brady, and Biddi, but Nerissa didn't return the pleasantry. It was false. She had seen people in Granitz on parade to the execution block; Trahern had the same waxen pallor, the slight glaze to his eyes.

She touched his arm. "Don't be afraid."

He patted her head absently. She jerked away and resisted the urge to bite his patronizing hand.

"I said, 'Don't be afraid,'" she commanded.

Brady shook a finger at the smith. "You've had your orders. See to it." He turned to Nerissa. "Now tell *me*."

His eyes twinkled, and she forgot her ire.

They were joined by more villeins, some cloaked, some not, waving to friends, promising them souvenirs of Kozabir. Some of the men, Nerissa was certain, were Swords. They wore Swords' boots, and the ones with Swords' boots also wore cloaks, useful for concealing weapons. But Rhu had said it was all right, and Andrin and Biddi had said Rhu could be trusted….

"We're off, then," said one of the villeins, and they moved in irregular formation across the upper bailey and onto the wooden ramp atop the tower motte.

Nerissa caught her breath at the pageant spread below: Landry and Corvina, with Rhu and a half-ring of Swords behind them; the Mayoress and Burgesses and people in livery marching in through the gate. Household colors glowed, even in the overcast. Pennants flapped in the damp breeze.

"Move on, down there!" said someone at the top of the incline. "Let somebody else see, too."

They continued into the lower bailey and edged around the courtyard.

They had just reached a shuttered building when Brady groaned. "They're closing the gate. We'll have to wait here a while."

Rhu was hard pressed to retain his impassivity. It was all going wrong! He had submitted his plans for the ceremony and Landry had approved them. The drawbridge being raised had not been part of the arrangements. He had seen Trahern and his attendants come down the motte like a company of shepherds with one sheep. He had exchanged complicit looks with Corvina. Then the bridge had been drawn up and she had not met his eye again, but only quirked a superior smile.

Landry turned to him with dark displeasure. "This was not agreed upon. This is a public ceremony – Why are you closing the gate?"

"The order was mine, Brother."

The new Chief Sword bowed jerkily, uncertainty in his speech and manner. "My Lord, I assumed you knew–"

"Brother, I understand you've ordered the rebel, Kinnan, to be brought here. I knew you would want to keep him, once you had him, and I was shocked to learn your order had not been passed on."

"I gave no order to turn a celebration into a siege. I have no doubt of holding anyone I want held. I have no doubt of keeping anyone where I want them."

By this time, the Procession had formed into its pre-determined ranks.

Kinnan stepped forward, his soldier's eyes and intuition reading the Sarpans' interchange. Having satisfied himself that Rhu had not betrayed him, he was grimly amused at Corvina's ham-fisted intrigue. She thought he was at her mercy. She would learn differently. His mandate bag was heavy in its pocket. *His* mandate bag? *His*…?

Nerissa saw Andrin reach out and stroke the smooth doorpost of the building beside them.

"You miss it?" Biddi asked.

The old man laughed quietly. "In many ways, yes. Yes, I must admit, there is much I miss about it. And much I do not."

The Procession drew into a semi-circle facing the one from the castle. Villeins and Swords mingled in any vacant space.

Nerissa watched in amusement as Brady surreptitiously increased his height so he could see over most of the crowd. She, herself, had no interest in Layounna's politics, except for a cheerful hope that all possible bad things would happen to Corvina.

The throng pressed back upon them. "Swords have drawn!" someone shouted. "Raiders!" came a second cry.

"Stay here," said Brady. "I'll see what's happening."

Nerissa dumped Chandler into Andrin's arms. "Hold her for me. I'm going, too."

Brady's exasperated frown met her defiant scowl, but held its own. "It isn't safe. Stay here!"

A woman in a Runners cloak faced about. "You stay here, too. You've done more than enough for the good of a country not your own. It's our turn, now."

"El–" his voice dropped to a hoarse whisper, but Nerissa caught every sound he made, "–Elsie! You're supposed to be–"

"Safe. I know. But if this goes awry, there is no safety for any of us. The only safety now lies on the other side of peril."

Landry's voice rang out. "Two mandates have been placed before you. One is offered by a man you know to be Karol beren Ada's chosen Consort, the man she trained to govern in her absences, the man who avenged her death with the fire of his own rage and the strength of his own hand. Who here remembers that? Yes, many of you! The other is offered by a man no one ever heard of until after Karol's disappearance, when he showed up with a doubtful piece of paper. Why, if he is truly the child of Ada beren Cinnie, was he not raised at court, as Karol and Sorcha were? Why, if Karol acknowledged him, did she not do so openly?"

Kinnan must have tried to interrupt, for Landry's voice rose. "Oh, I have no doubt he offers some excuse and calls it explanation, but we are not so gullible. Think, citizens. Think and decide."

A slave, a child, a victim of arbitrary abuse, Nerissa was extremely good at reading people. She saw anger and desperation in Brady's face and body, and the same in Elsie's. But, in Elsie's, she also saw resolve.

Elsie glared up into Brady's eyes. "Do not try to stop me. I warn you."

Nerissa stretched an arm across his chest, as if she could restrain him. Elsie looked at her, blinked slowly, lifted a corner of her mouth in a worried bit of a smile, and turned away.

"Before you choose," Elsie called, her voice clear and determined, "let me step forth."

The ranks of Raiders, Thanes and Burgesses parted, and she walked with regal deliberation to Kinnan's side.

As her cloak brushed against Nerissa, a thread shook free of her gown and fluttered to the dust. Nerissa picked it up. It rippled with colors in her hand.

"What's that?" Brady took it from her, then gave it back, not seeming to see its wonder. "That's from Elsie's mending. They were all over everything. Throw it away." He edged forward, unaware that Nerissa edged right beside him.

Elsie ignored Kinnan's glare. She only glanced at Rhu – Her purpose nearly shattered when she saw his ashen face, the sick terror for her in his eyes. She looked, instead, at Landry, and stood shoulder-to-shoulder with her kinsman.

"My little bride!" Landry sounded amused. He addressed the crowd. "We told you she was in the castle."

"I am not your little bride. Tell him who I am, Uncle."

Kinnan was shamed by his body's reluctance to draw breath, form words, make sounds that would undercut the birthright he had given so many years to affirm. Yet Elsie was part of that birthright. He could not repudiate her without denying his very self.

Kinnan's voice, Elsie was sure, could be heard in the street as he pronounced her true name: "This is Elsie beren Karol. The scrivener's *foster* daughter. The Roll-Keeper's *adopted* child. She is the daughter of Karol, daughter of Ada, daughter of Cinnie. She has proof and witnesses."

Rhu felt as he had when they'd told him his father was dead in middle age. *I knew,* he had thought then, *when I last saw him, something was wrong. I knew, from the way my mother spoke of him, the Way was leading him toward its center. This is only the signature on a letter I've already read.* Elsie's appearance here, Kinnan's announcement of her lineage – These only sealed a certainty he had been trying to push away. She had always been beyond his hopes. He had always known it. And now she had put herself beyond his help, as well.

Steeling herself not to look at Rhu, Elsie removed her cloak and handed it to Kinnan. The heir to Layounna faced her enemy as she had predicted, rough-shod and badly mended.

But it wasn't to teach me humility. It was to teach me pride.

"Look at her!" someone shouted. "She's Karol, to the life!"

The corners of Landry's mouth turned up. "Proof and witnesses? As convincing as those of the silversmith's boy?"

"He is Kinnan beren Ada. I am Elsie beren Karol."

Laughter from the crowd. "Aye, old Ada herself couldn't have said it haughtier."

Landry matched her stare for stare. "We will see your 'proof', by and by. But tell us: Who have we to thank for your disappearance on our bridal day? Who managed it? … Was it Rhu?"

She raised her chin, as if answering his question were a favor she granted a subject. "My mother managed it."

It wasn't until Landry turned a bloodless gray that Elsie realized – Though she had meant "Devona," Landry had heard "Karol." She chose not to correct his misunderstanding.

His attempted smile was a travesty. "And do you have a mandate to offer, too? Or will you share the throne with – Who is it? – Your uncle?" He seemed to speak to her, but addressed the crowd. "Or will the two of you struggle for it? Ada's youngest child against the child of Ada's eldest, both of them with very shaky claims, each of them a runaway?"

Over the ensuing mutters, before they could rise to arguments, Elsie spoke.

"It will be quite enough division for Onagros to unseat Sarpa from its stolen throne. If my uncle offers the mandate in my name or jointly with me, I am here. If he offers it for himself, I bow before him. I have no bag of precious things to offer my people as a pledge."

Nerissa didn't understand what was going on, only that Brady was intensely interested. Her own absorption sprang not from anything she knew but from a stirring in the root of her being. She had survived on the streets of Granitz by animal instinct as much as by human cunning. The same combination of blood and brain had caused her to trust the bright bird in the moonlit alley, the dragon on the heath, the unicorn in the woods – even Tartarus in his unsteady coracle. Now she found an unshakable trust in someone else. Herself.

"Here!" She ducked under the arm Brady threw out to stop her and dodged around Raider and Burgess to stand at Elsie's side. *This is right. This is what to do.* "You can have mine."

She gave Elsie the brown paper cornet. Landry laughed. Corvina joined him. Some others did, some others did not, but it all died quickly, oppressed by a tension none could explain.

Kinnan alone, of the principals, looked neither at Elsie nor at the rubbish in her hand. His attention was on the child. Her bruises were gone, she was clean and better fed, but this was the girl who had saved his life in Granitz, the child Trahern had failed to find. How had she come here? His mind, his body tingled with the sense one got in battle when the pattern of an engagement began to flicker into clarity.

Without condescending smile or hesitation, Elsie laid the cornet on the Lady Mayoress' golden tray. The Mayoress untwisted the ends of the paper horn and spread it open. A feather, four clay beads, a small comb, a pebble.

Solemnly, Nerissa put the shimmering thread of Moder's mending into Elsie's hand. Karol's daughter laid it atop the pitiful heap.

"I claim my right to rule," Elsie declared, "by these priceless treasures, the gift of a generous heart."

At Elsie's words, the tray trembled in the Burgess' hands. Landry's mandate bag and its contents smoked, the silk blackened and curled, the gems and alicorn chip malformed into cinders, which winked into coldness. In the same instant, Kinnan's faceted sack flashed as if the sun had come from behind its cloud cover. The mirrors melted, flowed like water and evaporated. The jewels and twist of alicorn collapsed into sand.

The wrinkled brown paper of Elsie's offering folded, corner to corner, softened in a silver glow. Within the space of a held collective breath, it became a bag of yellow crane skin, stained with a pattern of green stems and leaves and pink-tipped white flowers.

The Lady Mayoress held the crane skin bag aloft. "Know ye by this, the mandate bag of our people, this woman is our chief!"

chapter 22
CORVINA'S SACRIFICE

Corvina clutched Landry's arm. "Order the Swords to attack. We'll retreat to the tower."

"What happened to your sly plot of poison–"

"It's the winners who kill the losers, Lan! This is no time for subtlety."

"She's Karol's daughter. She won't kill me."

"Order the attack! Now, when they think they've bested us!"

When he did nothing, she nodded, as if he had spoken to her. She swept the bailey with a pass of her arm.

"*Attack! Swords, Thanes, attack!*"

"*No!*" His denial was lost in the roar of battle-cries, the hiss and clang of weapons drawn and countered.

Shoving her brother before her, Corvina headed for the motte. The clash of steel on steel behind her, of screams and shouts, made her heart lurch and thud. *It isn't over! If we kill the Onagrans, we can still claim possession of the throne.*

Up the motte, past the Swords streaming down. *Grasp one as he passes.*

"Stay with us! Guard us!" *Grasp another.* "Tell the lookout to signal the city gates. Close them. Bar them. If Swords or militia or Thanes flying our banner arrive, let them in. Hold the gate against Onagros." *Into the keep.* "Bar this gate! Let them fight it out below."

Landry allowed Corvina to marshal their withdrawal. His mandate was gone. His mother was dead, his Chief Sword was dead, Karol was alive, or as good as alive. Thanks to his sister's interference, their trap had sprung too soon and caught them inside it. Corvina – *the fool!* – had turned a game of chess into a brawl. There was nothing to do now but survive and make the most of what remained. Meanwhile, let her be seen giving the orders. Let any subsequent blame attach to her. She craved the burden of rule – Let her suffer it!

Under darkening skies, Sword fought Sword on the steps to the Great Hall.

Corvina tugged at him. "We'll go in through the kitchen." Villeins barred their way, holding stakes pulled from the garden, hoes, axes, rakes, barrel staves…. "Stand aside! You will let us pass!"

Their guard drew his weapon. "I'm taking them to the tower. Make way!"

The peasant ranks parted. Corvina stared into each face she passed, wanting to fix it in her memory.

The Thane and the Consort pattered down the kitchen steps, their Sword clumping behind them. Outside, the rain began.

A bulky, red-faced woman stood at the kitchen's central table, a cleaver in her hand and a smile on her lips. "Well! Snakes in the kitchen, whatever next? Welcome backstairs, you two. I've been waiting to see this for a long time."

Corvina trembled with the power of her wrath. "How dare you speak so to us?"

"I speak as I please."

"You'll not speak at all, with your tongue slit. Sword! See to it!"

The Sword didn't move.

"I gave you an order! Landry, tell him to obey!"

"I think not, Sister. But we will pass."

The woman didn't budge. She nodded to the Sword. "Hello, Farrell."

He nodded back. "Janet."

"Kill her!" Corvina shrieked.

Farrell went so far as to lay a hand on the pommel of his sword, but he did not draw. "I had a brother," he said. "Guthrie beren Melanell arrested him – on your say-so, Landry Oliva – and killed him for helping your bride run away from you. I think you knew he didn't do it. I *know* Guthrie knew. But my brother died in disgrace."

Landry smiled sadly, sweetly at him. "I am so sorry for you. So sorry about your brother. But you're wrong, you know. I did believe him guilty. I would never deliberately condemn an innocent man. I told Guthrie—"

Corvina snatched a knife from another table. The Sword drew, then.

Landry held out his empty hands. "The mandate has been passed, you know. There's no need for violence, and the new Kinninger will want to dispose of us herself. We place ourselves in your keeping–"

"Fool!" Corvina shouted. "Coward! Tortoise, deliver us! Give us the victory! The throne for my brother! The throne for my blood!" She plunged the knife into her own belly, and the kitchen whirled out of view.

As her vision cleared, she heard a man's rough voice.

"Oh, no, My Lady."

A calloused hand plucked the blade from her, but there was no pain, no blood on her fingers. There was no wound.

She stood in a blind alley lined with ramshackle tenements. The gutters ran black with rain. Men and women, hands heavy with clubs of broken wood and missiles of cracked paving stones, gabbled of her sudden appearance.

A large and filthy man with matted black hair and a beak of a nose blocked the only way out. He stuck her knife beneath his belt. "A quick cut and a self-righteous prayer – that's too easy an ending for you, 'Mistress'. Poison a Wayfarer, would you? Enslave a smith? Kill a cook? In Tortoise's name? I'm the answer to your prayer, Lady, and the answer is: Tortoise doesn't like you."

This is a death-scene, a dream, a test. Nothing to fear. "Out of my way, churl, and give me my knife! My Master waits for me!"

"So does your husband. So does your mother. If you hurry, you can catch up with them. Here, let me help." He stepped back, filling the exit passage. "Hey!" he shouted, pointing. "Look! It's her! That sister of Landry's! And she forgot to bring her guards!"

chapter 23
The final contention

As Corvina ordered slaughter, a contingent of Raiders funneled Andrin and Trahern into the abandoned temple. They had some difficulty with Biddi, who bounced a rolling pin off a Sword's head before she was shoved to safety.

Trahern slammed the door behind them.

Chandler squawked and thrashed until Andrin released her

"Grandmoder…," the old Waymaster whispered, "I beg you…." He fell silent, afraid to even attempt interference.

Outside, faces contorted with blood-lust screamed hatred under the towering thunderclouds.

"No!" Elsie commanded it. She pulled Nerissa close. *Not for me. Don't die in my name. Don't kill in my name. Oh, my people!*

"No!" Kinnan bellowed it as he slammed into a broadside of Swords. The Swords' first targets of choice had been Elsie and the Mayoress. That made it easier for him to shove a shoulder under the guard of the nearest attacker and domino him into the ones beyond. The weapon Trahern had made him seemed to leap into his hand, to thrust itself before him like a thirsty horse who scents water. It seemed drawn to flesh as iron is drawn to a magnet, and every blow added to his strength and speed.

"No!" Rhu cried it, pushing aside Swords with his bare hands, gathering Elsie and the child into his arms, desperate to shield them. He called to the Mayoress and Burgesses, "To me! This way!"

Anshar! The Raiders! Armed men and women surrounded Rhu and his non-combatants and convoyed them toward the closest shelter, the Roll-Keeper's post. The heavy door was locked, the key in the pocket of the Roll-Keeper.

Swords and Thanesmen loyal to Sarpa sought to fight through the rearguard, shouting *treason*, shouting *traitor*, shouting *kill them!*

"No!" Brady sprang into the air as a falcon. *Nerissa! Elsie!* At first he couldn't see them, sheltered as they were by Rhu's body. *Now's your chance*, a wheedling voice whispered in his brain. *Fly away. This is not your fight.* The falcon's voice shrieked *No!* and he dove into the fray.

A whirlwind caught him and he flapped madly, losing feathers as he struggled to recover and reorient himself on the wing. When he did, he found himself high and distant from the castle, outside the city walls. *Not your fight*, a voice hissed through the drizzle.

Brady cursed the wind currents that criss-crossed his path, giving him an unwanted tour of the city when all he wanted was to throw himself away in service to a filthy child and a once-despised grown-up brat.

Below him, the city walls, assaulted inside and out, swung wide, and the countryside streamed in, exiles and militia to the fore.

Townsfolk, thanesfolk from all corners of Layounna, countryfolk in for the Festival – the city swarmed. Weavers' doors, cloth merchants' doors, smashed open and anything red, yellow, gold, anything blue, green, pink, was cut into banners and badges, tied around arms, pinned onto bodices, stuffed into hatbands.

Death! screamed uprisen Kudasad. *Peace!* the new forces roared. *Peace, in the name of Onagros! Peace, by order of Elsie beren Karol!* Guildleaders, shopkeepers, the Town Watch, all who were sworn to keep order, all who wore the signs of Onagros, raised weapons and voices, joined the shout: *Capture them! Bind them! Spare them for the Kinninger! Save them for the justice of beren Karol!*

The wave of combat rolled below Brady, through the streets and alleys and washed around the palisaded castle compound.

Swords guarded the ramp to the upper bailey, Swords guarded the gate mechanisms. Swords attacked both positions. Lookouts on the wall hesitated, not knowing friend from foe. Some fired into the crowd outside, then fell as the crowd fired back. Raiders converged on the castle.

At last! Brady soared over the palisade. *There's Rhu!*

Rhu, taller than everyone around him, made an easy target for projectiles, though the Raiders kept hand-held weapons distanced. Blood ran from wounds on his head, his arms. As Kinnan's sword drank its way through the Chamberlain's attackers, a knife slid past, opening a gash in Rhu's neck, splashing Elsie with his blood.

Elsie cried out, and Nerissa echoed her.

The Brady-falcon screamed and aimed himself at the man who threw the knife.

Again, he was plucked out of the air.

Stay back, you idiot! a voice growled, and Brady, a sodden bundle of feathers, tumbled beak over claw to land on the floor of Andrin's darkened temple.

Across the yard, Kinnan fought his way to the cluster Rhu sought to defend, feet slipping on the ground wet with rain and gore.

"Do something, Uncle!" Kinnan saw Elsie struggling with her protector, each trying to shield the other. Her voice was not shrill with desperation, but strong with authority. "Stop this! Take the throne! Take everything, but stop this horror!"

"We're winning!" he shouted back.

"It's the same as losing, this way! This is wrong!"

His sword was warm in his hand, warm and red. But his side was warmer. His side was hot – burning.

His sword murmured: *Blood, blood, think only of blood.*

His left hand dug into his pocket and drew out a metal spiral. *I am here when you need me.* The bracelet Karol had given him lay in his left hand, and it outweighed the sword in his right.

What am I doing here? I'm a silversmith, not a warrior, not a Kinninger. I don't kill people, I coax beauty out of nowhere. He parried a blow, but did not return it. *If you're here when I need you, I need you now, whoever you are. If you can stop the slaughter, come!*

He threw the bracelet into the air, as high as he could.

An arrow intercepted its arc and struck sparks. Two sparks in the rain. Sparks that did not die, but grew. And grew. They were hummingbirds – long-tailed pheasants – firebirds! A Phoenix – two – one – searing through the sizzling rain.

Sometimes one, sometimes two, they circled Kinnan, blackening the blood on his blade. He lowered his sword, ashamed of having raised it.

The firebirds swirled through the bailey, their long tails shining like fireworks in their wakes.

Weapons fell from scorched hands; talons raked cheeks, and beaks tore ears if weapons did not fall.

They left the lower bailey for the upper.

In the lower bailey, hearts schooled in violence retrieved discarded swords and raised them again.

The clouds overhead boiled, shifting form, stretching, growing long, sinuous, bright-eyed, sharp-toothed, razor-clawed. The enormous figure rushed over the fray, dazzling fighters with flashes of yellow, green, violet, blue, shaking them with rumbles and crashes, scalding them with steam.

This was no translated grandmother. This was Dragon – the Spirit itself – strong, good, generous, and vigilant.

The Dragon storm howled and flared over all the city, blinding and deafening. The rain came harder, pounding, ending all possibility of striking a telling blow. Rain blistered warriors through cloth or armor, and splashed in cool comfort on the defenseless.

Knives and swords clashed onto cobbles. Even stones and wooden truncheons scalded until dropped.

The battle was over, but the storm raged on until every hand was empty and every head was equally damp and chill.

When the deluge eased and storm clouds thinned, when thunder grumbled into silence and lightning flickered and faded, the only sounds within the bailey were anguished moans and the sobs of the new Kinninger, mourning the dead and suffering.

Then came another sound. It was a hum, low-pitched, throaty, many-voiced. It came from all directions, pouring over the palisade in a slow tide, converging in an open spot near Kinnan and Elsie. It shimmered in the silver light and became the Unicorn, huge, monstrous, a beast larger than the largest warhorse, with a spiral horn like a lighthouse. It had legs like columns: thick enough to hold its mass, an ideal of power. Three of them. Three legs.

Yes, Elsie, Kinnan thought. *Yes, it is beautiful.*

"Help them," Elsie implored it.

"Help them." Nerissa spoke with her.

It is all the same to me. But I will help them, since you wish it, Tabby, Gosling. It turned its massive horn toward Kinnan. *And you, who have given your life to see this agony, this carnage. What do you ask?*

Kinnan shook his head. "I ask… not this."

The creature nodded. *Pick up your sword. Raise it to me.*

"No!"

Don't, then.

Slowly, he did as he was bidden. The hunger of the sword for flesh, for blood, ran from its tip to Kinnan's core.

Slay me with it.

Joy at the invitation washed over him, nearly drowned him. He clung to Elsie's and Nerissa's cries of protest as if they were lifelines.

"No."

My blood will free you. Without it, that sword and its appetite will come to rule you. You cannot put it aside, having once given way

He trembled, fearing a life of unappeased blood-lust, fearing much more a life of trying to appease it.

He found he could not force the sword to drop. But he could, with all his strength, with all the mulish contrary stubbornness of his mother's lineage, refuse to let it strike.

He ground out the words as if his jaws were millwheels. "I. Will. Not. Strike."

The Unicorn crossed the sword with its horn.

Kinnan cried out and dropped the weapon. His arm ached, from fingertips to shoulder.

Sheathe it. Onagros has returned to the Way.

He picked it up. There was no power in it now. It was only a sword. He sank it in its scabbard. His words rang with unnatural clarity through the bailey: "Let this hang in the Great Hall beneath the Onagros banner. Let it rust there before Onagros raises it against Layounna."

The last cloud evaporated. The Unicorn dissolved, leaving the land bathed in a honey glow and the sweet scent of clover.

As it disappeared, a disheveled Brady propped himself in the temple doorway.

"I told you, Kinnan," he whispered, trying to shout. "*Three legs!*" He collapsed into exhaustion.

chapTer 24
balance

Elsie and Nerissa sat in a darkened chamber, both in one large, soft chair.

After a great deal of persuasion, Nerissa had allowed Chandler to return to the new henhouse under Biddi and Andrin's supervision. She, herself, had been washed in perfumed water and dressed in a rich gown.

The choicest morsels will be yours, Elsie had told her, *and you will sleep in a bed stuffed with down between sheets of finest linen. You had the true mandate bag. The Unicorn called you Gosling. The name our birth-mother, Karol, gave you.* Elsie had scooped Nerissa into an embrace that fulfilled the child's most secret dreams of tender affection. *My sister. Grace's Gosling. My sweet baby-girl.*

Elsie, her spirit bleeding from lessons learned that cut more deeply than any blade, had allowed Raiders and loyal Swords to bear Rhu unconscious to the castle. Though the woman longed after her Tall Man, someone else must minister to him. The Kinninger had other duties.

She had taken Kinnan and Nerissa with her up the steep stairs and onto the lookout tower above the gate, where she had lifted the crane skin mandate bag and listened to wave upon wave of cheers.

At length, cheers still flowing, she had returned to the bailey, where she had passed among her attackers and defenders. She had taken each hand and pressed it, looked into each face, asked for and repeated each name. Many eyes had refused to meet hers. Onagros still had enemies among those Landry had pampered and elevated at others' expense. She held no illusions that this finished anything forever.

She had formalized her name as Elsie Devona beren Karol.

"Elsie Devona?" her foster father had objected. "It does you credit, honoring the woman who served you as a mother, but – two names together? No woman has a name like that, except...." He had entered it into the roll-book.

She had declared another week of festival, with bread and cheese distributed freely to the poor. She had instructed Thanes and Waystations and baby farms to send records of land exchanges, novitiates, refugees, and abandoned children from the past fifteen years.

With the people distracted and the officials busy, she granted herself the luxury of sitting by Rhu's bedside, her baby sister tucked under her arm, managing his recovery.

Always. It was always him I wanted, even when I thought I wanted something else.

He was sitting, now, swathed in bandages and a woolen night-shirt, a quilt tucked up under his arms.

Elsie stared at him as rudely as Nerissa, willing him to meet her eyes.

Instead, he looked at the child. "May I trouble you to unshutter the window?"

Elsie pressed Nerissa in place with a gentle hand and rose to let in the light.

"I beg your pardon, Your Grace," Rhu said. "I meant to ask the maid."

Nerissa laughed. "I'm a Grace, too!"

He turned his face to the wall, a wall no stonier than his expression.

"What are you thinking?" Elsie moved away from the window to where he could see her, if he would only look.

"I'm thinking you must choose a new Chamberlain."

A quiet knock drew Elsie to the door. The business of the realm must never find her unavailable, and she had left orders to that effect.

It was Kinnan and Anshar with a petition from the Thanes.

"My last service, Niece," said Kinnan, "before Trahern and I go back to the forge in Kudasad."

"You belong here!"

"I belong in a smithy. I've done what I set out to accomplish. It isn't what I *thought* I wanted, but it is. Now I want to go back to working metal, as I was raised to do."

Elsie nodded, and shared an embrace with her mother's brother. "I can't lose you, Uncle. We *will* visit, you here and I there."

"I'll come on the third Market Day of the month. You come when you can."

Anshar rattled the paper in his hand. "Petition," he said. "Who takes it?"

"Give it to my current Chamberlain," said Elsie. At least work would bring him back from the unutterable emptiness she felt in him.

"It's about Landry," said Rhu, reading the petition. "The Thanes want to know what you've done with him, and what you plan to do."

The former Consort was imprisoned in his tower room, where the Sword named Farrell had taken him upon Corvina's disappearance. He was guarded by Raiders, and his food was delivered and cleared away by Janet, herself. No one but she knew she concocted his meals out of kitchen waste and he, intent on being charming, never complained.

Elsie had considered the question, but had come to only a partial conclusion. "I will not take his life," she said. "I won't inaugurate my rule by killing my Consort-father. And I want my opponents to know I can be clement if I'm given the choice."

Rhu's expression changed very little, but her eyes read it: He approved her decision.

"Then, Your Grace, I suggest he be exiled to Oakwood, into his grandmother's keeping. He will be made comfortable and kept amused, and no one will be persuaded by his winning ways. They've known him from the cradle up."

Elsie couldn't help smiling. "If Brady is any measure of the insolence long acquaintance can inspire, Landry Oliva faces a life of set-downs. I could almost pity him."

Anshar regarded his fingernails. "Some of my Raiders and I will escort him. And I'll carry your formal letters to Oakwood, if I may, and deliver them to your aunt, Sorcha, and to the remnants of Sarpa. My parents live at Oakwood."

Rhu looked at him more closely. "There is something familiar about your features. Does your mother work in the kitchen there?"

"She's married to the Bailiff."

"But," said Rhu, "Hayward beren Oliva is the Bailiff at Oakwood."

In the astonished silence, Anshar explained. "My real name is Atwell. Atwell beren Sorcha. One of the many gifts of your ascension, Your Grace, is that I may go home, now that my....," he squinted, working it out, "mother's... sister's... oldest daughter has her house back."

Elsie followed the trail of kinship and said, "So, not only is my uncle a notorious rebel, my cousin is his chief lieutenant."

"As your oldest relative," said Kinnan, "I advise you to keep better company."

The Chamberlain's voice cut into their delight. "With your permission, Your Grace, I'll return to Oakwood with them. I've been of use at Oakwood; I hope I may be so again."

Her face as closed as his, she said, "You are not yet strong enough to travel." To Anshar/Atwell, she said, "You may be gone one week. Then you must return. I'll need your help choosing a new Chamberlain."

He bowed.

Heart thudding, she went on. "And I must have a Consort, as well. I was not raised as Kinninger; I need someone who understands the running of the realm. Someone wise, kind, just, respected by the people and by our neighbors."

Kinnan snickered.

Elsie cocked her head and looked up from under her lashes, in the way that could always win her foster father's approval. "Please, my Tall Man? Will you take my name? The first time I saw you, when I was four, I thought, 'I'm going to marry him some day.' May I?" She stamped a foot in mockery of her former self. "Say yes!"

Faintly, Rhu managed, "Yes."

~*~

Andrin was called up from the building that had once been his temple to perform the Joining of the Way. His hair and beard had been washed and combed until they shone. The smell of cinnamon soap rose from his dusky skin. His tunic and trousers were new, but as rough and common as his old ones. He had become accustomed to the feel and freedom of clothes it wouldn't hurt to stain.

"Now let your ways be joined. Now let your paths run parallel or let them separate and cross and cross again. Now let you share your travels. Let your journeys be one. Elsie Devona beren Karol, do you consent to give this man your name?"

"With all my heart."

"Rhu beren Robia, let all know you hereafter as Rhu Robia beren Karol. May you both live in the peace at the heart of the Way."

~*~

Biddi was waiting in the old temple when Andrin came down the motte.

"Tell me all about it. What was she wearing? Did he ever smile?"

Andrin had cleaned the place, and had been lent a pot. A fire burned in the hearth, but the building still had an air of the temporary, of the already-abandoned.

He answered all her questions, then they sat in companionable silence for a time. As afternoon filled the room with soft shadows, she spoke again.

"And what will you do now? Reopen your temple? Have them build you another one?"

"Why, no, I hadn't thought of that. No, I don't want that."

"What will you do, then?"

"Go back to my cottage by the river, I think. I liked living there. I liked living, there."

She pulled her braid over her shoulder and plucked at the ends. "A little cottage by the river would be nice."

"It is."

"I'd like it, too. Andrin.... We've been friends a long time.... I'd like to live in your cottage with you. I'd like to.... I'd like to give my name to you."

"...To me? But my dear girl, I'm ages older."

"In ten years, I've grown thicker, heavier, grayer; my skin is coarse and wrinkles have popped out like...like...."

"Buds in springtime."

Biddi laughed in spite of herself. "And you haven't aged a day. Just wait for me."

A soft, whispery voice blew past the door like leaves in a breeze. *Accept her, Andrin. The girl is a wise one.*

"The cottage, then," said the Wayfarer. "You won't mind if a relative of mine comes to dinner now and then, will you?"

~*~

Brady threw himself into the ascension holiday, and only made token protest when Nerissa demanded he squire her around. She was disappointed not to find Farukh or Salali in any of the squares, but adored the "story" Brady told to explain their absence.

The week ended with the Players giving a command performance of The Dragon Queen. When Brady proposed joining them again, Florian clapped him on the back and agreed.

Kinnan gave Brady Trahern's bottomless food pot, the wonderful lantern, and the loggerhead that could start a fire in water-soaked wood. "The boy has to bring something with him to justify your letting him tag along."

Brady found himself both eager and reluctant to go. He wandered the back of the upper bailey, where he had roamed as a cat. He got in the kitchen staff's way and was given the rough side of Janet's tongue. Inexplicably disconsolate, he drifted down the stairs into the store room, where he had heard Nerissa crying, where they had plotted Trahern's deliverance. He leaned on the edge of the well and peered in, enjoying its cool exhalation.

"Careful – Don't fall in."

He blinked, and stared again, and there was the woman he dreamed of – had dreamed of the night before, in fact. A white linen palla, embroidered with yellow, covered her head and was thrown back over both shoulders, just as he had first seen her. Roan hair strayed from under the cloth. Her eyes, the shape of her face... so like Elsie, but–

He turned, and Nerissa pulled the palla off her head, leaving her cropped hair in disarray.

"What do you think? Chandler just laid an egg and when I broke it this came out. Isn't it pretty?"

At last Brady understood. "How old are you, Gosling?"

"Eleven, I think."

"Eleven. Nerissa beren Karol, I don't have a bride-price, and only one skill – two, if you count playing the pipes. I know I'm not fit for a Royal, but – When you're sixteen, will you look at me?"

"Look at you?"

"He wants you to marry him when you come of age, Guttersnipe." Tartarus came from the shadows. "Which, by the way, is *fourteen* in Layounna. Tell him no."

Nerissa grabbed Brady's hands.

"I won't tell him no. I can't tell him no. We're married already, and I'm glad."

Brady, startled, tried to pull away, but Nerissa tightened her grip and fixed him with a scowl that pulled a chuckle from their old master.

She shook their joined hands for emphasis. "You shared my bed. That makes us married."

"I was a cat! Just for warmth!"

"It doesn't matter! We belong to each other, and you know it!"

Brady, master of masquerading, looked behind the savage insistence and saw the painful need, then looked behind the weakness and saw the strength.

"You were older in my dreams."

"I'll get older. Go with the Players now. When I'm *fourteen*, I'll find you. And you'd better not be married to anybody else."

Feeling as carefree as a boy who has never looked death in the eye, Brady nodded. "And next time I come through with the Players, I'll beg off a week and escort you and your sister to a little place in the Fiddlewood. There's somebody there who wants to see you."

Tartarus shook his head, as if baffled by the sheer perversity of life. "You'd think I'd dedicated my life to making you fit for each other." He flapped a broad, flat hand in dismissal. "Marry and live and die." In a voice rich with revulsion, he said, "Young love."

Then he was gone.

epilogue

Tartarus sighed and flopped full length onto the ground outside Moder's cottage. "I would suggest we make ourselves comfortable inside, but I doubt there's room in there for all of us."

Salali and Farukh, hand-in-hand, turned from the door. Salali wore a new ornament in a new hole in her left ear: a small silver stud, half of someone's worldly goods. Moder sat on the bench under the eaves.

Verrina joined her, giving Tartarus a scathing look. "I'd rather be crowded than sit on that ground. The goats and geese have free run of it."

Tartarus raised an arm, looked at its underside, shrugged, and relaxed again. "I hope you're all happy now. True heir restored, everyone two-by-two like the first day of mortality." He grimaced. "I did what I could."

"What ill you could." Salali seemed inclined to hold a grudge.

"Of course. Everyone running around trying to smooth a path for the House of Onagros – seemed only fair for one of us to throw out a few stumbling blocks."

Moder prodded him with her stick. "Yet you tripped the Roll-Keeper on the cliff. You gave him the chance to see what he was doing in time to save Elsie."

"I knew she–" he nodded at Verrina, "–was waiting below to rescue any living children and to Translate the rest to fish – fish no angler would ever catch. Thought I'd have some fun with that one's raising. Dropped in on her now and then in the form of a sweet little kitty, just to make sure her character was being thoroughly disfigured. And one day I come in, and there's my thieving protégé, safe in the bosom of the family, helping the mother undercut the father's spoiling. Imagine my disgust. It's been like that the whole way through. One thing after another. Nothing worked out."

"Of course, it worked out." Verrina's dark eyes crinkled with delight. "You misunderstand, Brother: None of us acted to smooth Onagros' return;

we each acted according to our natures. So did you. And what we did –
you, as much as we – worked in harmony with the Way. You helped, whether
you meant to or not, because you, above all, are true to your nature."

"You make me sick," said Tartarus.

END

CHARACTERS

(MORE OR LESS IN ORDER OF MENTION OR APPEARANCE)

Darcy Aminta beren Valda (unmarried name: Darcy beren Aminta)	Roll-Keeper of Eastern District, then of Layounna. Husband of Devona, father of Elsie.
Devona beren Valda	Public scribe, wife of Darcy, mother of Elsie.
Elsie beren Devona	Chosen second wife of Landry.
Salvia Zglaria called Moder Zglaria	Old woman who lives in Fiddlewood.
Landry Oliva beren Ada (unmarried name: Landry beren Oliva)	Consort to Karol beren Ada.
Karol beren Ada	Kinninger (ruler) of Layounna. Chief of the House of Onagros. Wife of Landry.
Rhu beren Robia	Landry's Chamberlain.
Guthrie beren Melanell	Chief Sword under Landry.
Ada beren Cinnie	Mother of Karol beren Ada, Kinninger before her. Mother of Sorcha and Kinnan.
Gils Nara beren Ailith (unmarried name: Gils beren Nara)	Heart-husband and child-sire of Ada beren Cinnie and Osa beren Ailith, father of Cameron and Kinnan
Cameron beren Osa	Son of Gils Nara and Osa beren Ailith, half-brother to Kinnan, heart-husband and child-sire to Karol beren Ada
Kinnan beren Ada (birn Matka, beren Osa, beren Moder)	Son of Gils Nara and Ada beren Cinnie, half-brother to Karol, half-brother to Cameron. In line for throne of Layounna
Sorcha beren Ada	Karol beren Ada's younger sister, half-sister to Kinnan, wife of Hayward.

Oliva beren Audre	Thane of Sarpa. Mother of Landry, Hayward, and Corvina. An Adept of the dark Tarkastrian Arts.
Hayward Oliva beren Ada (unmarried name: Hayward beren Oliva)	Son of Oliva beren Audre, brother of Landry and Corvina, married to Sorcha.
Corvina beren Oliva	Daughter of Oliva, sister of Landry and Hayward. An alchemist specializing in poison.
Andrin beren Tooli	A Waymaster.
Biddi beren Anna	A kitchen maid, friends with Andrin.
Farukh Suria'Apa-Dan	A storyteller from the land of Sule.
Fala Salali	A trinket-woman from the land of Nishi.
Verrina beren Unna	Andrin's grandmother.
Chandler	A hen.
Trahern birn Lona	A blacksmith from the land of Kozabir.
Brady birn Ilka	Devona's apprentice from Kozabir.
Nerissa birn Matka	A slave.
Isa birn Isa and Barand Tara birn Isa	Nerissa's owners.
Audre beren Oda	Oliva beren Audre's mother. Thane of Oakwood.
Edelin beren Cinnie	Elsie's male disguise.
Vevay beren Sorcha Atwell beren Sorcha Joia beren Sorcha Blaine beren Sorcha	Children of Sorcha and Hayward.
Brina beren Moder	Waymistress of Kudasad Waystation.
Anshar "The Divine Spear" Redhand	A Layounnan rebel based in the land of Istok.
Janet beren Lana	Cook in the castle in Kudasad, capital of Layounna.
Bryan beren Basha	Captain of Landry's Swords.
Robeard Caitlin beren Regan	Thane of Leven. Spokesman of the Southern Council of Thanes.
Robia beren Dela	Rhu beren Robia's mother.

GENEALOGY

ONAGROS BEFORE INTERMARRIAGE

husband (unnamed) + Ada beren Cinnie + Gils Nara beren Ailith + Osa beren Ailith

Karol beren Ada   Sorcha beren Ada   Kinnan beren Ada (Osa, Moder)   Cameron beren Osa

No shared blood

SARPA BEFORE INTERMARRIAGE

Otmar Sadira beren Oliva + Oliva beren Oda

Landry beren Oliva   Hayward beren Oliva   Corvana beren Oliva

INTERMARRIAGE OF ONAGROS AND SARPA

Landry Oliva beren Ada + Karol beren Ada + Cameron beren Osa

?

Sorcha beren Ada + Hayward Oliva beren Ada

Vevay beren Sorcha   Atwell beren Sorcha   Joia beren Sorcha   Blaine beren Sorcha